The Merest Loss

The Merest Loss

A Novel

Steven Neil

Matador
9 Priory Business Park,
Wistow Road, Kibworth Beauchamp,
Leicestershire. LE8 0RX
Tel: 0116 279 2299
Email: books@troubador.co.uk
Web: www.troubador.co.uk/matador
Twitter: @matadorbooks

ISBN 978 1788039 710
British Library Cataloguing in Publication Data.
A catalogue record for this book is available from the British Library.

Printed and bound in the UK by 4edge Limited
Typeset in 11pt Minion Pro by Troubador Publishing Ltd, Leicester, UK

Matador is an imprint of Troubador Publishing Ltd

My thanks go to: my wife, Carol, for her constant encouragement and support, my university tutors and fellow students for their guidance and feedback, and those kind people who read my drafts and offered insights and suggestions. This book would not have been possible without you.

CHARACTER LIST

Elizabeth 'Eliza' Ann Harryet (later Harriet Howard
and Comtesse de Beauregard)
Tom Olliver: jockey (later racehorse trainer)
Martin Harryet: son of Elizabeth Ann Harryet
James 'Jem' Mason: jockey
Francis Mountjoy-Martin: Guards officer
Nicholas Sly: civil servant
Prince Louis Napoleon Bonaparte (later Emperor Napoleon
III)
George Carter: huntsman
Jack Skinner: whipper-in
Duke of Grafton (4th)
Davy Gibson: stable owner
Squire Joseph Gawen Harryet: father of Elizabeth Ann
Harryet
Elizabeth Mary Harryet: mother of Elizabeth Ann Harryet
Allen McDonough: jockey
Will Pope: jockey
Queen Victoria
Prince Albert: consort of the Queen
King Louis Philippe
Lord Normanby: politician
Lady Normanby: politician's wife
Lord Palmerston: politician

Lord Melbourne: politician
Lord Russell: politician
Mr Ridley: school principal
Mr Dalziel: school deputy principal
Melliora Findon: friend of Elizabeth Ann Harryet
Lavinia Lampard: friend of Elizabeth Ann Harryet
Guillaume Macaire: riding instructor
Francie Strabally: school pupil
Duke of Grafton (5th)
Jean Mocquard: Louis Napoleon Bonaparte's private secretary
Jean-Gilbert Fialin (Comte de Persigny): Louis Napoleon Bonaparte's advisor
Colonel Vaudrey: Louis Napoleon Bonaparte's advisor
Doctor Conneau: Louis Napoleon Bonaparte's physician
Benjamin Disraeli: politician
Viscount Fitzharris: politician
Edward Bulwer-Lytton: politician
Margaret, Lady Blessington: society hostess
Count D'Orsay: dandy
Donald Treves: actors' agent
John Elmore: racehorse owner
George Dockeray: racehorse trainer
General Montholon: Louis Napoleon Bonaparte's advisor
Colonel Parquin: Louis Napoleon Bonaparte's advisor
Lieutenant Aladenize: Louis Napoleon Bonaparte sympathiser
Captain Col-Puygelier: garrison commander
Major Girardet: garrison commander
Charles Thelin: Louis Napoleon Bonaparte's valet

Lord Strathmore: racehorse owner
Lord Chesterfield: racehorse owner
Sarah Langdon: actress
Lady Willoughby: courtier
Lord Aberdeen: politician
Josiah Mason: father of Jem Mason
Emily Elmore: daughter of John Elmore
Lord Sefton: racehorse owner
Lord Beauclerk: racehorse owner
Will McDonough: jockey
Tom Ferguson: jockey
Sir James Graham: politician
Lord Stanley: politician
Lord Malmesbury: politician
Lord Cowley: politician
Lady Cowley: politician's wife
Nathaniel Strode: financier
Duke of Beaufort
Eleonore Vergeot: mother of two of Louis Napoleon
Bonaparte's sons
Princess Mathilde: cousin of Louis Napoleon Bonaparte
Lord Hertford: politician and racehorse owner
Lord Henry Seymour-Conway: racehorse owner and
founder of the French Jockey Club
Comte Achille Delamarre: head of the French Jockey
Club
Clarence Trelawney: Austrian hussar
Eugenie, Countess of Teba: Spanish countess
Armand-Jacques Leroy de Saint-Arnaud: military
commander
Lord Clarendon: politician

Georges-Eugene Haussmann: architect
Virginia, Comtesse de Castiglione: Italian countess
Princess Carola of Vasa: Swedish princess
Princess Adelheid of Hohenlohe-Langenburg: German princess
Felice Orsini: Italian nationalist
Lord Derby: politician
Sir George Lewis: politician
Sir Robert Peel: politician
Alphonse Toulon: chief of police
Raymond Fitzgerald: husband of Lavinia Lampard
Count Alfred van Nieuwerkerke: friend of Princess Mathilde
Marguerite Bellanger: actress
Freddie Adams: jockey
William Cartwright: racehorse owner
Count Frederic Lagrange: racehorse owner
Harry O'Brien: head lad to Tom Olliver
Thomas Aldcroft: jockey
Tom Chaloner: jockey
James Snowden: jockey
Eleanor Strode: wife of Nathaniel Strode
Beatrice Findon: mother of Melliora Findon
Dr Villeneuve: physician
Marianne-Joséphine-Caroline de Csuzy: wife of Martin Harryet
Marie-Anne Mocquard: wife of Jean Mocquard
Amédée Mocquard: son of Jean Mocquard
Marie-Emilie Mocquard: daughter of Jean Mocquard
Tom Leader: assistant trainer to Tom Olliver
Sarah Clare: friend of Melliora Findon

CONTENTS

Part One

ONE
A French Accent
Newmarket, England
1862

The young man who walked into my Newmarket racing yard that red-skied spring morning was tall, slim and blessed with all the charm that a faultless command of English, with a strong French accent, bestows. At first, I gained the impression of a certain arrogance in his character, but I warmed to him as he spoke. He told me he would succeed to the French nobility and gave his name as Martin. He knew his English mother, although his relationship with her was strained, but he never knew his father. I couldn't quite understand how these facts held together, or how his story could conceivably be connected to me, but I assumed this would be revealed in due course.

He explained he was born in England, but grew up in France. Having almost reached his twentieth birthday, he was back in England to solve the mystery that followed him all his life: his father's identity. He said he possessed a piece of paper with five names written on it. My name, Tom Olliver, was one of them. He waited as I finished with the horses and we went into the house to take some breakfast. He asked if I would be prepared to help him. I swallowed hard at this, but I couldn't help being intrigued.

'Go ahead,' I said. 'Tell me the names. What do you need to know?'

'Just tell me about them,' he said.

The first name on the list was Jem Mason. I knew Jem well. We rode together as jockeys in the early days, but I saw him less in recent years. I knew he suffered some bouts of ill health. He was a fine man on a horse and it set me thinking about our adventures together. I remembered when he won the Grand National on Lottery in 1839 and, later, the years when we rode in France. They were happy times. Looking back, I think I already knew who Martin's mother must be, but my mind rejected the obvious line of thought. I stuck to the logic that trying to narrow down the women who were known to both Jem and me in those days would not lead to a shortlist. We were young men then and we enjoyed ourselves.

I noted Martin looking at me closely as we talked together. It struck me he was trying to gauge my reactions: to see if I would betray anything in my speech or my actions that would give him some clue.

Before we went any further, I asked what seemed to me to be the obvious question.

'Have you asked your mother who your father is?'

'If it was so simple, I would not be here,' he said.

The second name was Francis Mountjoy-Martin. At the mention of his name, any lingering doubt about the identity of the young man's mother disappeared. I met Francis a few times. He always appeared the perfect gentleman: a rangy, thin Guards officer. I liked him.

'Your mother is Harriet Howard,' I said. 'I am sorry I was so slow. I really am very pleased to meet you. Is your mother still very beautiful? I hope so.'

It was a naive thing to say and I felt my face flush.

'The years have been kind to Mama,' he said. 'People say she has retained all her elegance. I am not the best one to judge these things, but I believe this is correct.'

The third name was Nicholas Sly. I never met him, but I knew his reputation. An enigmatic figure: something to do with the government and the military, but no one really knew. Harriet spoke about him several times. He had some hold over her, but I never discovered it. I thought she seemed afraid of him. I knew a story went with the name, but it eluded me at that moment.

I felt uneasy about the way things were going.

'I am puzzled,' I said. 'May I speak plainly?'

He nodded.

'This seems to be rather an elaborate charade. Have you considered just asking me the question? As I understand it, you believe I am one of five men who could be your father, yet you are vague about your mother's identity, preferring that I deduce it from the hints you make. Then, when I do discover who she is, you continue with a discussion about someone else on the list. If you ask me the question, I will tell you what I know.'

He pinched the bridge of his nose and cast his head down. I felt embarrassed again, as if I was wounding him with my directness.

'Sir, I appreciate your candour,' he said. 'I will also speak plainly. There is one name on the list who I have asked.

He refused to discuss it. I know he is a liar, so even if he answered me his reply would be worth nothing. I prefer to make my own judgement. I have grown up not trusting others. I cannot even trust my own mother to tell me the answer to a simple question. You may be an honest man, but I cannot know that. I am grateful you have agreed to help me. I will understand if you terminate our discussion, but I hope you will not.'

'Thank you,' I said. 'Let us continue.'

The fourth name was Louis Napoleon. I knew we would come to him: Louis Napoleon, now Emperor Napoleon III of France; the most public of Harriet's acquaintances. I met him once and found him a strange fellow. He spoke perfect English, but with a vaguely German accent, tinged with American. He seemed very enthusiastic about horses, I remember. I have seen many portraits of him since, invariably mounted on a horse and, indeed, a dashing figure he cuts. However, when I met him, I thought him weedy and unimpressive. It occurred to me that if Louis Napoleon proved to be his father, Martin was fortunate to inherit his looks from his mother.

I rambled on about the "suspects" at length. I suppose I was just thinking out loud, but, of course, not everything came out. Some of it I kept to myself.

'I am sorry. I am not sure if I am helping you,' I said. 'You will already know much of this.'

'Yes it is helpful, but I have not come to you unprepared. Everything is building a picture for me. I have done my research.'

'Will you share some with me? It may jog my memory.'

It emerged that he was a skilled detective. He knew, for example, that Harriet could be placed at various addresses in London during the 1840s: in Oxford Street with Jem Mason in 1841; with Francis Mountjoy-Martin in Rockingham House in 1844; with Louis Napoleon in Berkeley Square in 1847. He told me the problem he faced: the more information he found, the less helpful it was. Most of the facts and figures had the effect of ruling the men in rather than out. They might all have been his father, but obviously only one could be. It struck me he was being remarkably calm and businesslike about his quest, as if looking for a long-lost book, rather than the truth of his own life. As he spoke, images came into my mind. I recalled a glamorous occasion at Gore House, in Kensington, many years back and I pictured the young, flame-haired Harriet in a striking blue dress.

'And the fifth name is Tom Olliver,' I said, 'if I understand you correctly.'

I certainly knew Harriet. I think she must have been about fourteen when I first met her in the hunting field, although we called her Elizabeth Ann or Eliza then, and memories flooded back. She was the daughter of a Norfolk family: the Harryets. The name change came later. I told him about the times we spent together and how Jem and I competed for her attention. I talked about myself. I enjoyed good luck through my riding career and I achieved enough success to set up as a racehorse trainer. It was all I knew and the wealthy friends I made in racing were happy to support me when I retired from race riding. I met Harriet many times over the years. We became good friends and

I told him as much as I could about my recollections. I felt awkward, though, as if I was somehow betraying her, but by now I liked him and I wanted to help him. I had my own suspicions, but I respected his honesty and his diligence. I could see how important it was for him to know the truth about his father, but it was also clear that the discovery must be his own. He would be a son to make someone proud.

Our conversation seemed to reach a natural conclusion and he sat back in his chair and closed the black notepad in front of him. He thanked me for my help and I checked my pocket watch. Time seemed to speed past and I wondered what his arrangements were for transport and lodging. He was staying at The Golden Lion on the High Street and I agreed to ferry him there later, if only he would agree to stay on for lunch. I asked him if I could put some questions of my own to him.

He filled in some details of his mother's life for me. I realised I had not seen her for almost five years, although we had exchanged letters and a great deal had happened in that time. I remembered more about her relationship with Emperor Napoleon. How could I not? For a while during the forties and fifties, Harriet was often in the newspapers. In 1848, she appeared by Louis Napoleon's side in a carriage on the Champs Élysées. Just before Louis Napoleon became Emperor, the society writers called her "The English Empress".

'Would I be correct in thinking that the man to whom you asked the question, and who you say is a liar, is the very same man: the Emperor?' I said.

'Exactly so. I grew up with two of his sons as brothers. Now, he will not see me.'

'And your mother?'

'She and Louis have a complicated relationship. There were arguments about money. She was made Comtesse de Beauregard and installed in a château, just outside Paris, but there were holes in the roof.'

'The French nobility is a mystery to me,' I said. 'Can you inherit the title from your mother?'

'I will become the Comte de Béchevêt on my twenty-fifth birthday. It is a gift from Louis. I consider it a farewell present.'

Finally, I was reminded that Harriet later married Captain Clarence Trelawney, a Cornishman serving in the Austrian Hussars, by all accounts.

'The man is a charlatan,' he said. 'I have nothing to do with him.'

'At least we can probably rule him out of your calculations,' I said.

For the first time, the serious young man beside me relaxed his shoulders and the flicker of a smile played around his lips.

We talked on into the late afternoon. Martin seemed comfortable with horses and he came with me to deliver the teatime feed. It was my habit to do the last feed of the day myself. This gave me a chance to check on the horses' well-being and to see if there were any changes to their behaviour, which might be a sign of a problem. Some horses whickered and whinnied, some stamped, some weaved. If they changed their patterns, I knew I needed to be on my watch.

When eventually we parted in Newmarket, I felt sorry to see him go. He went without asking the obvious question that hung in the air. He would come to his own conclusion about his father's identity. I offered to help him further if I could and I wondered if I would see him again. I hoped I would.

Later in the evening, as I made my final check around the stables, I thought over the day's events. I spoke the names out loud: Jem Mason, Francis Mountjoy-Martin, Nicholas Sly and Louis Napoleon. I thought about Martin and replayed some of our conversations. At one point, I asked him why it was so important to him to know who his father was. How could I have been so crass?

'I am not just solving a puzzle,' he said. 'I am trying to find out who I am. Is that hard to understand?'

And what of Harriet Howard? What were her circumstances now and why was she putting her son, Martin Harryet, through this ordeal?

TWO
Mystery Boy
Northamptonshire and Norfolk, England
1836

Tom Olliver doesn't know he is going to make a new acquaintance out hunting in Grafton country, but he soon will. Tom arrives at the meet at Farthingstone early, well mounted on a strapping grey gelding. He is a short, muscular, broad-shouldered man with dark, alert eyes, a leathern complexion and a sharp jaw-line. It lends him a roguish look. His appearance, coupled with his reputation with the ladies, earns him the nickname Black Tom. When he is not racing, if the invitation comes to go hunting, he never refuses. Time spent on a horse, jumping fences, is never wasted as far as he is concerned.

Hounds arrive and the field moves off promptly at eleven o'clock. Carter, the huntsman, gets a fox away from covert and they make a good point over the meadows up along the vale behind Maidford, before their quarry goes to ground in some badger setts. Carter blows that funny doubled toot-toot on his horn to signal he is not for dallying with the terriers and cracks on.

It is a fine crisp day, with a frost along the top of the hedgerows. A pair of buzzards circles overhead, calling to each other as the mounted field canters up the headland towards Mantle's Heath. The usual set is out: farmers and local gentry, alongside a few jockeys, like Tom. The Duke of Grafton is field master on his chestnut horse with the jagged white blaze. He has some guests from London and a party from the West Norfolk are staying locally and riding out on hirelings from Gibson's yard at Weedon. A group of almost fifty riders kicks on, including a young fellow, no more than thirteen or fourteen years old, who Tom has not seen before, riding a coloured pony. He catches the boy's eye as he jumps an awkward ditch off the Maidford road, rather than waiting to follow the field through the gateway. It runs through Tom's mind that he is either brave or foolhardy. Given time, a day across Grafton hedges has a way of resolving that one way or the other, without the need for speculation, and Tom waits and watches to see what will happen.

Carter's confidence that he will soon find another fox is not misplaced. Almost as soon as he puts hounds into covert, a black dog fox jumps into the lane and slips down the hill along the gorse bushes. Hounds fly in pursuit with Skinner, the whipper-in, close on their heels as they go out of sight beyond the crossroads. Everyone follows in behind, clattering down the lane; sparks flying from the metalled hooves. Carter and the Duke see the line the hounds take and, cantering on, they go side by side at a wide hawthorn hedge and ditch off the lane. Both horses refuse and hit the hedge chest high, leaving the riders hanging around their necks in a rather ungainly fashion. There is much merriment and stifled sniggering from the onlookers, as the two foremost horsemen in the county struggle to regain their composure.

'Can someone get a bloody gate open?' shouts Carter.

Two riders trot along the lane about fifty yards, jump down from their mounts and make to open up the six bar gate. Meanwhile, the young man who Tom noted at the Maidford road spins his pony around, gives him a kick in the ribs with his spurs, lands him a hefty blow on the backside with his whip, jumps the hawthorn hedge and ditch off two strides, and goes off hollering and whooping down the hill like a demented cur. A nervous moment's silence ensues as everyone waits to see how the Duke reacts. He has a temper on him and they never rightly know when it might emerge.

'Who the blazes is that boy?' he splutters.

It turns out no one recognises him. The regulars assume he is one of the guests and the guests assume he is one of the regulars. Carter breaks the tension.

'Well, he can bloody well ride whoever he is. Best catch the bugger and find out.'

And with that, they all file through the gateway and gallop on after the mystery boy and the coloured pony.

After the escapade at Mantle's Heath, there follows a great run up across the back of Everdon church to the ridge and hounds swing left-handed. The fox takes them over the bridges and across the sheep pasture at Fawsley. All the while, they are about two fields behind hounds and they can see the red coat of the whipper-in and the brown tweed of the new young thruster close behind. They are skimming

13

the fences and what a lovely sight they make, moving stride for stride in perfect rhythm. Eventually, the fox retraces his tracks and hounds are stopped in the deer park. Carter counts in his pack and the "mystery boy's" identity is about to be revealed.

∽

Squire Joseph Gawen Harryet comes to his senses around mid-morning, having had a glass too many when the port was passed the previous evening. His wife is on hand to tell him his darling child has been missing since breakfast time – about the same time the hunting party left. Harryet blusters and shouts a good deal before the innkeeper offers him the use of his gig and pony, and Squire and Mrs Harryet set off on their search, first to Weedon and then, by way of the lanes and tracks, to Fawsley by about two o'clock. As they trot up the lane along the dog-leg bend by the church, the steaming field of around thirty remaining horses clank and jangle their way down the hill, past the hall, to meet them.

A minute earlier, Tom canters alongside the young fellow in the tweed hacking jacket.

'Well ridden,' he says, 'though I think an apology to the Master might be well advised.'

'And who might you be?' comes the reply.

'Tom Olliver. At your service.' He removes his hunting cap and draws a low, wide arc with it, finishing at his horse's quarters, while making an exaggerated bow.

As the field meets Harryet's gig head-on, he stops, ties in the reins and stands up to survey the riders.

'Elizabeth Ann, get down off that pony this instant,' he booms.

Tom volunteers to lead the now-famous coloured pony back to his stable, which turns out to be Davy Gibson's yard at Weedon. The "mystery boy" feels the sharp end of her father's tongue.

∽

Later, it is learned that when old man Harryet doesn't appear at breakfast that morning, his daughter, Elizabeth Ann, more familiarly Eliza, realising her father's absence, borrows some breeches and a hacking jacket from the innkeeper's son, tags on to the hunting party heading to Weedon and rides on the back of the second carriage to avoid detection. Hanging back as the group mounts up and waiting for them to set off for the hack to the meet, Eliza presents herself to Gibson and asks for the horse Harryet had originally booked as a hireling.

'We have no horse ready for you, young sir,' says Gibson.

'Harryet is the name. Be so kind as to find my horse straight away,' says Eliza, in the lowest pitch she can muster, which still sounds like a strangled squeak.

'We had a big hunter ready for a Mister Harryet, but we were told he wouldn't be coming, so we turned the horse out in the field. He wouldn't have done for you, sir, in any event.'

'Well, find me something else and be quick about it. I am Squire Harryet's son and he wishes me to hunt in his place. We are guests of the Duke and I am keeping him waiting. And you, sir, are keeping me waiting.'

Gibson smiles and calls his groom to saddle up Hotspur. Minutes later, the groom leads out a coloured pony, which plunges and bucks on the end of a lead rein.

'Is that the best you can do?' says Eliza.

'Hotspur will take you anywhere and jump any fence off any stride,' he says, 'if you can ride as well as you can talk.'

Eliza gives him her version of an imperious stare, vaults onto the pony and canters off down the track from Gibson's yard, without a backward look.

There is great amusement as the full story of Eliza's acting performance emerges and variations of the tale, with all manner of embellishments and attributions, begin to circulate among hunting folk in the Midlands from that moment on. Elizabeth Ann Harryet makes her inaugural impression and it is the first story of a series about the wild, red-haired girl with the waspish tongue who can outride any man. Tom is embarrassed to say he is probably responsible for a good many of them.

∽

Eliza stays silent all the way back home to Aylsham, where she shuts herself in her room and refuses to eat. Back in Northamptonshire, the Duke of Grafton sends his first footman to ascertain where the Harryets stayed on their visit, which turns out to be the Plume of Feathers in Weedon. He then instructs him to drop into the hostelry to make enquiries about their address in Norfolk. Armed with this information, he sends his estate manager on a trip to find out more about the family and, in particular, the daughter.

Squire Harryet is not speaking to his daughter. She wouldn't answer even if he was. As his wife Elizabeth Mary points out, however, he only has himself to blame. Eliza has been indulged since birth and her father is reluctant to punish what he sees as her "spirit". Nevertheless, he is at a loss to know what to do with her. She cannot be contained at the local school and she has seen off three governesses in quick succession in the last year. The most recent incumbent still resides at the county asylum, near Norwich, pending further assessment. Even the squire himself admits his daughter "jiggers his nerves" and the hangover he inflicted on himself when staying at Weedon is hardly an uncommon occurrence. Eliza's mother is the only one, it seems, who has her measure, but the constant fighting wearies her and she confesses she is "at the end of her tether".

When the invitation comes, a few weeks later, to visit the Duke of Grafton at Euston Hall, near Thetford, Squire Harryet thinks one of his neighbours is playing a trick on him. He has been the butt of jokes ever since his daughter's adventure with the Grafton pack and he is not a little sensitive to the unwelcome fame his family has attracted. While the Duke has his hunting estate in Northamptonshire, the ancestral home of the Duke's family, the Fitzroys, has always been Euston Hall and the fourth Duke splits his time between the two estates and his London residence in St James. Eventually convinced of the veracity of the coat of arms on the invitation and the accuracy of the signature, Harryet sends an obsequious acceptance. He is, not to put too fine a point on it, somewhat down on his luck. Living beyond his means, courtesy of excessive drink and gambling, has resulted in some drastic changes. The Harryets have already moved from the main farmhouse to a smaller farm cottage, land has been sold off and the bank is threatening foreclosure on what remains. Whatever the Duke has in mind, there is no doubt that Harryet senses salvation, in one form or another. Quite why he thinks this so strongly he is not able to explain to his wife, but on the day of the journey from Aylsham, via Norwich to Thetford, it is fair to say no one has ever travelled more hopefully.

THREE

Education
Aylesbury and the Isle of Wight, England

1837

Dairy Farm Cottage
Shepherd Lane
Aylsham

My dear Eliza

I know you will hate us, but it really is for the best. It is very fortunate that we have a kind benefactor who has taken an interest in your education and is paying all the fees for your tuition and boarding. It is something your poor, dear parents simply could not afford to do. As you well know, there are few such schools for girls and this is a rare opportunity. I hope that you will learn a great deal at Carisbrooke. Please work hard at your lessons and do your best. I hope that one day you will be able to see the value of what has been provided and will be grateful.

Mama

Carisbrooke School
Isle of Wight

Dearest Mama
You are quite right. I hate you and Papa more than you can possibly imagine. Please don't think that I will ever be grateful. The whole place is beastly. I will probably die of pneumonia and you will be to blame.
Eliza

∾

Tom Olliver and Jem Mason meet at the bottom of a ditch. Not a ditch by the edge of a field, that is, but the ditch in front of a steeplechase fence. It is at the Aylesbury racecourse, a bright May afternoon, with skylarks spiralling into the air across the water meadows and a buzzing crowd up from London on the hillside. They are both riding novice horses in the last race and they take off a whole stride too soon, coming to the third last fence and fairly whack the boards on the way up. They twist in the air, deposit both riders in the ditch, come down the other side and gallop off. Jem, seeing Tom is unconscious, drags him sideways off the track. Allen McDonough, following on a good twenty lengths away, matches their fall, only, this time, his horse lands in the ditch where Tom had lain and catapults him right over the top of the fence, to land about six yards down in the mud. Will Pope follows him at a similar distance on old Madgwick's bay gelding, jumps ditch, horse and McDonough and canters in to win by a distance from only one other finisher. Tom comes to his senses a few minutes later, with the metallic taste of blood in his mouth and his head pounding like a farrier's hammer.

Tom always says that Jem saved his life, because when half a ton of horse lands on you at full pelt, there is usually only one result. Jem makes light of it.

'You'd have done the same for me, Tom,' he says. 'We are learning our trade. You have to know how to fall, to know how to win.'

⌒

While young Tom Olliver and Jem Mason make their way in horse racing in England and worry about where their next winners will come from, there are weightier matters concerning the politicians of Britain and Europe. In Britain, Queen Victoria accedes to the throne on the death of William IV. Victoria is just eighteen and there are doubts that she will be up to the task. There are those who think that the monarchy itself is under threat. In France, King Louis Philippe is just about holding the monarchy in place. The July Revolution of 1830 gives France its "King of the French", but after a brief honeymoon period the French become rather lukewarm about his reign. As usually happens in France, apathy eventually gives way to outright dissatisfaction and Louis Philippe survives several assassination attempts.

Waiting in the wings is twenty-nine-year-old Prince Louis Napoleon, son of the former King of Holland and nephew of Emperor Napoleon Bonaparte. The King of the French doesn't take the Prince very seriously. The year before, Prince Louis arrived in Strasbourg with a contingent of armed supporters. He expected to be carried on a wave of public support, all the way to Paris. Unfortunately for him, the great French public seemed unaware of their role in this popular revolution and the Prince and his conspirators were arrested and exiled.

The British Government takes a keen interest in events across the English Channel. It is twenty-two years since the British and their allies finally defeated Napoleon Bonaparte and banished him to Saint Helena. Relations between Britain and France have been uneasy ever since. Lord Palmerston, the foreign secretary, receives the news of Louis Napoleon calmly and discusses it with the home secretary, Lord Russell.

'It was a shot across the bows. No lasting damage is done. The King has given Louis a slap on the wrist and sent him to America. I think he will regret his leniency. The young pretender will learn from this, no doubt.'

∽

On the Isle of Wight, Elizabeth Ann Harryet's residence at Carisbrooke School, "dedicated to the refinement of gentlewomen", is proving a challenge to everyone. The school is an imposing, mainly limestone set of buildings with sandstone ornamentation. Rumoured to have been an old military hospital but derelict for many years before the present owners embarked on their project, it marks a new development in education and something of an experiment, based on the principles of Mr Pemberton's Gough House establishment in London – an attempt to put girls on an equal academic and social footing with boys and a response to the demand from wealthy, military and diplomatic parents, serving the British Empire overseas, to have their daughters, as well as their sons, educated in England. The buildings have an austere presence and this is reflected in the disciplinarian tone set by the principal, Mr Ridley, a former military man himself. Eliza's end of term report from the deputy principal, Mr Dalziel, to Mr Ridley, marked For Your Eyes Only, reads thus:

Sir

Miss Harryet has fully lived up to her reputation as "difficult". While we pride ourselves on our ability to deal with girls of all types of character, this young lady is of a different order altogether. She has been in detention more times than any of the other girls in her year put together. On the academic front, she has managed to fail all of her exams, in two cases omitting to write a single word on the answer sheet. I think if we continue with her, we will have to go back to basics. She seems rather unclear about the essential difference between right and wrong.

While there are some positives, they have unfortunately been coupled, in every case, by an equal and opposite negative facet.

Even her sternest critics on the staff agree that she is possessed of an extraordinary energy. One might say she is boisterous, but I think the adjective does not quite convey her behaviour accurately enough. Nevertheless, if it could be bottled and channelled into her studies, it would give us some hope for the future. She is intelligent – there is no question about that – but whether we will ever be able to persuade her to match her ability with discipline and application is a moot point.

She has a great gift for mimicry. Although this can, on occasion, be tolerably amusing, it also has a rather cruel side to it and such is the effect on some of her fellow pupils, not to mention members of staff, that we have had to place a ban on this activity, although this is proving quite difficult to police. Miss Harryet's uncanny impersonation of Mr Rogers was attributed by her to a "very bad touch of tonsillitis".

She can, when the mood takes her, be quite engaging, but it must be admitted that this mood comes upon her infrequently. She seems to have made few friends, although she is on good terms with Miss Melliora Findon and Miss Lavinia Lampard. Unfortunately, their own record of bad behaviour, though not in the same league as Miss Harryet, means we have had to separate them. The fire in their dormitory may well have been an accident, but it is not a risk we can take.

She has a tremendous talent as a horse rider; however, we have also had to curtail this activity. While she is the only one to have mastered some of the more complex equitation techniques taught by Monsieur Macaire, her habit of jumping out of the ménage and galloping off round the grounds at the end of her lessons has had disastrous consequences. Once she rides our horses, none of the other girls can hold them, even in a gag bit. Poor Miss Strabally was run away with so badly that she was found in a ditch six miles away in Newbridge. The horse was found swimming off Yarmouth towards the mainland and had to be recovered by the lifeboat – put out from Cowes, as the Yarmouth boat was already in service.

You have asked me to consider whether we can, in the interests of retaining our staff and our other pupils, continue to persevere with Miss Harryet. While all the evidence points against it, I am inclined to see if we can make some progress over the summer break and look again at the situation at the beginning of next term. I am suggesting, therefore, that we do not send her home for the summer, but keep her here under my supervision and put together a programme aimed specifically at her.

I am sure the Harryets will readily accept this idea and, provided her benefactor, the Duke, is prepared to meet the additional costs, I think it is worth trying. We have never failed with a pupil yet in our short history and I don't want to give up on our record and reputation.

Dalziel

While this document is under consideration on the principal's desk, Eliza takes matters into her own hands. She decides that Carisbrooke School is not for her.

There is a full moon and the pale shapes of two barn owls can be seen hunting up and down the hedgerows when Eliza emerges from the shadows of the stables behind the school buildings. It is just before the church bells chime six o'clock. She knows that the dairy cart will come by promptly. It always does. The carter picks up at the dairy farms at Brook, Limerstone and Bowcombe and comes past Carisbrooke each morning. He drops off the school delivery, then carries on to meet the boat to Portsmouth at Ryde. There has been no rain for weeks and the ground is baked hard. Eliza can see dust swirling in the distance to the south, long before the cart rumbles into the courtyard. When Jenkins arrives, he finds Eliza sitting beside the mounting block. She has raided the school dressing-up box and is reprising her "mystery boy" appearance.

'Good morning, sir,' she says. 'I walked up from Newport. Mr Trinder says I'm to come on with you.'

'Where would that be to then?'

'I'm to be cooper's boy at Trinder's place at Fishbourne.'

'No one's told me nothing about it. Bessie's got enough to pull.'

Eliza conjures up tears. 'Begging your pardon, sir, but if I don't get this job, my poor, dear parents and my six little sisters won't eat.'

Jenkins pushes his hat back on his head and rubs his chin. Eliza senses he is weakening.

'We buried Lottie in the churchyard only last week. It was the starvation that finished her off,' she adds.

He jerks his head towards the cart and she needs no further sign. Soon, they are jolting their way along the track eastwards, Jenkins clicking his teeth to move Bessie on a pace and Eliza gazing backwards to the school for a few moments, then closing her eyes and settling down to dream of freedom.

Meanwhile, a breathless Francie Strabally rushes around the school in search of Mr Dalziel. Eventually, she tracks him down in the senior staff breakfast room.

'What is the matter, child?' he asks.

'Please, sir, Eliza Harryet's gone with the milk churns.'

'Gone where?'

'Please, sir, I don't know, but I saw her.'

'How long ago was this?'

'Not more than twenty minutes, sir.'

'Very good. Thank you for letting me know. Leave it with me.'

Eliza makes it all the way to Fishbourne, where the carter drops her off at Trinder's. As soon as he is out of sight, on his way to Ryde, she makes for the harbour. As she rounds the corner onto the quayside, Mr Dalziel, whose part-thoroughbred pony has managed the direct trip rather more quickly than Bessie's indirect route, waits in his phaeton.

'Very cleverly done,' he says. 'Now, I think you had better come back with me, don't you?'

The next morning, Eliza meets the principal in his office. The room is spartan, to say the least. Ridley sits at a large, padded leather chair, his ample black gown concealing any physical shape. His hands are spread wide apart, with his fingers resting on the edge of the broad desktop, empty save a single document, a blotter, an inkwell and a pen. He is a balding man with an elaborate moustache curled at the ends. A facial tick at the corner of his mouth gives the moustache the impression of a small furry animal quivering under his nose. Eliza wants to giggle, but even she recognises that sometimes it is better to stay quiet.

'Miss Harryet, this will not be tolerated,' he says. 'You have been given an opportunity to make something of yourself. Please don't waste it. We are giving you one last chance.'

FOUR
No Finer Sight
Towcester, London and Bedford, England
1838

When Tom Olliver sees Elizabeth Ann Harryet again, the transformation takes him aback. Apart from her riding skills and her rudeness, she left Tom with the impression of a waif-like, whey-faced urchin the last time they met. Tom is back hunting with the Grafton after the summer break and hounds meet at Wakefield Lodge. He is talking to George Carter, the huntsman, as staff from the house cautiously make their way between the riders, proffering glasses of sherry from silver trays. A mist hangs in the rides and down the long drive from the gatehouse, turning in off the Paulerspury lane. A thin sun tries to get through and the whole scene has a strange, ghostly quality about it.

Tom notices three shapes moving towards the field, down the mist-shrouded drive. They start off as little more than dots in the distance, but gradually the dots turn into tall, black smudges. Soon, he can make out horses and riders and as they come closer he sees that the shapes are ladies, riding side-saddle on three very handsome bay hunters. As they draw near, the throng of chit and chatter stops abruptly, and heads turn to view the new arrivals. It is a most arresting image. There can be no finer sight than three elegant ladies, sporting silk top hats and black veils and sitting ramrod-straight on mahogany-polished, thoroughbred horses. One lady, in particular, seems vaguely familiar to Tom. They ride straight up to the Duke of Grafton, seated in his carriage, dip their heads and draw their hunting crops by their sides in a most pleasing greeting.

'Good morning, Master,' they say, in unison.

'A pleasure to be with you today,' says one.

'The pleasure is mine entirely,' says the Duke.

The Duke has not only forgiven Eliza for her earlier misdemeanours; she is positively feted by him and Tom discovers, as the morning progresses, that Eliza and her two friends are staying with the Duke as his guests and are mounted on hunters from his own stable. Clearly, Eliza's social ascendance is progressing well and Tom is anxious to find out what else has happened to her since their first brief meeting. It is not until they stop at Easton Neston, after a skip across the paddocks at Plum Park, that he has a chance to speak to her. He moves in beside her and repeats the elaborate cap doffing and bowing greeting with which he first introduced himself two years earlier.

'Tom Olliver. At your service,' he says, grinning.

'Yes, of course, Tom. How lovely to see you again.'

Pleasantries are exchanged with Eliza's associates: Melliora Findon and Lavinia Lampard. When the field moves off, Tom and Eliza fall to riding upsides for the rest of the morning, conversing like old friends. She explains that her earlier adventure has not gone unpunished by her father and that she has endured almost two years at a mercilessly strict boarding school, with extra History, Latin and French lessons from a private tutor at evenings and weekends, as well as a disciplined fitness regime and no opportunity to ride. It has been torture.

It has not, however, been without effect. The new Eliza is all grace and poise. In place of the bumptious arrogance of her earlier incarnation, here is a demure young lady with impeccable manners and the most disarming and captivating smile. Piercing brown eyes shine through her veil. Tom is quite overwhelmed by her and begins to imagine their life together. It is a habit that sometimes afflicts a young man who is besotted by a becoming young woman, and he finds himself in exactly that position.

'What will you do with all this education?' he asks.

'I shall be an actress. My mind is set on it.'

That day, the Duke arranges a stop for second horses at half past two and instructs Carter to make his way back to Wakefield for tea at six o'clock. Foxes are in good supply and he wants to put on a show for his attractive young guests. The fourth Duke, George Henry Fitzroy, is well in his seventies now and in the final years of his mastership. His son, Henry Fitzroy, is being groomed to take over the reins when the time comes. Father and son could not be more different: the old Duke witty, outgoing and charming; his heir shy, laconic and diffident. These differences are never more evident than in their dress sense: the Duke stylishly attired, typically in a top hat, red frock coat and neatly strapped trousers; his son happier in a Norfolk jacket, breeches and top boots.

A new rider appears at second horses: Jem Mason, Tom's friend and colleague, who is schooling some horses locally that morning. He borrows a mount to hack on to intercept the field at change of horses and to enjoy the afternoon's sport.

The sun has burned through by this time and the morning riders wait for those with fresh horses to join in. Hounds are scampering about on imaginary trails, nose to the ground. Other hounds are rolling on their backs, feet in the air, enjoying the warmth of the autumn sun.

The two jockeys draw alongside each other. Jem looks as immaculate as ever. He is always fitted out in the finest that Jermyn Street can supply and, from the highly polished tan-topped boots to the silver-handled hunting crop, he looks quite the gentleman. He has the blackest head of hair, with thick curls, just visible beneath his hunting cap and he affects long, bushy sideburns, as is the fashion these days.

'Are you going to introduce us?' says Jem to Tom, looking towards Eliza.

Tom is sure he sees a tangible spark fly between them. His visions of romance are snuffed out rather harshly, with Jem and Eliza inseparable for the rest of the afternoon. Everyone trails in their wake, as they both display the easy elegance that only the most naturally talented riders possess – as if horse and rider are one flowing entity. Wherever Carter goes, however severe the fences, Jem and Eliza can be seen close behind, topping the hedges like birds.

At the hunting tea laid on by the Duke, talk is of little else than the beautiful Elizabeth Ann Harryet and the dashing Jem Mason. As the assembled riders take their places at the tables, Tom looks around the room. There are two notable absentees. Tom shrugs. Even so, he can't quite reconcile why he wakes that night with an image of Eliza in his mind and struggles to get back to sleep.

∽

At around the same time, Prince Louis Napoleon arrives in London. He stays at Fenton's Hotel in St James's Street, but also takes up residence in rented rooms in Leamington Spa. He ferries between the two, seeking influence where he can. He has four associates with him: Jean Mocquard, Jean-Gilbert Fialin, Colonel Vaudrey and Dr Conneau, his physician, along with three servants and several horses. He is intent on making friends in England, preferably in high places. Since he already has one failed coup to his name, he is reluctant to risk another – at least until he can be sure of success. He sees himself as the natural heir to his uncle: Napoleon Bonaparte, Emperor Napoleon. He has an unshakeable belief that France awaits his triumphant return. It is just a matter of timing, political support and finance.

Jean Mocquard is his private secretary and he goes everywhere with him. He has sharp features, a long aquiline nose, thin lips, bushy eyebrows and a high forehead under wispy, unkempt hair, giving him the look of a distracted professor. He is as fluent in English as in French. He has as many friends in London as in Paris. In short, he is a good man to know.

Jean-Gilbert Fialin, who prefers to be called Comte de Persigny even though no one has given him the title, is a former cavalry officer and, alongside Vaudrey, Louis Napoleon's advisor on political strategy and military matters. If Mocquard is the brains, Fialin is the enforcer. He has a full moustache and thinning hair, combed over to the left. Beside Mocquard, he is a slight figure, with darting eyes. He is not such a good man to know.

Between them, they arrange meetings with men they deem to be the politicians of the future. Louis meets Benjamin Disraeli, new MP and bright young man of the Conservative Party. He meets Viscount Fitzharris, another prominent young Conservative and son of Lord Malmesbury. He meets Edward Bulwer-Lytton, author and MP for Lincoln. The social calendar is arranged by Lady Blessington and Count D'Orsay, who seem to have the requisite access to the upper echelons of the aristocracy and to the more pleasurable diversions of London society. Lady Margaret Blessington married into her title and is regarded as not quite "the right sort" in some circles, but what she lacks in breeding she makes up for in energy and her list of contacts cannot be bettered. Count D'Orsay is quite the man about town and knows everyone.

Louis expresses satisfaction with the friends he is making and his excursions to London are made more permanent by taking the lease on a house in Carlton Gardens. He is convinced that Number One Carlton Gardens will advance his case in England and, ultimately, France. The Grecian

Doric columns, balustraded parapets and stuccoed façade provide the grandeur appropriate to his ambitions. On a more pragmatic level, the proximity to The Mall, St James, Haymarket and the parks of St James, Green Park and Kensington Gardens gives him access to his primary interests, namely: ostentatious promenading, conspicuous wining and dining, carousing with the leading actresses of the day and riding out with the rich and famous.

∽

The present British Government cannot make its mind up about France. This may, in part, be due to the fact that Lord Palmerston, the foreign secretary, is rather disinclined to express an opinion about the French in case they prove him wrong within the day and, also, that Lord Melbourne, prime minister but in the twilight of his career, is reluctant to make a decision about anything. King Louis Philippe believes himself to be on good terms with them both and is confident that Britain will not want a French monarchy challenged, with Britain's own young Queen's position so fragile. Things can change quickly in politics, though, as he well knows.

∽

Louis Napoleon is not the only arrival in London. In October, Elizabeth Ann Harryet leaves her parents' home in Norfolk. She packs a bag and a few possessions, and stays with her friend Lavinia Lampard in Kensington. Squire Harryet tells his daughter he will disinherit her if she doesn't return home immediately. 'You won't get a penny,' he says. Given his circumstances and the rate at which he is spending money, this seems to Eliza a rather hollow threat. She pays her way by working as an usher in the theatres around Shaftesbury Avenue. An acting career is her only aim. She secures her first part in James Sheridan Knowles's play, *The Love Chase*, at the Haymarket Theatre. She plays Constance, daughter to Sir William Fondlove. She manages to pester the stage manager to let her understudy the part of Lydia, lady's maid to Widow Green, but when the actress who is to play Constance is taken ill and her understudy cannot be located, Eliza steps forward. She knows the part well.

'I know all the parts,' she says.

It is not the ideal role for her. She is too young for Constance. However, she brings an unexpected vibrancy and guile to the role and draws excellent reviews. The play's run is extended and the "house full" signs go up. Offers of more parts come in. The producer finds her an agent: Donald Treves. Everything moves quickly.

'We shall have to find a stage name for you,' says Treves. 'Elizabeth Harryet Howard, perhaps. Even better, what about Harriet Howard? It has a ring to it, does it not? Wonderfully alliterative. And, of course, Howard is so aristocratic. It will do no harm.'

'Are you sure?'

'Trust me. You will not go wrong. We'll leave it until the end of the run here. Next year will see a new actress take London by storm.'

∽

Tom Olliver meets Jem Mason one day at Bedford. They walk the new layout of the steeplechase course. They come to two options: a tall, black, five-bar gate and a bullfinch hedge, set about with thorns. Tom asks Jem whether he will have the gate or the hedge.

'I'll be hanged if I'm going to scratch my face, Tom. I'm going to the opera tonight with Eliza. I shall have the gate, forty miles an hour and defy any man in England to follow me,' he says. He is as good as his word.

After the racing, they talk. They are both young jockeys making their way in a competitive world.

'I've moved up to town,' Jem says. 'Contacts is what racing is all about now.'

'I don't suppose Eliza has anything to do with it?'

'That's a bonus. I'm working on it. As you well know, I'm not the only one showing an interest.'

'I thought you liked to play the field. No ties.'

'She's worth more than all the others put together. There's no one like her.'

◌⁄◌

One evening, late in December, Louis Napoleon visits the theatre at Haymarket. He is quite captivated by one of the actresses he sees. His eyes are fixed on her throughout the performance. He looks through the programme for a name: Elizabeth Harryet.

'Have that girl sent to my rooms,' he whispers to Fialin at the end of the final act. He is used to getting his way. Fialin is usually very persuasive.

FIVE
Perfect Match
London and Liverpool, England
1839

London Weekly Chronicle,
Saturday 23rd February 1839

JULIET ENTRANCES

This week, we were fortunate enough to see the arrival of a startling new talent on the London stage in Mr Macready's new production of William Shakespeare's Romeo and Juliet, at the Sadler's Wells Theatre, which commanded an exceedingly large audience.

Miss Harriet Howard shone as Juliet and we forecast an illustrious future ahead of her. Seldom have we seen such a combination of vivacity and grace. She is young and charming and altogether presents a most elegant appearance. She was entirely believable as the innocent, star-struck lover of Romeo, but it was the poise and style of the performance that so captivated the audience. The play was well performed throughout and we must pick out for special mention Mr Samuel Phelps, for his sympathetic and finely executed portrayal of Romeo, and Mr Robert

Walden, for a flamboyant interpretation of Mercutio. In addition, we should say that we were much pleased with the simple and judicious acting of Miss Kitty Hopkins as Nurse. Similarly, Mr James Roper, as Tybalt, certainly gained a laurel, to which we hope he will have many additions.

The theatre has recently undergone an extensive renovation and this new production of the play was beautifully mounted, having had the advantage, accordingly, of new scenery and decoration.

At the end of the play, the crowd made their affection known and the whole cast was warmly applauded by a house equally overflowing in enthusiasm and numbers. Miss Howard excited extraordinary adulation and it was five curtain calls before her admirers would let her go. Even then, the cheers rang on into the night. If you can find the means to obtain a ticket, we urge you to go and see this wonderful play, performed with much effect, for yourself. It is indubitably destined to be a decided, indeed a remarkable, success.

∽

Liverpool Chronicle, Wednesday 27th February 1839

GRAND LIVERPOOL STEEPLECHASE

Yesterday saw the running of the Grand Liverpool Steeplechase and what a fine race it turned out to be. A sweepstake of twenty sovereigns each, five sovereigns forfeit and one hundred sovereigns added, for gentleman *riders, each to carry twelve stone over four miles and a few hundred yards of the new Aintree racecourse, it lays claim to being the most prestigious steeplechase of the racing calendar.*

The race was started promptly at three o'clock. All the horses ran away quickly, with Conrad ridden by Captain Becher and Daxon ridden by Mr Ferguson leading the way. The race went on through fields, where the horses encountered deep ditches and high banks. More imposing fences followed and no problems were seen until a rough, high, jagged fence, coupled with a six-foot wide brook, claimed the first victim. Captain Becher was first at the fence, but his horse Conrad hit the top and rolled over into the brook, throwing his rider off. Lottery and Mr Mason cleared the fence along with Seventy Four, ridden by Mr Olliver and The Nun, ridden by Mr Allen McDonough and these three led the field off into the country.

Captain Becher remounted and set off again after the main group. Soon, they were at a high hedge bank with rails and another water ditch, which was six feet lower than the take off. By this point, Captain Becher was back at the head of the field. The captain was again to be unlucky, when Conrad crashed through the fence, throwing him into the ditch and then gave him the indignity of rolling over him and running away. Rust and Mr William McDonough was next at the obstacle and he also fell but remounted.

The race continued and the next obstacle to be jumped was a fence where the landing side was higher by four feet in some places, but this did not catch out so many. The race continued on with a series of easier fences and back to the straight towards the wall. At this obstacle, Barkston and Mr Wilmot was in front, but simply refused to jump at the first attempt and was passed by Lottery, who jumped the wall fluently, as did The Nun and Paulina, with Mr Martin. Barkston was given a second chance and this time cleared the fence from a standstill. Out on the second circuit, the remaining runners negotiated the course without further major incident, although some of the stragglers fell or were unseated.

As the leading horses turned into the home straight, there was a line of hurdles to be jumped before the run in and these were crossed with ease. Lottery, who was still full of running, won the race by three lengths from Seventy Four, who was three lengths in front of Paulina and True Blue. This was a very encouraging success for owner Mr John Elmore and trainer Mr George Dockeray from Epsom. We also saw the emergence of young James (Jem) Mason, as a jockey of the first rank.

❦

'I'll have you back in London by lunchtime tomorrow, Jem. Are you game?' says Tom Olliver. 'We catch the last train from Liverpool to Manchester, change trains at Newton Junction onto the Grand Junction Railway and hitch the overnight mail train to Birmingham. I'll leave you there at Curzon Street. I'm riding at Stratford. You walk across the platform and jump on the train into Euston, arriving early afternoon.'

'I can barely make sense of it. Will it work?'

'Nothing ventured...'

∽

The green and gold liveried steam engine of the London and Birmingham railway, pulling twenty carriages, wheezes into Euston at exactly thirty-two minutes past one in the afternoon. Jem is jolted awake. He has been dozing and dreaming all the way down from Birmingham, with a brief stop to change engines at Wolverton, and he feels remarkably refreshed after all the travelling. Tom was as good as his word and the afternoon awaits. London is warm in the spring sun and Jem decides a stroll is in order to shake off the stiffness of the journey. He looks over his shoulder at the Grand Arch as he walks into Drummond Street and sees two doxies across the road, eying him up and down and whispering to each other. The bolder of the two approaches him.

'First of the day to the fine sporting gentleman. No charge for you, my lovely. No funny business, mind.' she says, her eyes darting towards the two race whips sticking out of the end of Jem's bag.

'That's very kind of you, but I've other plans today.'

'There's two of us, if you like,' she says, gesturing to her friend. 'What do you say?'

'I say take the afternoon off and buy yourselves some lunch on me.' He tosses her a coin, winks at them both and walks on.

He leaves Drummond Street, crosses Euston Road and

strides along Warren Street. The street vendors call out to him and he stops to talk to some of the hansom cab drivers. Jem is well known about town and word has already reached London about the previous day's success. He turns into Cleveland Street and then south into Great Titchfield Street. His pace quickens and by the time he reaches Oxford Street, he is running.

When he enters the door at number 106, Eliza has heard the key in the lock. She leaps at him and tears at his clothes. They don't reach the bedchamber. They lie together for a long time, their limbs entangled. When he wakes, he nuzzles at her neck and strokes her stomach, but she pulls away. There is a flounce and a furrowed brow, which tells him that something is brewing. She wraps a blanket around herself and pulls her knees up to her chest.

'We are alright together, you and me, Jem? Aren't we?' she begins.

'Of course we are. Why do you ask?'

'I worry that this won't last. We have everything. We are both doing well.'

'Lucky us.'

'You always make a joke of things, Jem. As if you can't be serious. You won't talk about feelings, but it's important to me. I always tell the truth, I…'

'Is that because it's easier to remember?'

'There you are, doing it again. I want to know where we are; how you feel about me.'

'We are together; we are doing well, as you say. Life is good. You and I are different. I don't want to narrate my life, I just want to live it. You are an actress. A good one. You live your life in words. I live in action. I'm only as good as my last ride. Every ride is a risk.'

'We are not so different. I am only as good as my last performance. There are other actresses. I am talking about commitment. Action and words, if you like. Am I another affair, like all the other girls, or is this something more substantial? I need to know.'

'I don't know how to answer you. We are both young. You, especially. How can you talk about commitment? You hardly know yourself.'

'If there is one person I know, it is myself. I know what I want. My only problem is finding out whether you want the same.'

'Alright, let's talk about it. Tell me exactly what you want. Everything. Then, I'll tell you what I want. And I'll tell the truth. I won't make jokes. But then what? What will we have achieved? It's just dreams. No one knows what is round the corner. I might break my neck. You might get stage fright or forget your lines.'

'How did you get to where you are now, Jem?'

'What do you mean?'

'I mean, how did you become the best young jockey riding today? Better than McDonough. Better than Pope. Some say you will be the best of all. Better even than Tom Olliver. Did that just happen? Was it just luck? I'll tell you, Jem. It happened because at some point, you said: "I want to be the best." Maybe you didn't say it out loud. Maybe you just thought it in your head. But, at some point, you had that ambition. It's not just dreams. It's the way we start to achieve things.'

'You have thought this through, haven't you? But what if I had no talent? Could I still be the best?'

'Of course not. But it distinguishes you. There are plenty with talent, but you have something extra. It's ambition that counts. I see it everywhere. I don't want to live in someone else's dream. I want to live in mine. And yours. I want us to build a dream together and live in it together. Is that hard to understand? That is what I mean when I talk about commitment. I mean describing how we want things to be, reaching an agreement and going after it.'

'Alright. You first.'

She gathers herself and stands up, as if she has stepped forward, centre stage, to deliver a soliloquy.

'I want to be independent. I want to be my own woman. I want to be the best actress on the London stage. I want people to say, "There goes Harriet Howard. She is a wonderful actress." I want to have enough money to live a comfortable life. I want to look after my parents and make them proud of me. I want to share my life with someone who I love and admire. One day, I want to have children. I want Jem Mason.'

'By the Lord, Eliza. You make me ashamed. From now on, we'll do it together. You and me. Jem and Eliza. Eliza and Jem.'

'Promise?'

'Promise.'

'Now you.'

'Now me?'

'What do you really want?'

He considers his reply. He lights up a cigar. 'I never want anyone to look down on me. I learned that from my father. He is the best horse dealer in the country. He finds the best horses. If a horse doesn't suit, he takes it back for another one. If a horse is found to have a problem, he gives the money back. He is honest. He can be trusted. He is a fine man; the best of men. But people still talk down to him. He is a tradesman, a dealer. They are gentlemen, toffs. I won't ever have that. I will be the equal of any man alive. Do you understand that?'

'I do. Is there any room in that world for an accomplice? Someone who feels the same?'

SIX

In the Stars
London and Gravesend, England
Boulogne and Ham, France
1840

Dairy Farm Cottage
Shepherd Lane
Aylsham

My dear Eliza

It is all very well being an actress, but of course no good will come of it. As your father says, actresses are never more than two steps from the gutter. As for the rumours we hear about you and Jem Mason, it shocks me to think you would bring such shame on your poor dear parents in this way. It really is making your father most unwell with the worry of it all. The best thing would be for you to come home and settle down among your own kind, rather than putting on fancy London airs.

There are many suitable young farmers here in Norfolk and I'm sure a match could still be made for you, despite the sinful acts you are involving yourself in. We are a long way from town here and news travels slowly. Our new neighbours, the Waleses, have two fine sons and although they would not be the brightest apples on the tree they will inherit good acreage and one of them would probably be grateful to have a girl with your looks, even with your reputation.

By the by, this silly nonsense about you changing your name is most upsetting, but I can see, in some ways, it is probably for the best if you are set on living a life of debauchery.

Please let us know your intentions.

Mama

༄

106 Oxford Street
London

Dearest Mama

Thank you very much for your letter. I am so sorry to hear about dear Papa. I hope you won't disown me. I am working hard to make a success of my acting and I want to make you proud of me. I'm determined to follow my dreams, here in London. I have an agent now and he is helping me get the right parts. I hope you will come up to town and see me on the stage one day soon.

Please don't fret about Jem Mason. He is the best of men and very ill treated by the newspapers, who thrive on made-up stories.

God bless you.
Your loving daughter.
Eliza

∝

Harriet Howard's star is in the ascendant. She determines that she will be a serious, dramatic actress. Her agent sends a selection of her reviews to London theatre producers and directors. Within days, the offers come in. If the play is written by William Shakespeare, she takes it. Her work rate astonishes those around her. She throws herself into every part and the results speak for themselves. Her Miranda is judged "luminescent", her Desdemona "spine-tingling" and her Cleopatra "captivating". Treves makes sure it is her name at the top of the bill postings and that she is the best-paid member of the cast.

'After all,' he says, 'she is the one they are coming to see.'

∝

Harriet's success is matched by Jem Mason, who rides no end of winners. He and Tom Olliver are among the first of the group called "professional" riders. They earn their living riding horses. Up until the beginning of the century, all jockeys riding in steeplechases are gentleman-riders – that is, they are riding their own or their family's horses. But the gamblers won't wear incompetent amateurs. It isn't sufficient to be a gentleman. The gentleman must ride well, too. It is soon realised, of course, that it is easier to turn a great rider into a gentleman than it is to turn a gentleman into a great rider. As one sage commentator puts it, "You can't put in what God's left out."

"Get Mason" is the familiar shout, when owners are discussing who should ride their horses.

Owners and gamblers alike come to know that not all of the jockeys are trying to win all of the time. There is as much money made stopping horses as winning races, as the stakes in gambling get higher and higher. Jem Mason won't ever do that.

'Get someone else if you want the brakes on,' he tells them.

He has the gift of it on a horse, there's no doubt. When he wins the St Albans Chase on The Poet, few observers think anyone else could have won on him. The Poet is a difficult horse and a lary jumper, but Jem rides him on a nice long rein and has him relaxed and in a rhythm. That is the quality that sets him apart. There is never any fuss or effort with him. He just knows the right thing to do and gets on with it. Less is more.

There is always a unique look about him. He is a reed of a man and he wears a frock coat as elegantly as any dandy. He spares no expense with his tailor and his boot maker. He can often be found at the end of a day's racing with a cheroot in one hand and a glass of champagne in the other, smiling that crooked smile of his.

'If you walk like a gentleman, look like a gentleman and talk like a gentleman, then you are a gentleman,' he says.

It is almost inevitable that Jem's friend, Tom Olliver, and Harriet's friend, Lavinia Lampard, find themselves often in each other's company. A strong bond forms between them and, like their mutual friends, they draw back from the easy relationships to which they are accustomed in favour of a more permanent arrangement. Equally inevitably, they talk about Jem and Harriet and swap stories about their friends' adventures. There is no doubt that the relationship between Jem and Harriet has been what might be styled "tempestuous" in the popular novels of the day, but Lavinia detects a change.

'They seem to have settled down, don't you think?' she asks.

'I do,' says Tom. 'Jem is used to his freedom. It is in the nature of the jockey's existence to be away overnight often. There were opportunities. Sometimes he took them. All he wants to do now is get straight home after racing. And Harriet?'

'She was impetuous. If she thought Jem was misbehaving, she felt she had the right to even things up. She is calmer now – happier. There is a touching tenderness between them.'

✍

It is Harriet's character to be suspicious of their good fortune. She confesses her fears to Jem.

'I am nervous. Can our run continue?'

'I thought you had everything organised. Wasn't this in your plan? Why be nervous?'

'You are mocking me. I know we are here because we have worked hard for it. But I don't discount fate. Sometimes chance can cast a shadow.'

'Then why make plans at all? Do your best. Let fate take care of the result.'

'That is not enough for me. If I hadn't made the decisions I have made, I would not be here. I know I can make things happen. So can you. Don't deny it.'

'You can make some things happen. The rest is luck. If this wasn't so, there would be no need to be nervous. You must give me that.'

'No, not even that. My nervousness is not to do with luck. It is a fear of complacency: that we will ease off when we need to work harder.'

'All we can do is carry on as we are,' he says. 'Work hard. Practise our skills. Hone them. Our future is in the stars. No one knows what is in store.'

∽

Prince Louis Napoleon and Jean Mocquard return to London after a trip to Italy. They take up their accustomed residence at Carlton Gardens. There is the usual round of parties, theatre attendances and soirees. Count D'Orsay and Lady Blessington are only too happy to host and accompany their old friends. Louis has a new look about him: his countenance more glowing; his hair more vigorous and shining; his swagger more confident. A man whose time has come, perhaps. Underneath the veneer of a summer holiday, plans are afoot for the inevitable, victorious return to France. Lord Normanby, the home secretary, and Lord Palmerston, the foreign secretary, are fully aware of the scheme, though perhaps not the detail, and are happy, unofficially, of course, to give it their blessing. It is rather hard to imagine, however, that if key members of the British Government know what is going on, there is not comparable intelligence available across the English Channel.

Nevertheless, the plan goes ahead and on the appointed date in August assorted men in greatcoats, collars turned up, make their way to Gravesend. There is sometimes much in a name associated with an important event. The British still talk about someone "meeting their Waterloo", recalling Emperor Bonaparte's ignominious defeat. Gravesend hardly breeds confidence. Inauspiciously and unseasonably, it rains steadily through the night. A deluge becomes a torrent, as the downpour intensifies towards morning. Slowly, the clouds clear and, just before dawn, moonlight emerges and casts reflections in the deep puddles. As dawn breaks, a sliver of red sky bleeds across the horizon. As the early morning lightens, a zephyr wind gets up, filling the sails of the trawlers, putting out to sea. The pleasure steamer, the *Edinburgh Castle*, hoves into view. The captain, at this point, is still under the impression his vessel has been chartered for a group of tourists on a trip to Hamburg. She grumbles and thumps her way alongside the jetty, where the men assembled there begin boarding. The leaders are a random group of Louis Napoleon's confidantes, advisors and hangers-on. Notable among them are Dr Conneau, General Montholon, Colonel Parquin and Jean-Gilbert Fialin. Fifty men are recruited in total. They are a motley crew of Italian mercenaries, zealous Bonapartists and other sympathisers.

The ingenious plan is for them to land at Wimereux and make their way to the city of Boulogne and the barracks of the 42nd infantry regiment. Here, Lieutenant Aladenize, a long-time supporter of the cause, has arranged for the commander of the garrison, Captain Col-Puygelier, to be away for a day's duck shooting. The lieutenant will let the invading group into the barracks, by which time they will be dressed in 40th infantry regiment uniforms and be fully armed. The 42nd infantry regiment will immediately row in with the popular uprising and the garrisons from there to Paris will fall, like a set of dominos. The rest will be history.

All goes well for a while. The captain of the *Edinburgh Castle* readily accepts the generous additional payment for the rescheduled trip. The crossing is smooth. All the men get ashore without incident. Lieutenant Aladenize meets Louis Napoleon and his "troops" as planned and they make their way to the garrison, where the sentry opens the gates, as instructed by Aladenize. Fundamentally, however, the scheme is flawed and naive in the extreme. French agents track Louis Napoleon all the way from Carlton Gardens to Wimereux and alert Captain Col-Puygelier, who waits inside the garrison. He arrests the conspirators as soon as they walk through the gates and onto the barrack square.

Put on trial for treason, the men involved fear that the King is unlikely to be as generous with his response as he was following the earlier Strasbourg fiasco. They are right. When the Court of Peers announces their verdict, Louis Napoleon is sentenced to perpetual imprisonment at the Château de Ham fortress in northern France. The other ringleaders are sentenced to between five and twenty years. Fialin pleads illness and secures a sentence in a military hospital rather than a prison. Mocquard is the only one to escape completely, having been sent ahead to Paris, to await news of success.

ல

Lord Normanby and Lord Palmerston meet to discuss the news.

'Impetuous, wouldn't you agree?' says Normanby.

'Quite. He seems to have learned nothing from Strasbourg.'

'Strategy not his strong point?'

'Indeed. King Louis Philippe is hardly quaking in his buckled shoes. Louis Napoleon may be a Bonaparte, but he has all the hallmarks of a lunatic. A few years cooling his heels in prison will do him no harm at all.'

'I assume we are reconsidering our position?'

'For the time being, yes, but France cannot be assessed using logic. She has her own special music – even the French don't understand it, so we have little prospect. Yet we must take a position. Events so close to home cannot be left to chance.'

'It does rather upset our plans, though.'

'Let's keep things moving. It does no harm.'

ல

The prisoners take time to adjust to life at the Château de Ham prison. The château is a nondescript, rambling set of buildings, with no dominant style or architectural merit. When Louis Napoleon first sees it, he shudders visibly and has to lean on Dr Conneau's arm for support. It serves a dual purpose as infantry garrison and occasional prison for high-security "guests". As grim as it looks on the outside, it has a curious charm inside. The courtyard gardens in summer are fragrant with roses and alive with verdant climbers. Local villagers join soldiers and prisoners in maintaining the gardens and vegetable plots. It is said that Major Girardet, the garrison commander, turned down several promotions so that he can stay where he is.

On arrival, Dr Henri Conneau and General Montholon are assigned adjacent rooms to Louis Napoleon and a further room houses Louis's valet, Charles Thelin. Thelin is not charged following the failed Boulogne coup, but he is accommodated anyway. There is also a sitting room, fitted out with tables, chairs, lamps and clock, with a library, albeit very small, and a dining room. Coffee and croissants are served at half past eight in the morning, lunch at midday and dinner at six o'clock in the evening. The prison chef ensures that the men receive a strict diet of meat, chicken and green vegetables, with only very occasional variation and while there is always a soup or consommé to commence dinner and a cheese course and a choice of desserts to follow, Conneau thinks some of the cheeses are not always in the best condition. Burgundy or Bordeaux wine is provided, although Montholon is rather critical of the vintages.

During daylight hours, time is taken in the gardens if the weather is fine or in the sitting room, reading and debating. Evenings are spent in a game of contract whist or piquet. Mass is only allowed once a fortnight. Louis Napoleon finds the regime quite intolerable and writes a letter of complaint to the King. Major Girardet forgets, unaccountably, to send it on.

SEVEN
The Proposition
London, England
1841

London has a gloom over it and it has been like this for some weeks. It is late May, but the flowers in St James's Park are slow to bloom and there is a grey pallor on the lake. In Whitehall Place, carriages come and go, dropping off and collecting a steady stream of visitors. A man in a filthy greatcoat and a battered bowler hat scurries between the horses' hooves and does his best to scoop up the tide of horse droppings and urine in a wide shovel, before depositing the foul mixture onto a low cart. A woman walks by with her nose pushed into a handkerchief, her head pulled to one side. Later in the afternoon, the sky brightens and some thin shafts of sunlight slant between the tall buildings, fastening themselves to the stark stone walls, but a biting wind prevails. Poverty and wealth go hand-in-hand in this part of the city and the local ruffians follow the well-heeled gentlemen and their ladies at a discreet distance, looking for an easy opportunity to fall their way. Two peelers take a turn about the street, keeping an uneasy order in place, their hobnailed boots crunching gravel on the metalled pathway and echoing in the alleyways.

In Nicholas Sly's wood-panelled office, two people sit across from each other at a large, plain desk. There is a fire laid in the fire grate, but it has not been lit. The room is chilled. There has been a brief exchange of words. Sly looks at Harriet Howard over his half-moon glasses. He is a big man, thick-set and heavy-jowled. He is dressed all in black. His stomach protrudes and the thin, stockinged legs sticking out from his frock coat give him the appearance of a plump black cockerel.

'You're asking me to be a courtesan,' she says.

'I am asking you to be a patriot,' he says.

'You're asking me to spy for a secret government service?'

'Oh, Miss Howard, don't be so melodramatic. Her Majesty's Government does not have a secret service and it does not employ spies. We are asking you to place yourself in our care and to be available to entertain the company of certain distinguished gentlemen when we require it. Otherwise, you are free to proceed as you wish… but with certain restrictions, of course.'

'And what would these restrictions be?'

'So you are accepting our proposition and we are now discussing the arrangements. Is that correct, Harriet?'

'No, sir, I am not. You've apprehended me without warning and brought me here against my wishes. My answer is no. I would be grateful if you would allow me to leave. And you may not call me Harriet.'

'Ah, Miss Howard,' he says. He lets out a long sigh.

Minutes pass. He looks at her more closely. She is

young, slim and elegantly dressed. He is struck by her red hair, which hangs in ringlets and frames a pale face, with piercing brown eyes and high cheekbones. He notices that her features are not augmented with the powder and rouge that are the order of the day. He considers that she is not quite what he expected.

'I rather hoped all this would be unnecessary,' he says. 'It is most irregular that you need persuasion.'

'I have nothing further to say.'

He sits forward at his desk and rests his chin on his hands, which he has clasped together, as if in prayer. She looks towards the window and sits upright. There is a slight pout at her lips.

'I want you to think about this carefully,' he begins again. 'We have taken an interest in you for some time now. We know a great deal about your situation. You have received an excellent education, you are an accomplished horsewoman, you speak French tolerably well and I am told that men of a certain type find you attractive. The Duke of Grafton and Lord Normanby speak very highly of you. I rather hoped that you would wish to use your talents in the service of Queen and country. It is an honour to be asked.'

'I will not be at anyone's beck and call. I will not be bullied.'

'You will have a great deal of freedom – rather more than might be imagined. We can arrange somewhere superior to live. There will be a dress allowance. You will be able to attend all the balls one could wish for. Lady Blessington will look after you and introduce you properly into London society. It is a wonderful opportunity for a young lady in your position.'

'You know nothing about my "position" as you call it. I have a career as an actress. I am making my own way in life. I wish to make my own choices.'

'An actress, Miss Howard. Are we talking in euphemisms now?'

'Do not patronise me, sir. I have made my reputation through hard work.'

'Oh, my word. Reputation, is it? Hard work? I have no doubt your efforts are appreciated.'

'My answer has not changed.'

'You drive a hard bargain, Miss Howard. Time was when a young lady like you would be happy to join us. I always find it quite distasteful to talk about money, but you are rather forcing my hand on the matter. You will receive a generous personal allowance on top of the arrangements I have already explained. I cannot name a figure, but it will not be unacceptable, I believe.'

'I am not interested. I have nothing more to say.'

'Come, come. It is not as if I am asking you to do something you have not done before. We are simply improving the terms, so to speak.'

'Do not press me. You have my answer.'

'You are beginning to test my patience. We can, perhaps, see our way to the provision of a personal maid if that would help, but really we are reaching the end of our negotiation on the matter.'

Nicholas Sly's brow creases. He is accustomed to acceptance. He wonders where the young woman, little more than a girl, is finding the confidence to cross him like this.

'I am going to give you one more chance. There is nothing more on the table. If you resist our offer, you will not find us so convivial the next time.'

The light at the windows fades and a servant arrives with a taper to ignite the oil lamps. Sly holds up his hand, palm outwards, and the servant backs away through the doorway. He snaps a match into a sulphurous flame and lights one candle on the desk in front of him. He watches the candle sputter and smoke, as the tallow begins to burn off. He waits.

'I will not bow to threats,' she says.

'You and I are going to meet again and I will not be so conciliatory. You are a very foolish young lady. I see that you do not have the wit to understand what is being offered. I am very disappointed.'

'Perhaps I am not what you are looking for.'

'Do not test me. This is not a game you are playing. There are consequences.'

'Then I shall live with them.'

She tosses her head and flicks her hair to the side. She can see that the man in front of her is rattled and she senses she has the upper hand. She looks him straight in the eyes.

'I am finding this tiresome. Please call your man and have him arrange a cab for me. I have other appointments.'

'You do not dictate terms to me. You come here with your airs and graces, and you tell me what you will and will not have. Well, I tell you, you have picked a fight that will end badly. Despite your privileges, as we see you now, you are little more than a gutter harlot.'

She rises, walks the two paces between them and slaps his face with all her strength. He stands, then staggers back, one side of his face reddened, but he recovers quickly. He moves around the desk and pushes her backwards into her chair. He grabs one of her arms and forces it behind her. With his other hand, he grasps her face between his thumb and forefinger and jerks her head back. He forces his knee between her legs and leans into her, pinning her into the chair with his weight. He brings his face close to hers. He is salivating as he speaks.

'I could do anything with you. Anything. Do you understand that?' he shouts. 'No one would lift a finger to help and no one would believe you.'

Her body is rigid and she cannot breathe. He steps away from her.

'I will be back,' he says. 'It may not be next week or even next month. But I will be back, be in no doubt of it. Never imagine that your life will be as it was. I will make sure of that. You will live to regret your pride.'

He regains his composure. He rings a bell, turns on his heels and walks out of the room. The oak door slams shut behind him.

✑

She is on the street, gulping air into her lungs. The encounter has shaken her, but she senses her heart pumping and she feels oddly elated. She tastes blood in her mouth as she makes her way to Trafalgar Square. She decides that she needs to walk. She travels along Cockspur Street and crosses into Haymarket. Theatre crowds are on the move, and there is a mood of expectation and excitement in the air. All the street lamps are glowing brightly and noisy groups of drinkers spill out of the taverns. She crosses Shaftesbury Avenue and over into Wardour Street.

At the north end, she turns into the wide-open spaces of Oxford Street and breathes more calmly. She notices the cooling night air, which always seems to feel cleaner here after the grime and stench of Soho. She walks west towards Oxford Circus. She paces along in her haste to return to her rooms, but she feels her stride shorten as she reaches her doorway and fumbles in her wrist bag for her keys. The energy seeps from her.

She stumbles into the hallway, pulls herself up the stairs into the bedchamber and falls onto the bed, burying her face into the pillows. Her right fist smashes into the fretwork of the headboard, splintering the wood. She lies like this for over an hour. Her mind races. She knows Sly has turned the tables, but she must not let him win. She will need all her reserves of strength, but she will work this through. She will overcome this. Blood from her hand seeps into the damask bedcover. Eventually, she rises, goes to the sink in the kitchen and bathes her knuckles. She heats some water on the range and then dabs at the inside of her lower lip with a warm, soaked cloth. She winces.

She hears the sound of a cab drawing up in the street and then a sharp rap on the front door. She looks through the window, but can see no one. She is not expecting Jem. He is racing at Huntingdon and is staying with his parents at Stilton tonight. She wants to obey the rule never to answer to visitors when she is alone after dark. She knows it is a sensible precaution, but something panics her. What if Jem has had an accident? She runs downstairs and slips the latch, putting the chain across. She opens the gap a couple of inches. She can see nothing and there is no sound, no footsteps. Then she hears something heavy crash into the lock from outside. The chain rips away from the frame, taking part of the jamb with it. She loses her balance and drops to her knees. The door gapes open to reveal a man, resting a sledgehammer on his shoulder. He smiles at her. He steps aside and Nicholas Sly moves forward into the hallway, his bulk blocking out the light from the streetlamps.

'I was just passing,' he says. 'I thought I would drop in. I don't think we are finished yet.'

༄

In the weeks that follow, Harriet tells Lavinia something terrible has happened, but she does not elaborate. It is not discussed again. The summer goes well for Jem and the winners flow. Harriet continues to establish herself in her acting career. She almost persuades herself that the episode with Nicholas Sly was a passing incident and she does her best to banish it from her thoughts, but, of course, that is easier said than done. Lavinia is attuned to Harriet's moods and realises she needs help. She tries to coax Harriet into sharing what is on her mind.

'I know you are unsettled. I see it. I am here if you want to talk.'

'Thank you. I have to cope with it myself,' says Harriet.

'Whatever you do, don't punish Jem. And don't punish yourself.'

Lavinia is not the only one who senses all is not well with Harriet and her relationship with Jem.

'I'm confused by them,' says Tom. 'It is obvious they are well matched, but they seem to drift in and out of love.'

'I spent time with Harriet, Eliza as she was then, when we were younger,' says Lavinia. 'She was as wild as a goshawk. I never knew a girl like her. She was always fighting everything around her: her parents, authority, the world. Yet she was the kindest, dearest friend to those she trusted. From what you say, Jem shares many of those traits. I think, in some ways, they are too alike. They are both wilful and there is a recklessness simmering just below the surface, ready to explode. But never question that they are in love. That will remain constant, whatever happens.'

'Will they succeed, do you think?'

'I don't know. I hope so. They deserve to.'

༄

By the autumn, Tom and Lavinia, together with Jem and Harriet, begin to make their marks on the fringes of London society. The four friends may not have the background, although Lavinia's parents are said to be "well connected", but in dress, manners, style and expenditure they are indistinguishable from the aristocracy with whom they mix. Everything seems more relaxed and on an even keel. As the year moves on, Jem and Harriet draw ever closer and Jem purchases a diamond ring. They still have their disagreements. After all, as Lavinia says, they are two strong wills, but when they are alone together, cocooned under a fur pelt, with the doors and windows shuttered against the outside world, a log fire crackling in the grate and candlelight throwing shadows around the room, there is nowhere else either of them would rather be.

Tom confides in Lavinia one evening.

'I think Jem is going to ask Harriet to marry him. I probably shouldn't have said that.'

'I think she will probably say yes,' says Lavinia. 'I probably shouldn't have said that either.'

∽

In December, however, things start to unravel. Jem misses out on some winning rides when the owners replace him with other jockeys. Harriet doesn't secure parts Donald Treves promises are hers for the asking. She wonders if Sly is behind it. She does not forget his threats. Just before Christmas, Jem and Harriet have a blazing row. Neither of them is quite sure how it starts, but it escalates quickly and accusations are made on both sides. Jem spends the Christmas period with his parents. He has rides at Northampton on Boxing Day and Bedford the day after. He explains it as a sensible practical arrangement, but really he needs time apart from Harriet to think. Something is happening to them that he doesn't begin to understand.

While Jem is away, Nicholas Sly calls on Harriet again at Oxford Street – his second visit to the house. Lavinia knows something is wrong when she and Harriet meet the next day. She knows her friend well, but Harriet, typically, won't talk about it.

A day later, they are both invited to a masked ball in Mayfair. Lavinia is unenthusiastic. Tom is also away and she is not in the mood for socialising. By contrast, Harriet feels the need for distraction and persuades Lavinia to accompany her. When they meet that evening, it is apparent that Harriet has already been drinking.

'Are you alright?' asks Lavinia.

'I am going to drink wine until I drown and the devil take the consequences,' says Harriet.

'I don't think that is wise.'

'I don't want to be wise. I want to be drunk.'

❦

When Harriet wakes the following morning, the door to her bedchamber has moved to the other side of the room. The window drapes are not the familiar blue silk damask. It takes her a while to realise she is not at home in Oxford Street. A drumming headache pulses at her temples. A tall, slim, shirtless man in white breeches comes into the room, smiles across at her, tosses a blue and red tunic across the back of a chair and begins to pull on his jackboots. She groans and turns over.

EIGHT
On the Verge
London, England
1842

O n New Year's Day, Tom and Lavinia talk again about
Jem and Harriet. Tom says Jem has told him he thinks
they are on the verge of breaking up, but he doesn't know
why. Tom says he has never seen Jem in tears before. Lavinia
is more guarded, but Harriet's apparent descent into self-
destruction worries her.

'I fear for them,' she says. 'I don't think they realise what
they have.'

⁓

Haymarket Theatre is the jewel in the crown of London's
theatre district. Everyone wants to play here. Elizabeth
"Harriet" Howard is no exception. She enjoyed a brief
run here in her young career, but there is a bigger prize
in view. She is making her way in Shakespearean theatre,
but this is the one she wants. Walking left out of Coventry
Street, the famous portico of six Corinthian columns
comes into view and imposes its status on the street. The

grandeur continues inside. There is not one chandelier where two will do. Red, plush velvet is everywhere. She taps her foot on the back of the seat in front of her, as she waits her turn at the audition. In other circumstances, she would be confident, but her recent setbacks unnerve her slightly.

'Can we have Act 5 Scene II, please?' says the producer. 'Katharina's final speech: The Taming of the Shrew. Quiet, please. When you are ready.'

Harriet steps forward on the stage. She looks up.

∽

'*Fie, fie! unknit that threatening unkind brow,*
And dart not scornful glances from those eyes,
To wound thy lord, thy king, thy governor:
It blots thy beauty as frosts do bite the meads,
Confounds thy fame as whirlwinds shake fair buds,
And in no sense is meet or amiable.
A woman moved is like a fountain troubled,
Muddy, ill-seeming, thick, bereft of beauty;
And while it is so, none so dry or thirsty
Will deign to sip or touch one drop of it.
Thy husband is thy lord, thy life, thy keeper,
Thy head, thy sovereign; one that cares for thee,
And for thy maintenance commits his body
To painful labour both by sea and land,
To watch the night in storms, the day in cold,
Whilst thou liest warm at home, secure and safe;
And craves no other tribute at thy hands

But love, fair looks and true obedience;
Too little payment for so great a debt.
Such duty as the subject owes the prince
Even such a woman oweth to her husband;
And when she is froward, peevish, sullen, sour,
And not obedient to his honest will,
What is she but a foul contending rebel
And graceless traitor to her loving lord?
I am ashamed that women are so simple
To offer war where they should kneel for peace;
Or seek for rule, supremacy and sway,
When they are bound to serve, love and obey.
Why are our bodies soft and weak and smooth,
Unapt to toil and trouble in the world,
But that our soft conditions and our hearts
Should well agree with our external parts?
Come, come, you froward and unable worms!
My mind hath been as big as one of yours,
My heart as great, my reason haply more,
To bandy word for word and frown for frown;
But now I see our lances are but straws,
Our strength as weak, our weakness past compare,
That seeming to be most which we indeed least are.
Then vail your stomachs, for it is no boot,
And place your hands below your husband's foot:
In token of which duty, if he please,
My hand is ready; may it do him ease.'

'Oh bravo, bravo. Wonderful,' says the producer. 'That's a bonny Kate.'

Applause ripples from the few people dotted around the theatre. Even the stage hands join in.

'There will be no arguments this time,' says Donald Treves.

❧

Jem and Harriet are at home in Oxford Street, together. Their relationship has been strained for some time. There have been tears and tantrums. Tonight, she sits with a book on her lap, but she seems to spend more time staring into the embers of the fire. He watches her. No pages turn.

'There is something wrong,' says Jem. 'I know it. Something you are not telling me. What is it?'

'It's nothing.'

'Remember. You and me. Eliza and Jem. Jem and Eliza. We tell the truth. No secrets. Following the dream together. What happened to that?'

'Maybe you were right. It's just dreams.'

'Do we give up that easily?'

'I didn't get the part.'

'What? You said it was yours. They said you were the obvious choice.'

'The producer said I was exciting, enchanting. He said I perfectly captured the essence of Kate. It was a formality. Today, they sent a message saying they were offering the part to Sarah Langdon.'

'Why?'

'Something is going on. I have gone for five parts. I

didn't get any of them, even though they said I was ideal. Treves says that the producer at the Haymarket had a visit from someone, a woman, after the auditions. Later on, he said he made a mistake in casting me; he was reconsidering.'

'It goes that way sometimes.'

'You are not so cool when you lose a ride, Jem.'

'That's not the same.'

'Isn't it? It's easy for you to say.'

'No, it's not. Strathmore says he's not putting me up anymore. He says it's nothing personal. He just wants a change.'

'So much for loyalty. You turned down better mounts to ride his horses. And now he does this.'

'I'm starting to think there is more to this than coincidence. You are losing parts you should walk into. I'm losing rides for owners I've always ridden winners for. Who could have it in for both of us?'

'I don't know, Jem. I really don't.'

Deep down, of course, she does know. But she doesn't want to take it in; doesn't want to believe it. She hopes against hope that everything will blow over.

Jem seems the more philosophical, perhaps because he doesn't know what Harriet knows. He carries on riding because that is what he does. It is not that he is getting no rides, it's just that they are fewer and less competitive. When he talks with his main trainer, George Dockeray, though, the doubts he has been suppressing come out.

'We'll keep you going, Jem,' says George. 'There are plenty of other owners.'

'Tell me the truth, George. Have I lost it? I would rather know. If others can see it but I can't, you have to tell me.'

'You're riding better than ever, believe me. But something's afoot, that's certain. Seems you've made a few enemies in high places. They have the hack writers in their pockets. There's barely a week goes by without some story in the newspapers about you.'

'But hasn't that always been the case with jockeys? They build us up, then knock us down.'

'This is different, Jem. Yes, there has always been a bit of that. This looks like it's been planned. There's a slow drip. Most of it is suggestion. The drafting is careful: "it is alleged that…", "sources believe that…", "one steward was heard to say…" – that sort of thing. If they would come out with it, you could get the lawyers on the case. This is much harder to deal with.'

'But mud sticks.'

'Exactly. Keep at it, Jem. Your friends will stay by you.'

☙

Harriet perseveres and auditions for another part, as one of the weird sisters in Shakespeare's Scottish play. Count D'Orsay plans to cast and produce his own play for the first time at the Drury Lane theatre. Lady Macbeth is already cast. He takes his time over the remaining female characters. No one who knows him is at all surprised. The doe-eyed dandy has charm to spare and money to burn, it seems.

'You have a very good résumé,' he says. 'In a way, I worry you might be overqualified for this part.'

'I am keen to extend my range. It is not all about the leading roles.'

'I understand, but this would be a step down and, of course, the remuneration would not be what you are used to.'

'That is not my priority. I have researched this role and I think it would suit me.'

'I'm hopeful of a long run. How can I be sure you will not leave us if a better offer comes along?'

'I'll sign a binding contract.'

'You would not be the first to walk away from a contract. I am really not convinced.'

'I know I can play the part, sir. I just need an opportunity. I would be very grateful.'

He senses the desperation. He walks to the bookcase and takes a text down. He leafs through it. He is not really reading anything, just expending time. He folds his arms and sits on the edge of his desk. He leans forward and puts his face close to hers. She can smell the eau de jasmine.

'I will need to think about this. Perhaps we could discuss it again this evening over dinner?

'If you wish.'

'No, my dear. It is if you wish. I have many actresses who would like this part.'

∽

A few days later and a change in fortune finds Jem more his

old self. He rides two winners at Hendon and Tom has news for him. He can hardly wait to tell Harriet.

'Tom Olliver's put me in for the ride on Lord Chesterfield's Vanguard. He says he is a particular type of horse, more suited to my way of riding.'

'We still have people who will help us. That is good to know.'

'And you, Eliza. What news?'

'The part is mine. It is something, at least.'

'Maybe it's a turning point. Come on, Eliza. We won't let them beat us. We are better than them. New year, new start. You'll see.'

The two of them embrace and Harriet realises that it has been a long time since Jem has shown her any affection outside the bedchamber. She struggles to hold back tears. She senses their slow slide away from intimacy.

∽

Nicholas Sly does not forget about Harriet Howard. He has other things under consideration, but today she tops his list of subjects requiring attention. His instructions have been carried out, but he is shouting at the two men in front of him. The colouring in his face reaches the purple end of the scale and one of the men flinches every time Sly bangs the table.

'I want more,' he says. 'This is intolerable. This woman plays us for fools. I want her backed into a corner. The softening up process is one thing, but we need something that clinches our deal. She has proved remarkably resilient.

And so has her sideman, Mason. I don't just want them on the ropes, I want a knockout blow, do you hear me? Do whatever it takes. Time is still on our side. Developments abroad are moving more slowly than we thought. Nevertheless, I want to be sure that next time I invite her to a meeting there will be no room for error. Keep me informed of your progress.'

༄

The year does not improve. At the beginning of March, the Grand National Steeplechase comes round again. Jem rides Lottery, out of loyalty to the old horse, but he is not the horse he was and the handicapper gives him thirteen stones, four pounds to carry. It is too much and Lottery pulls up. To add insult to injury, George Dockeray trains Gaylad to win, owned, like Lottery, by John Elmore and ridden by Tom Olliver. Later in the month, Jem has a bad fall at Leamington. Inexplicably, the girth leathers split on his saddle. No one has ever seen such a clean break before. He proves an ill-tempered patient. Men usually are. When he doesn't ride, he doesn't earn. The Scottish play goes badly. The reviews are poor. The leading actress is not up to it and there is talk that the run will end early. The more time Jem and Harriet spend together, the more they bicker. And now there is a new development. She thinks she may be expecting a child. No, she knows she is. She spends a restless night considering her options, but in the morning she feels there is only one course of action open to her.

My dearest Jem

I am sorry to write like this but I can't say these things to you face-to-face. I couldn't stand it. You deserve better than me, Jem, and I can only say that I hope you will forgive me.

We can't see each other again. I am going away for a while and when I return you mustn't contact me. I can't tell you everything, but please trust me that what I am doing is in both our best interests.

We've had good times together and bad and I'm truly sorry that I can't carry on. We have both been foolish and our habit of punishing each other when we fall out has taken its toll.

My career has faltered and I've taken the decision to give up acting, at least for the foreseeable future. I've always wanted to be independent and to pay my own way and it's clear that I don't have the means to achieve that. I won't be a drain on you, Jem. I couldn't bear it.

You will be better off without me. I fear that your relationship with me may have cost you some support among the owners and I won't be responsible for that. You are the best of the best and there is no one who can ride a racehorse like you.

I want you to know that I love you more than I can say and always will. Sometimes we have to accept that destiny is against us and we have to choose another path. Please don't hate me.

Your Eliza

❧

A note arrives for Lavinia from Harriet along similar lines. Harriet is sorry for everything. She is going away to deal with things herself. Within the week, Lavinia is sent to Ireland by her parents. Her father is unhappy with the company she keeps and wishes to make a match for her as far from London as possible. Where Harriet's father's threats to disinherit her amounted to nothing, Lavinia's parents have more leverage. A small but not insubstantial trust fund hangs by a thread. Lavinia is fond of Tom, but she knows he strays occasionally. With Harriet beyond help, she feels she can leave without guilt. In the end, the decision to accept her parents' wishes is the only sensible course.

NINE
No Way Out
London, England
1843

Of course, Her Majesty's Government does not have a secret service. That would be absurd. It is rumoured, however, that there is an organisation called State Services. And State Services' role and reporting arrangements, even its existence, seem to be, well, secret. Home Secretary Sir James Graham thinks that State Services, if it exists, probably works for the Ministry of War and the Colonies. A similar enquiry of Secretary of State for War and the Colonies Lord Stanley would draw the opinion that State Services, if it exists, probably works for the Home Office. And so it goes.

In the meantime, Nicholas Sly, who would be the head of State Services, if it existed, gets away with a lot, which is convenient for him.

In a secret location, on a secret day, with a man whose identity must remain secret, the following conversation takes place.

'What do you have for me concerning Miss Howard?' says Sly.

'I think you will be pleased.'

'I will judge that.'

'We have news about her situation with Mason, a child, her parents and her attempts to revive her acting career. It will be enough.'

'And if it is not enough?'

'If we need more, we can arrange for Mason to have another accident. We put him out for three months last year. His future is in the balance. But it won't be needed. The threat is enough. There is no way out.'

'Very good. By the way, I wanted to ask you about Mason's accident. It was a very pretty piece of work. Credit where it is due. How was it done? I'm interested.'

'You want me to give up our secrets?'

'Just between us.'

'It is straightforward. Security varies between the racecourses. Leamington is weak and what exists there can be bribed. There is always an opportunity when the jockeys weigh out. The weight cloths are made up with the lead weights and the jockey stands on the scales. The stewards verify the weight to be carried and the saddle and weight cloth, with number cloth, where used, are passed to the valet. In turn, the valet passes the whole tack to the trainer, or trainer's assistant, who saddles the horse up, before it goes into the parade ring. The saddle is out of the jockey's possession from the time he weighs out until he is legged up on the horse, just before the race. Here is the opportunity.'

'I see. So it is the valet who is bribed?'

'Yes. We need the saddle for only a few minutes. It

is a delicate operation. The girth strap is sawn almost through on one side with a blade. It is a matter of delicate judgement. The straps must hold the girths in place and must be robust enough to canter to the start and be retightened, without breaking. Once the race begins, the combination of the movement of the horse, the pressure from the rider and the brushing of the girth on the top of birch fences conspire to weaken and then split the strap. It usually takes five or six fences, which is no problem in a three-mile chase of twenty or so fences. There is a margin for error. Our man learned his trade in Ireland. He is a fine craftsman.'

'Excellent work. Having said that, I must ask how you knew our target would be injured, rather than killed.'

'We didn't.'

∞

February sees London in the snow. A phosphorescent whiteness gives way to muddy brown, as the drifts stack in the lanes and a few carts and carriages spatter the doorways, walls and windows. It is impossible to navigate on foot without garments taking on the stinking sludge of horse droppings and snow-melt as it turns to slush. A fog drifts up from the Thames and shrouds the rooftops along Whitehall Place. At some of the entrances, swathes have been cut through the snow and two men in oversize greatcoats are pushing wide brooms in an effort to clear away the slurry. The normally busy thoroughfare is quiet today, with only a few visitors. A solitary hansom cab clatters in the lane and draws up at one of the buildings. Harriet Howard is met by a footman and escorted to the door.

In Nicholas Sly's office, a few dying embers glow in the fire grate. Neatly chopped kindling and logs flank the hearth, but Sly makes no move to use them. A single candle flickers on his desk and lights up his face. He has the look of a man with a brag hand with three threes. He knows he must win, but he is determined to savour every moment of the game. In his excitement, though, he opens boldly.

'Shall we cut to the chase?' he says. 'I will make you the offer I made when we met before and you will refuse me. Is that correct?'

'You are,' she says.

'Very well, then, Miss Howard,' he begins again. 'There is a gentleman acquaintance of yours, a certain Jem Mason. We believe he is, how shall I put it, someone with whom you have had a rather intimate liaison. I do not wish to be indelicate.'

He looks for a response but there is none.

'We understand that this liaison began some time before your sixteenth birthday. I know it is the fashion these days to overlook such detail. The law appears rather vague on the subject, as I am sure you are aware. But attitudes are changing. I know Her Majesty wishes her government to take a stronger lead on the matter. At the very least, this information could attract some scandal and some of Mason's well-connected patrons might decide to withdraw their support. The word "kidnap" has been mentioned. We believe he has a promising career as a jockey, but, of course, he follows a very dangerous profession. I understand he was unfortunate enough to have a fall last year, which lost him some important rides. One never knows when these things could happen again. It would be a shame, would it not, Miss Howard, if his career was cut short for some reason?'

She does not respond, but there is a visible colouring at her cheeks and the hint of a tear. He looks her up and down and thinks back to the young woman he met two years earlier. The elegance and poise are still there, but now her clothes are frayed and stained in a few places. She is only in her twentieth year, but there is something careworn in her face, an emptiness around the eyes. He smiles inwardly and warms to his task.

'Then we come to the self-styled Squire Joseph Gawen Harryet. He is your father, we believe. We understand that he has spent his way through a not inconsiderable fortune and can now be found residing in two rooms above the Black Bear in Norwich. Your mother, Elizabeth, keeps your father and herself from the poorhouse by working as a maid. Your father is a drunkard, Miss Howard.'

She weeps openly now and her shoulders drop. She picks at the stitching of the muffler in her lap.

'Sir, can you show me no mercy? I have a child.'

'Ah, yes. I was aware of that. I must admit we were somewhat disconcerted by this news. It seems you have gone to great lengths to conceal the fact. There is a Martin Harryet, born on the sixteenth of August last year. The registered parents in the parish records are your parents, Joseph and Elizabeth Mary Harryet, yet you now wish us to believe that he is your son. Am I correct?'

She nods and looks away.

'While unfortunate, it does not disqualify you from helping us. In fact, we see a way that this can provide us with a credible alternative background for you. There are some aspects of your family history that we may wish to, how shall I say, reconstruct.'

'It seems I'm to lose my freedom.'

'Freedom, you say. Why it is the merest loss when set against the life that will be before you. Let me elucidate for you, Harriet. We will make any problems that young Jem Mason might face go away. We will rescue your parents from their current unfortunate circumstances and restore them to a comfortable living. We will provide you with a house, where you and your son will live under the guardianship of my colleague, Major Mountjoy-Martin. It may be imagined that he is the father of your son. It is serendipitous that you have named the boy Martin, I think.'

'Are there conditions?'

'Yes, there are two. They are not onerous, given your present circumstances. You will not see Jem Mason again and you will give up the folly of your so-called career as an actress. We understand that parts are harder to find, your star a little faded. Is that not so?'

'You are contemptible. A disgrace.'

'I think that a trifle unnecessary. The newspapers are a very reliable guide, I always think.'

'When you have told them what to say.'

'Bitterness is such an unattractive quality. Our conversation is at an end for now. As I explained to you before, we will arrange for Lady Blessington to look after you. We will be in contact when we need you. Think of it as the closing of one chapter of your life and the opening of another. Good day.'

Harriet feels defeated, as if nothing she could do could alter her situation. Perhaps Jem was right, she thinks. Fate is against me.

∽

Sly wastes no time in moving things along. In the afternoon, another meeting takes place in his office. A thaw is under way outside and carriages are moving more freely again. He sits in a leather armchair in front of a blazing fire, his feet resting on the edge of the fire surround, his hands clasped across his stomach. He is smiling and he hums tunelessly to himself. When Lady Blessington comes in, he rises abruptly to his feet and makes a low, extravagant bow. She joins him and they sit opposite each other at his desk.

'Our bird is caged. Now we need to teach her to sing,' he says.

'And you would like me to take this on?'

'If you would be so kind. She will need work, but I think she can be whipped into shape, so to speak.'

'And the timetable?'

'It is not urgent. Send her away for a while. We will need to sort out the details.'

'Do you have any news from France?

'Lord Malmesbury tells me that diplomatic moves are still continuing. That must be the preferred route. Our

Frenchman remains imprisoned at Ham, but we detect a softening of attitudes. If all else fails, he will have to be sprung.'

'And the practical arrangements for Miss Howard?'

'We won't trouble you with those. Major Mountjoy-Martin will be her guardian. He is new to the role, on secondment from a Guards division. Unofficially, that is.'

'I know him, of course. I would not have thought this was his line of work.'

'No, indeed, he took some persuading, but his wife has been very sick and we helped him understand the benefits.'

'As only you can.'

'How kind of you to say so.'

And that signals the end of Nicholas Sly's appointments for the day. He relaxes into his fireside chair and begins to whistle to himself.

TEN
The Choice
London, England
1844

St John's Wood is rather "up and coming" these days and the new stuccoed "town villas", with their regular features and symmetrical doors and windows and pristine white paintwork, glisten in the sunlight. Blue and white lavenders are planted in neat rows along the entrance paths. The warmth of the summer air draws the scent from the lavenders, and bees and butterflies hover and flit between them.

Rockingham House is larger than the other houses and is also marked out by the additional columns, flanking the main door and the carved balustrade above. Wrought iron gates and railings add to the feeling of exclusivity. There is a flurry of activity at the entrance. Hansom cabs come and go and a number of mounted gentlemen arrive, one in uniform, their horses led away by grooms to the stables in the mews beside the house.

Inside the spacious drawing room, introductions are made. It is clear that the house is not yet a home, devoid, as it is, of any personal items or ornamentation. After a brief exchange, one man signals an end to the discussion, instructions are issued to the servants and the group of apparent strangers breaks up. Eventually, only two people remain. The woman is young, early twenties, elegantly dressed and quite strikingly beautiful. The man, in Guards officer's uniform, is in his early thirties, tall, slim and fair-haired.

'You,' she says.

'Do not say anything here, Harriet,' he says. He puts a finger to his lips. 'I will explain everything. This is awkward, I know.'

The two figures move away into the gardens at the back of the house. Lawns and newly planted perennials combine to bring the country into the town – at least that is the intention.

'You are not quite what you seem,' she says. 'Is Mountjoy-Martin your real name or is it the name you gave me before?'

'You have the truth now and you will continue to have the truth. But we can never discuss the time we met before and, in particular, Sly must never know.'

'Oh dear. Would that be inconvenient for you?'

'I think it would be inconvenient for both of us. I want to be honest with you. I am to be your guardian. That is my job. I am under orders from Her Majesty's Government. Nicholas Sly is my superior. You and I will be taking instructions from him. If I disqualify myself from this task – and an admission that we know each other, especially under the circumstances of the meeting, would surely achieve that – you will be assigned someone else. It will be bad for me and my career, but bad for you as well. I am on your side. Be sure of that. If I can help you, I will. I know that you didn't want this and neither did I. This is our fate and we must make the best of it. You can do this with me or with someone else, who will not be as sympathetic. It is your choice.'

'A fine speech, sir. I almost believe you.'

'It is true.'

'Truth. You seem very much taken with the idea. The truth is, Major, you are to be my pimp. Mr Sly will be my procurer. I will be "entertaining the company of certain distinguished gentlemen". Do you know what that means? I will be the Queen's prostitute. I will be available to any old lecher with whom the government wishes to curry favour. It is disgusting.'

'I cannot argue with you if you wish to describe it in those terms, but the reality will be somewhat different. I cannot tell you everything at this point, but you will need to trust me.'

'Trust you? A man who I met once before, some three years ago, and who told me his name was Captain Margarson. Is that what you are saying?'

'I am sorry. That was wrong of me. When you know my situation better, I hope you will understand me. I hope you will think better of me. In the meantime, we have few choices in the matter. I want to work with you to protect your interests. I genuinely intend to be your guardian.'

'I need more than that. How will things be different? Why should I trust you?'

'All I can say is that we are engaged in a long game. I think you will be called upon very little, if at all, for the time being.'

'Is it a game we are playing?'

'I'm sorry again. My choice of words may be ill advised. What I mean to say is that there is a long-term strategy in place. You are an important part of that strategy.'

'I am intrigued. What is this strategy?'

'I have already said too much. I must leave it there. On the question of trust, you must trust me because there is no one else. I will earn your trust, believe me.'

'And we both answer to Sly?'

'Yes, we do. He is not the ogre you think him. In my dealings with him, I have found him a hard man, but a straightforward one.'

'I cannot share your enthusiasm. I loathe him.'

'I understand you may not like him. We are all obeying orders. He does what is asked of him. That is the way of things.'

'I loathe him for reasons you cannot begin to understand, sir. If I have the chance to put a knife into him, I will. Do you understand that?'

'I see. That would be unwise, but I think we have said enough for now. I must tell you, though, that you will live a very comfortable life here. It would not be sensible to compromise your situation. Your son, Martin, will be well cared for. I will look after him as if he was my own.'

'Perhaps he is.'

'What?'

'Perhaps he is your son. I don't rule it out. You know his birth date, I think. How is your counting?'

'That is enough, Harriet. I will call your maid. We will talk again later.'

∽

Gore House dominates the scene, looking south across Kensington Gardens and, as Harriet exits Lancaster Walk, she feels apprehensive about her meeting. She has been in grand houses before, of course, but the size and scale of this house seem to lean in on her, as she walks up to the heavy door and surveys the assortment of polished brass door furnishings. While she is considering which bell to push, the door opens noiselessly and the butler signals her to follow him down a long, wide corridor to the left, which opens out into a vast drawing room, decorated with floral wallpaper and festooned with various family portraits. Lady Blessington is seated on a red buttoned sofa, the broad skirts of her pink dress spreading almost the width of the sofa itself. She is, perhaps, in her fifties, but she is lent a more youthful appearance by her long black hair, arranged in coils, and her prominent roseate cheekbones.

She indicates that Harriet is to sit on a high-backed chair, with a view out through wide, floor-length windows to an orangery beyond.

'I am so pleased to meet you. You are every bit as beautiful as they say.'

'Please spare me the flattery. I know what I am,' says Harriet.

'And every bit as curt.'

'I am sorry. I am not adjusting well to my new life.'

'I sympathise. We women have always to adjust to survive. I know you were not always Harriet Howard, but now you must learn how to be her in her new role. It may help you to know that I was not always Lady Blessington. That had to be learned. I can help you. You were a much more talented actress than I. I saw you.'

'I was happy then. Now, my life is ruined. I cry myself to sleep, but in the morning I wake up angry. I cannot shake it off.'

'You have suffered a bereavement. It is natural to feel the way you do. Your old life is gone, but "Harriet Howard" is alive. You can still have another life.'

'That is easy for you to say.'

'No, it is not. You presume too much. Let me tell you about my life. I was born Margaret Power in Ireland. My father was a waster. He married me to an English army officer, when I was fifteen, in order to pay his debts. My husband was a drunkard and a gambler. He beat me every night. The beatings only stopped when he was sent to the debtors' prison. Fortunately, for me, he died there. I was left with nothing, but I was still alive. That is not easy for me to say and it never becomes any easier.'

'I apologise. Forgive me.'

'Do you see that painting over there? That is me when I was twenty-nine, not long after I married the Earl. I rode my luck, as you might say.'

'You were very beautiful. You still are.'

'Please spare me the flattery. I know what I am.'

'You have me, Lady Blessington. I am put in my place.'

'The Earl died in 1829 when I was forty years old. By

then, I had expensive tastes. I followed my intuition in matters of the heart and my judgements were not always wise. I have squandered several fortunes and scandal has followed me all my life. Yet, I have survived.'

'Thank you. I am grateful for your honesty.'

'I understand the choice you have had to make. I made it myself. Among other things, I arrange introductions for Her Majesty's Government. I provide guidance for young women who do not have my experience.'

'I think I will need your guidance. I am finding it hard to come to terms with everything that has happened.'

'Come, Harriet. We can be friends. We are not so different, you and I. You must learn to trust me. When we are alone, you must call me Margaret.'

❧

London Gazette, Saturday 12th October 1844

FAMOUS JOCKEY MARRIES

This week saw the marriage of James (Jem) Mason, son of Mr & Mrs Josiah Mason, of Stilton in Cambridgeshire and Miss Emily Elmore, daughter of Mr & Mrs John Elmore, of Edgware, Middlesex, at St Mary Magdalene Church in Stilton. Jem Mason is, of course, well known to all racing followers as the winner of the Grand Liverpool Steeplechase in 1839 on Mr John Elmore's Lottery and he now becomes Mr Elmore's son-in-law, as well as his retained jockey. The guest list was a virtual "Who's Who" of the sport of kings and Lord

Sefton, Lord Chesterfield and Lord Beauclerk were in attendance. Jockeys Tom Olliver, Allen McDonough, Will McDonough and Tom Ferguson formed a guard of honour for the bride and groom as they left the church.

ELEVEN
Making the Best of Things
London, England
1845

Rockingham House
St John's Wood
London

Dearest Mama

I'm so pleased to hear that you are well and that Papa is more settled now. It is always a worry that he will slip back into his old ways, but I trust that he will realise he has been given a second chance and will keep to the path.

I'm very busy these days with entertaining and Francis is such a sweet man and indulges me far more than he should. Martin is growing up quickly and is running, after a fashion. It is my greatest pleasure to be able to spend time with him. I hope I will be able to bring him with me the next time I come to see you.

It was lovely to have a visit from Tom Olliver recently. He brought me up to date with all the hunting gossip and made me laugh with his tales of racing skulduggery.

I realise how much I miss that life and the people in it. Tom is quite the gentleman these days and making a name for himself as one of the very best riders. He has won not one, but two Grand National Steeplechases at Liverpool.

Your loving daughter
Eliza

∽

2 Ferry Lane
Norwich

My dear Eliza

I do so love to hear from you and I look forward to your little notes with snippets of news about this and that. It makes me so proud that you are doing so well. I can only imagine now what it is like attending so many wonderful parties and wearing such beautiful gowns. Your father and I had our time in society but it was all too brief. I have to pinch myself when I read in the London magazines that Miss Harriet Howard has attended this or that fine ball, to remember that this is our own little Eliza being talked about.

My only regret is that Francis is not able to marry you yet. Just imagine, a Guards officer for a husband. They say that poor Mrs Mountjoy-Martin is confined to her bed and may not have long to live. We will just have to hope for the best.

Please do be careful about Olliver and his

associates. It troubles me that you should be pining for that time in your life when you have so much more to be grateful for in your new life. I was reading only last week that Olliver and his friend Mason had been involved in some new mischief at Bedford races. Remember that underneath the veneer of gentlemen they are little more than gypsy ruffians. You know very well your father's view about Mason. You must not do anything to jeopardise your position.

Please write to me again when you can.
Send my love to Martin.
Mama

oxo

There is a tranquillity about Rockingham House. Harriet Howard and Major Francis Mountjoy-Martin live an unexceptional life – for all the world, they are a comfortably wealthy married couple. Neighbours think little about them. The major must have a good job, behind a desk, somewhere in Buckingham Gate, or perhaps Queen's Walk. He is every inch the Guards officer. His wife is always well turned out and smiles graciously at anyone who catches her gaze. The little boy is full of energy and has a newly acquired hobbyhorse to amuse him. The major must have an important social role, as well as his military duties, since there are always cabs and carriages at the gates in the evenings and sometimes well into the early hours.

On this evening, Mountjoy-Martin and Harriet sit either side of the marble fireplace in the drawing room. Young

Martin is in bed and the servants have been dismissed early. Harriet reads a book, but she fidgets in her chair and occasionally lets out a sigh. Mountjoy-Martin rifles through a pile of papers on a desk, makes some adjustments to a clock, adds a log to the fire, but can't settle at anything.

'I would like to talk about us,' he says.

'I won't deny you that. I have reason to be grateful to you.'

'We have been through a lot together, wouldn't you say?'

'You have been as good as a father to Martin. I cannot ask for more.'

'You are coy about that,' he says. 'You talk about the truth, but you won't tell me the truth about Martin.'

'I am not telling you any lies,' she says. 'I am unsure. Besides, if it was you, how would that help either of us? You are married. You have enough to contend with. I am to answer to the requirements of Her Majesty's Government, as they see fit. In case you haven't noticed, I am not at liberty to elope with you and seek my freedom elsewhere. Was that what you were going to suggest?'

'You know I cannot do that. We are both constrained. But it won't always be like that, I believe. We could think about the future.'

'Ah yes, the future. Let us make plans. Only to have them dashed? I was a great optimist once. I thought I could shape my life. I was wrong. You would do well to understand this truth above all others. It will save us both disappointment.'

A long silence ensues. Mountjoy-Martin is attuned to Harriet's moods. He can tell there is something else on her mind.

'You seem pensive, Harriet.' he says. 'Have I not been as good as my word?'

'You have, Francis. I am thankful for it.'

'We have made the best of things, have we not?'

'More than that. You and Margaret have been very kind.'

'Is something troubling you?'

'I am called to Gore House tomorrow. Do you know about this?'

'I do. I don't know the details.'

'Were you going to mention it?'

'I heard about it today, probably at the same time as you. I will tell you what I know. Don't chide me, Harriet. I am doing my best for us both.'

⁓

Gore House sparkles under a light morning frost. Kensington Gardens soaks up the sunlight and the Serpentine shimmers silver between the trees. Elegantly caparisoned riders and their horses move through the shaded paths.

Lady Blessington bustles into the library in riding habit, casting off clothes as she goes. Two maids follow behind her, gathering the crumpled items as they fall.

'What a wonderful morning it is,' she says. 'I do so love riding out in the gardens at this time of year. I hope I didn't keep you waiting. Do you know why you are here?'

Harriet is bemused by the sight before her. Lady Blessington strips to her undergarments and is transformed before her eyes as the maids fuss around her, fitting new clothes and spraying great waves of eau de cologne. She is reminded of her own scene changes at the theatre in the old days and, for a few moments, she is distracted.

'Harriet, are you alright?'

'Yes, of course. I imagine something important is afoot. I have been expecting your invitation.'

'I hope you are happy with the arrangements we have made for you? The price to pay not too onerous?'

'Thank you. You have been a true friend.'

'We have called on you very few times, I think, and the assignments have not been unpleasant ones, I believe. Francis tells me you are very settled together. Your new background is well established and very credible. Miss Harriet Howard has her position in society and you play the role very well. We are ready for the next assignment and I must tell you that it is the one we have been preparing for. It is a challenge, but I think you are ready.'

'Yes. The long game.'

'I don't quite follow.'

'Forgive me. It is a term Francis used once. Something to do with a long-term strategy. An important political alliance, if I understand the clues correctly.'

'You are well informed.'

'Perhaps. May I be better informed?'

'All in good time. Others will deal with the detail. In the meantime, my remit is to provide a broad outline of the plans being made. There is a certain French person of interest to Her Majesty's Government. He is being detained at present, but we understand that he will be free to travel in the near future. He will make his way to England at the earliest opportunity and he will find that he is welcomed here as a friend.'

'And my role in this?'

'I will introduce you. It is to be hoped that there will be an attraction on his part, perhaps even a mutual attraction.'

'I see.'

'We'll send you away for a while to the country. You will learn everything that you need and we can put the final touches to the character of Miss Harriet Howard. I think it is all rather exciting.'

'I will try to share in your enthusiasm.'

'Come, Harriet. We have gowns to view. And shoes.'

∾

The new Palace of Westminster looks as if it rises up out of the Thames on days like this, when there is a mist lying on the water, swirling at the base of the buildings. Inside his temporary office, where it feels as if the building work has been going on forever, Sir James Graham greets the Duke of Grafton.

'Thank you for seeing me, Home Secretary,' says the Duke. 'It is very good of you. I am sure you have important matters of state to deal with.'

'Yes, but I am never too busy to see you, Your Grace. I have taken the liberty of inviting Lord Normanby to our discussion. He knows some of the history of what you have told me and is a wise counsel.'

'Excellent. How are you, Henry?'

'Very well, Your Grace.'

Sir James Graham and Henry Normanby are old friends and share a love of clothes. To say that they are vain men, dandies, barely covers it. By contrast, the Duke looks as if he has just come from a farmers' lunch. Perhaps he has. It is he who curtails the small talk.

'This is all most unfortunate. I have been rather taken up with family matters since I succeeded my father last year. It has been very time-consuming and I have only just got around to this subject. Apparently, the old boy rather took a shine to one Elizabeth Ann Harryet a few years back. It now appears that he was intent on making a match with my son, William. Not that he consulted me about it. I don't know what he could have been thinking. Her family was of no consequence, as far as I can tell. But it seems she could ride like the devil and was something of a beauty, which commended her enough in father's book. The poor girl rather scuppered her chances by running off with some jockey fellow, but father didn't seem to mind. I understand she is currently in the service of Her Majesty's Government, although it all seems a bit odd, from what I can find out. I'm not sure exactly what she does. She now goes by the name of Harriet Howard.'

Sir James looks like a man who would rather be somewhere else. He glances towards Lord Normanby for help.

'Can you shed any light on this, Henry?'

'Well, yes. As a matter of fact, she works for you, Sir James. Indirectly.'

'Oh, heavens. Does she?'

'There is a chap called Nicholas Sly in State Services – used to work for me. Dreadful man. I think he got his claws into her last year. She is on our register of escorts.

Lady Blessington looks after her, along with another of our chaps, Major Mountjoy-Martin.'

'Oh dear. We have a register of escorts?'

'I'm afraid so, yes.'

Sir James gazes out of the window, apparently lost in thought. The Duke fixes his gaze on Lord Normanby.

'Well, the thing is, the old boy let it be known in his papers that he wanted her "looked after". What is the form?'

'Are you saying she is named in his will?' says Normanby.

'No, nothing of that sort. It came to light in his hunting diaries. I just feel rather honour bound to ask what can be done. Do you see?'

'I have met her. By God, she is something. Your father was a good judge.'

'Yes, I have often heard it said. He had a sound eye for the three aitches: hounds, horses and harlots.'

'Shame you couldn't have let us know sooner. We might have been able to call off the chase.'

'Damn it, Henry, don't rub it in. I feel guilty enough as it is.'

'Sorry, Your Grace. I spoke out of turn.'

Sir James strokes his chin and looks from the window towards the ornate, carved ceiling. He is looking for inspiration, but none comes.

'Leave it with me,' he says. 'We shall just have to make the best of a bad job, I think.'

TWELVE
Executing the Plan
London, England
1846

In Nicholas Sly's office in Whitehall Place, arrangements are being made. Today, Sly is smiling, cheerful almost, although it is as well not to relax in his company.

'Is everything in order, Major?' says Sly.

'I believe so, sir,' says Mountjoy-Martin.

'You believe so, is it? Major Martin, you are a military officer. I need more precision from you. Yes or no will suffice.'

'Yes, sir.'

'Very well. You will escort Miss Howard to Gore House at nine o'clock this evening. The Frenchman will be in attendance. You are required only to make the normal introductions and then to withdraw. Lady Blessington will take over from there.'

'How can we be sure the plan will work, sir?'

'Miss Howard will do what Miss Howard does. The Frenchman will do what Frenchmen do. I have no doubt of it.'

⌀

Evening sunlight still filters through the windows at Gore House, striking the chandeliers and diffusing light into the corners of the rooms. Large arrangements of fragrant pink and white roses greet the guests as they enter through the marbled hallway and make their way into the ballroom. A string quartet plays one of Signor Donizetti's latest offerings. Liveried footmen stand by, offering drinks and canapés.

Prince Louis Napoleon arrives, accompanied by an entourage of four gentlemen, who are encased in a great deal of ribbon and other frippery. For his part, the Prince wears a blue evening coat, with gilt buttons and a velvet collar, and a white waistcoat in the *"style Anglaise"*. His only concession to decoration is the Garter, a blue ribbon crossing his waistcoat, a star on his left pocket and the belted band below the left knee.

There is much head-turning and murmuring as he moves alongside Lady Blessington. He returns her greeting with a curt bow, a kiss on the hand and an audible clicking of his heels. She catches him firmly by the elbow and marches him towards the assembled throng, where various introductions are made and several repeat performances from the Prince ensue. He makes an imposing first impression at his first soiree back in England – of that, there can be no doubt. There are those in attendance, however, who feel that on closer inspection the impression does not quite carry through. Lady Willoughby thinks the Bonaparte nose a distraction and feels that his eyes are rather too close together. She wonders whether his somewhat mouse-brown hair is entirely his own. Moreover, and there is no avoiding this, when Louis Napoleon stands alongside Lord

Normanby, the new British ambassador in France, he barely reaches his shoulder. Subsequent reports have it that Louis Napoleon speaks only in English, eschews any opportunity to speak French and, if anything, affects a vaguely German accent. Lady Normanby comments later, to Nicholas Sly, that she is not at all sure what to make of the man.

'How long has he been in London, exactly?' says Lady Cowley.

'I understand from Malmesbury that he has been here just three weeks,' says Normanby. 'I am told he has taken rooms at King Street, near St James's Square.'

Just at the point when the evening achieves the desired level of dullness and Louis Napoleon is seen to check his half-hunter, Lady Blessington raises her fan to her face and nods to the footman standing on the right of the main staircase. Moments later, the string quartet ends their performance with a flourish and the polite applause that follows gives way to silence. Harriet Howard makes her way down the long upper gallery at the north side of the ballroom and then, very slowly, descends the stairs, the silk skirts of her vivid blue dress swishing as she moves. An ornate diamond pendant glitters at her neck. All the while, she keeps her gaze ahead of her. At her side, Major Mountjoy-Martin provides a suitably straight-backed aide. They reach Lady Blessington.

'I am so pleased you could find time to attend our little party,' she says.

'It is our pleasure. I am so sorry we were delayed,' says Harriet.

'May I introduce our distinguished guest from France.'

Prince Louis Napoleon dips a brief acknowledgement to Mountjoy-Martin and focuses his attention on Harriet.

'Enchanted,' says the Prince.

He lingers over the introduction and seems reluctant to give up Harriet's hand. Mountjoy-Martin gives a small cough, which breaks the attachment, leaving her free to respond with a long, low curtsey. Once she has reached her resting position, she looks up, fixes Louis Napoleon with her piercing eyes and smiles at him, her lips parting just slightly.

'How lovely to meet you,' she says.

All the attention follows the newly attached couple, as the music strikes up again.

'Who is that girl?' says Lady Willoughby to one of the ladies-in-waiting.

'I understand she has just arrived in London herself. She is a Howard. They say she has been educated in a convent. The Prince seems quite taken with her.'

'Really? A convent? I think I may have seen her before.'

It is not long after the dancing commences that Prince Louis manoeuvres Harriet onto the terrace, where they remain deep in conversation under the dimmed gas lamps.

∽

Mountjoy-Martin reports back to Whitehall Place. It is almost midnight. He thinks that Sly looks as if he has been sitting in the same position since he left him that morning. A single candle lights the room.

'How went the evening?' says Sly.

'Exactly as you said it would, sir,' says Mountjoy-Martin.

'Excellent.'

'Could I ask a question, sir?'

'Of course. Out with it.'

'Louis Napoleon, sir. If we are to support his cause, well… is he reliable?'

'He is a Frenchman.'

Nicholas Sly chuckles to himself as if he has just recalled the punch-line to a rather excellent joke.

'Sir, you are playing with me. You know what I am asking. If Britain chooses to support the Bonapartist cause, how do we know they will co-operate with us?'

'It is a fair question. In fact, Britain will offer nothing and will ask for nothing. Our politicians rarely agree about anything, but Palmerston and Aberdeen are agreed on one thing. We must not be seen intervening directly in French politics. However, we do have a clear cross-party policy and preference. We find that we cannot trust King Louis Philippe. He has no backbone. We need a strong alliance against Russia. On balance, the Bonapartists are more likely to deliver that than the current monarchy. It is a matter of judgement.'

'Would it not be feasible to reach some arrangement with the Russians as an alternative?'

'That has been considered. The French are unreliable, but they do occasionally do the right thing. The Russians can always be relied upon to do the wrong thing. That is the lesson of history.'

'And Louis Napoleon?'

'He is the natural heir to the Bonaparte legacy and France is bored again. If we can oil the wheels a little, then we shall. Unofficially, of course.'

'And Miss Howard?'

'Ah, Miss Howard, our secret weapon.'

'I worry about her, sir. I know it is not my place… but I think we expect a lot from the young lady.'

'Your concern is touching. Might it be that it is not just the Frenchman who is falling under Miss Howard's spell?'

∽

At Gore House next morning, the sunlit orangery is alive with bougainvillaea and oleander. The plumbago is just starting to flower. It is a little Mediterranean oasis. It is enough to put everyone in a good mood, but this is not the only reason Lord Normanby feels pleased with himself. He greets Lady Blessington with a beaming smile. She, however, does not reciprocate.

'Our Frenchman didn't know what hit him. What a joy to watch,' he says.

'We must look after her. She seems tough, but she is fragile.'

'We are fortunate we still have her.'

'We are, but why do you say that?'

'I thought you knew about the intervention.'

'You will need to enlighten me. It seems I have been overlooked.'

'The Duke of Grafton wanted us to pull her out of service.'

'When did this happen?'

'Last year, if my memory serves me. He came to see the home secretary. I was there. There was some story about the old Duke wanting her "looked after", whatever that means.'

'You mean we could have put a stop to this?'

'Well, yes and no. Strictly speaking, we could have done, but Sly kicked up a hell of a fuss and Sir James was not really on top of his brief sufficiently to overrule him. I did what I could, of course, but, frankly, the direction was already set and having seen the magic at work last evening, well… who can say we chose the wrong track?'

'Men are so weak sometimes. I fear Harriet is a victim of her own success. You should all be ashamed.'

'I think you are overstating things somewhat, Margaret. The home secretary came up with a very sensible compromise, I think. Miss Howard stays as she is, but we make a much improved financial arrangement with her. Strode will deal with it.'

'I suppose that may be some recompense for her loss of freedom.'

'That old chestnut again, Margaret. Who among us is really free? We all have a role to play in life. You are always harping on about freedom, but you have not done too badly. Watch out our young beauty doesn't eclipse you. Don't underestimate her.'

'I don't, but we are asking a great deal from her.'

'We ask because there is a great deal at stake. Europe's politics are finely poised. France can be an enemy or a friend. I would rather the latter.'

∽

Harriet is asked to call on Lady Blessington at teatime. When she arrives at Gore House, however, it seems that she is not expected and she is asked to wait. When she does enter the drawing room, there is someone else there. He is tall, over six feet and rather exotically handsome. If anyone ever oozed attraction, it is he. The scent of eau de jasmine lingers in the air.

'Allow me to introduce Count D'Orsay.'

'Good afternoon, sir.'

'We have met, I think?'

'I don't think so. I am sure I would have remembered.'

'As would I.'

D'Orsay is clearly in a hurry to leave and Harriet hears whispered farewells in the hallway before her hostess returns to her. Lady Blessington fans herself. It is no longer a warm day, but her cheeks seem unusually red and she looks as if she may have been crying.

'Have you known each other long?' says Harriet.

'Yes, Alfred and I have enjoyed a long relationship. We fight all the time, of course. He is the most terrible young man with money. He knows where to find me, though. He quite made me forget you were coming this afternoon.'

'But I am here now.'

'Yes, yes… of course.'

'And you wish me to bring you up to date with developments?'

'Yes, yes… I'm sorry I am not myself today.'

Harriet provides her report, as she knows she must, but her mind is racing. She is starting to tie the strands together.

THIRTEEN
Playing the Cards
London, England
1847

Whitehall Place has few visitors today. A nearby clock strikes ten times and Harriet Howard is back in familiar territory. She has several engagements and is anxious to get the first appointment over with.

'To business, Miss Howard,' says Nicholas Sly. 'You have done all that we ask so far. We are about to entrust you with a great deal of money and a great deal of responsibility. You will not let us down, because the consequences, for those close to you, would be unthinkable. Do you follow me?'

'Please don't threaten me.'

'It is as well to have things clear, I always think. No room for doubt, as it were.'

'I am clear.'

'You will share a house with the Frenchman in Berkeley Square. I am sure Mountjoy-Martin has explained things. It will be very congenial. The financial arrangements will be taken care of by Mr Nathaniel Strode. We have arranged a meeting with him later today. He has already been working on your behalf. The Frenchman will believe the wherewithal comes from you. He is gaining the impression that you are a wealthy heiress and that you may be prepared to help him in his ambitions. We will do nothing that might dissuade him from that view. When the time comes, money will be made available. All you need to do is continue playing your part. Are there any questions?'

'No.'

∞

Rockingham House is a comfortable family home in a desirable, new part of town and Harriet is sorry to leave. Martin is happy there and so, in many ways, is she. Still, she feels awkward about the last two years. They are an elaborate sham, of course, and although she feels apprehensive she also feels spurred on by the new circumstances, however uncertain the outcome.

'I will miss your company, Francis,' she says. 'You have been a good friend. Now I must face the next part of the journey on my own. I am nervous.'

'Don't be. You are extremely capable. Everyone is impressed. You will have help. I will be close by. If I am ever needed, I will come.'

'Thank you, Francis.'

'You will always have my support. As will Martin. This is beyond my role. This is a personal pledge. You understand that, don't you?'

'I do.'

'I wanted to say that when this is over I would like to

make our relationship more permanent. I think we could be very good together. Can I hope for that?'

'Let's not make plans. I cannot promise anything. I am resigned to my situation now. You have helped me see that. My parents' living is secure and Martin is growing up in pleasant surroundings and with a good education. I am thankful for that. This is not the life I wanted, but it is a life I can accept. Perhaps one day my assignment will be complete and I can have my freedom back. If that day comes, we will talk about the future then.'

'Very well.'

༄

Berkeley Square is something altogether different. Here are grand buildings. Here is history. Here is a small piece of English countryside, nestled beside the seething mass of London. Here is Number Nine Berkeley Square and here is Nathaniel Strode, a new entrant in Harriet Howard's world. At first glance, he looks like an accountant, she thinks. He carries a well-worn document case. Yet there is something else about him. His hair is slightly unkempt. His waistcoat is rather garish – a sort of dirty, salmon pink. She searches for the word. Raffish comes to mind.

'I am so pleased to meet you. I have heard a lot about you,' he says.

'Some of it may even be true.'

'I hope we will know each other better in time. I understand that you will have reservations about me. I recognise that my proximity to Nicholas Sly will not commend me. However, I can give my assurance that, while I will do my duty by Her Majesty's Government, I will also do my best to look after your interests.'

'That is thoughtful, sir, but what am I to you?'

'I have heard that you cut through to the heart of the matter.'

'Indeed.'

'I am sorry that I must remain ambivalent about some things at the moment. I can do nothing about the essential details of your situation. Some things cannot be undone and I understand that you have accepted your role and everything that it entails. Suffice it to say that there are friends who will look after you, as far as is possible. The road to the Élysée Palace is not straightforward, but that is the destination. It may not be achievable. Should you become surplus to requirements, or should the strategy change, my task is to ensure that you are not disadvantaged and that your future is guaranteed. I cannot ask you to trust me, as there is no basis to do so. Nevertheless, my actions will prove me worthy of your trust. Don't judge me yet.'

'You are also straight to the point, sir. I am grateful.'

'I am at your service.'

'Francis has spoken about you. He was very complimentary.'

'Francis is a good man. He cares about you. Don't doubt him.'

'I don't. But tell me, how will my future be guaranteed? I am intrigued.'

'That I can say. I will explain as simply as I can. Louis Napoléon will need resources to support his campaign.

You will provide the money. Her Majesty's Government will provide the money to your account. Once the draft comes across, the government will see that budget as spent and the treasury will write it off. They will lose interest in how it is managed. Questions will only arise if it does not produce the desired effect. I think you will be motivated to succeed.'

'Go on.'

'We will not be passing gold coin to Louis Napoleon in large sacks. That would be vulgar. Instead, the money will go into a trust in your name. The trust will purchase property. I will be the sole executor of the trust. Loans will be advanced to Louis Napoleon, secured against the properties. Provided Louis Napoleon succeeds in his ambitions and he is in a position to repay those loans, the proceeds will come back to you.'

'I see.'

'Good. It is an elegant arrangement, even if I say so myself.'

'What if he does not wish to repay the loans?'

'We think he will. It will be a matter of honour. The only reservation would be if he failed in his ambitions or if he fell out with you. As I say, I think there will be motivation enough to ensure that neither of these situations arises.'

'Indeed. What is in it for you? Do you mind me asking?'

'I would be surprised if you did not. I will take a management fee for my services, as trustee and executor. It will be quite modest. And, of course, I will have the great pleasure of our regular meetings to update you on your portfolio.'

'That is very gallant. But tell me, this does not seem to have Sly's mark on it.'

'That is correct. He knows nothing of this. He is inclined to favour the stick, rather than the carrot. I think we are beyond that now. I trust you will not tell him if I don't?'

'Of course.'

'Now, the matter in hand. I hope you will like the house we have found. We have taken a lease on it. Have a look around. I will take my leave shortly. Once you are ready, send word to the Prince. If there is anything more, send a message through Francis. I will be in touch.'

✑

Louis Napoleon moves around the drawing room at Berkeley Square, taking in the ambience. He looks closely at some of the paintings adorning the walls. At one point, he moves back to take a closer look at one of the signatures in the corner of a large hunting scene. He nods approvingly, so it seems to Harriet. He stares at a portrait of Horace Walpole. Walpole stares back. Eventually, Louis admits defeat and turns away.

'You told me you were looking for something more suitable,' she says. 'Somewhere the boys could be with you. I have taken the initiative. You will find me very direct. Please take a look around. There are three floors. If it meets your requirements, we can move in straight away. If that is what you wish, of course.'

'Have I not said so? You can be assured of my feelings.'

'I am pleased. Men can be capricious. They say one

thing upstairs and another downstairs. I don't want to press myself.'

'You are a remarkable woman, Harriet. I am indebted yet again.'

'Don't feel that you should be. We enjoy each other's company and I am in a position to make our arrangements more comfortable and to help you. That is all.'

'Your generous nature does you great credit, but what of your needs? What is important to you?'

'I am happy to live a modest life. Family is important to me. My son is my first priority. We share that view, I think?'

'Completely. We are in accord.'

'I have arranged for my son, Martin, to be educated nearby. He will have a tutor. Your sons could join him there if that was convenient for you.'

'Thank you again. That would be most agreeable.'

'I do my best.'

'You seem able to secure everything you want. I am impressed.'

'My trustees are there to look after me and they abide by my expressions of wishes. There is no obstruction. If I wished to advance something to a friend, I could arrange it without delay. Is there something more I can do for you?'

'I have ambitions, Harriet. France is in disarray and my associates tell me that I would be welcomed back in Paris. France needs stability. I can provide that. As you may know, the call has come before, but we have not achieved success. Next time, there must be no failure. Timing will be all important. Preparations will need to be put in place. I will need resources. Those who feel they can help me will be rewarded, of course.'

'I know little of politics. I am simply following my intuition. You will find me constant in my affections. I ask for nothing in return.'

'May I?' he says. He points to the staircase in the hallway. 'Take your time.'

⁂

It is dusk by the time Harriet reaches Gore House. She is familiar with the layout and the rooms now, and she comes and goes as she pleases. She does not wait to be formally received and introduced, and Rogers, Lady Blessington's butler, indicates, with a wave of his gloved hand, towards the orangery. Margaret and Harriet have, despite the essential inequality of their relationship, achieved a certain ease together. D'Orsay appears not to be in favour and is never mentioned by either of them. They both enjoy visits to the opera, although Harriet cannot bear the theatre now. They often ride together in the mornings and sit together talking in the evenings. The older woman, some thirty years Harriet's senior, has a fund of scurrilous stories about famous people and a ready wit. It would be hard not to enjoy her company. There can be no doubt that Lady Blessington has done her best and more to make Harriet's situation as bearable as possible. Sometimes, Harriet almost, but not quite, forgets why she is invited to Gore House. At some point, it always begins "Forgive me, Harriet, I must ask...", by which Lady Blessington means "You need to tell me what is going on because Sly needs my report".

'Forgive me, Harriet, I must ask. Did everything go well today?'

'Louis was very enthusiastic about our plans.'

'Can any difficulties be foreseen?'

'None at all.'

'He suspects nothing?'

'No.'

'Then the cards are dealt. We must see how they fall.'

FOURTEEN
The Return
London, England
Paris, France
1848

Lord Normanby and Lord Palmerston meet at the Reform Club in Pall Mall to review the situation in France. It has been a worrying time for Britain, with revolution so close at hand.

'Are we seeing the end game now?' says Normanby.

'I believe so. It has been an extraordinary year.'

'Indeed. I suppose once the King abdicated there was an inevitability about how things would turn out.'

'Yes and no. Once the mob takes charge, the outcome is impossible to predict. I think, however, that once the general parliamentary vote elected Louis Napoleon, in the department of Paris, the course was set.'

'But that was not the end of mob rule.'

'True enough, but the June riots were not a popular movement. More a case of extremists and anarchists flexing their muscles. Actually, it played into Louis's hands. It meant the executive committee resigned and a state of emergency was declared.'

'Meaning he had the chance to be elected a deputy under new elections?'

'Exactly so. And once he is a deputy and the new constitution is approved, all roads lead in the same direction. I think we will have our man.'

ℊ

In the drawing room at Number Nine Berkeley Square, Louis Napoleon paces. He bites at his nails. His face looks more than usually puffy and pale, and his hair sticks to his forehead in small curls. He rakes the fire. He sits briefly at the desk in front of the window and peers out into the street. Leaves swirl around the square and the few people taking the air are swathed in heavy winter coats and furs against the cold. A knock at the door brings the long-awaited messenger and seconds later, Louis rips at the envelope. His face lights up in a wide smile.

'Good news from Paris?' says Harriet.

'The news from Paris is extraordinary. We are elected president. I leave for France immediately.'

'Immediately?'

'France speaks. She will have what she wishes. I stand ready to serve.'

'Naturally.'

'I must answer first to my people now.'

'Can you spare the time to drink some champagne? We should mark the occasion. France has waited long enough. She can wait a little longer, perhaps?'

'Yes, certainly. You will not be forgotten. I will send for you.'

'You do not wish me to travel with you?'

'Not yet. There are arrangements I must make. Trust me, Harriet.'

'I hope I have been of help. In a small way, of course.'

∽

No sooner has Louis Napoleon's carriage disappeared into Bruton Lane than another liveried carriage draws up in the square. A tall gentleman, wearing a very tall, silk top hat enters the door at Number Nine.

'Lord Normanby,' says the footman.

'I trust I am not disturbing you?' says Normanby to Harriet.

'No, I am alone. Louis is travelling to Paris now. You have just missed him. He says he will send for me.'

'I know. He will. We have our own informants inside his entourage. He intends that you should be in Paris within the week.'

'Thank you for taking the trouble to let me know. You have always been kind. I am grateful to you. You seem to be taking a special interest in matters.'

'We will be seeing a great deal of each other. My role as ambassador to France is about to take on an even greater importance. If all goes as we expect, we will be neighbours.'

'I see.'

'I hope you do see. I wish to make some things even plainer. Her Majesty's Government is in your debt. You have done well with our mutual friend. Louis Napoleon is as good as president of France. Only the formalities have to be put in place and we are already in discussions with his people about an alliance. I must tell you, though, that there was a view in some quarters that you had served your purpose and that you could be disengaged from your current assignment.'

'Thank you for letting me know that, also.'

'I and others take a different view. We think there may be further to run. We want you to go to France and see where the relationship will take you. You will continue to live very comfortably. I understand that Martin gets on well with Louis's sons, Eugene and Louis Alexandre, and that they live as brothers together. There is even talk in France that all three are your sons. There will be some opposition to an English mistress, of course. However, we have little to lose.'

'Am I to have a say in this?'

'I was coming to that. I cannot pretend that you have complete freedom in the matter. Nevertheless, I am interested in your view. I will try to take it into account. I rather assumed that you wanted the adventure across the channel.'

'You speak as if there is no danger in going to France. Do not the French still have the guillotine for spies?'

'We will look after you. Quite apart from any arrangements the president will make, you will be invited to the embassy at receptions and ball, as befits an Englishwoman of your status and independent wealth. Lady Normanby will guide you. If there is any hint of suspicion, you will be withdrawn immediately.'

'Can you influence events so readily? Am I not under the direction of Mr Sly?'

'Sly cannot be completely ignored and yes, he continues in his role. However, there is a bigger picture here and he is a small cog in the wheel. You must trust me that you have friends who will continue to look after your interests. Mr Strode is taking care of things. He is most diligent. Now, what do you think: shall you join me in Paris?'

⸎

France has its president. Britain has its ally. In the Hotel du Rhin, on Place Vendôme, Louis Napoleon sets up an interim headquarters, while preparations are made to arrange the Élysée Palace to his liking. A rather battered portrait of his illustrious uncle hangs on the wall behind him. Louis is in his finery today. A public appearance is planned later. The dark blue jacket of a general is deemed suitable. It is rather flamboyantly set off with gold epaulettes and a gold sash, and matched with red trousers with black side stripes. His private secretary, Jean Mocquard, makes a note of requirements, as the president walks backwards and forwards, his hands crossed behind his back.

'There is an English woman named Harriet Howard. Please grant her every wish. She will arrive shortly with our three sons. She is a great friend. We could not have achieved this return without her support. Find somewhere near to the palace,' says Louis.

'I will see to it,' says Mocquard.

In fact, Mocquard has already anticipated the requirement. A townhouse in rue du Cirque, between avenue Gabriel and rue du Faubourg, and within tiptoeing distance of the Élysée Palace, is currently undergoing an extensive redecoration. Mocquard looks forward to meeting the incoming occupant. Normanby has told him a lot about her.

Not everyone is so enthusiastic. As Mocquard leaves, Louis Napoleon's first cousin, Princess Mathilde, arrives. He has not seen her since before he was imprisoned. The pretty young girl he remembers has grown into a beautiful woman and he is pleased to see her. They engage in polite reminiscence and she congratulates him on his appointment. It does not take her long, though, to give her esteemed relation, not to mention sometime fiancé, the benefit of her opinion of his English mistress.

'She is an adventuress, a courtesan. I am surprised you could be so easily duped.'

'She is a wealthy heiress.'

'Is that what she says? Do you believe her?'

'She has been constant throughout. There is no reason I should doubt her.'

'I think you will one day regret that woman.'

'Without "that woman", you and I would not be here today. You will learn to appreciate her as I do.'

'We will see.'

⚬⁀∽

On the rue de Rivoli sits the elegant Hotel Meurice. Locals call it "L'hotel de l'Anglais", on account of the favour it finds with the English aristocracy. Harriet enjoys the irony of her situation. She recalls visiting her grandfather at his hotel, the Castle, in Brighton when she was a little girl. She remembers it smelled of boiled cabbage. She receives Lady Blessington in her own suite of rooms. The tables are turned somewhat when compared with Gore House. Harriet is now the more expensively dressed. She positively ripples with jewellery. Here, it is Harriet who waves Lady Blessington to her seat. It is Harriet who commands the attendants and who asks the questions. She presses for an assessment of her situation, now she is in Paris.

'I would say that you are in a powerful position,' says Lady Blessington. 'Nathaniel has ensured that you will have your own wealth. Your parents are safe. Your son's future is secure. Normanby takes a great interest in you. Louis Napoleon is in love with you. I would advise you to follow the inclination of your heart, as I did. You may be an empress one day.'

'Empress?'

'Louis will not stop at president. Mark my words. His course is set. It would suit you very well.'

'I think not. Louis Napoleon is in love with me, as you say, but there are several others with whom he consorts. I make no waves and I make no demands. He is a considerate lover. The arrangements meet both our needs for now, but I have never really loved him. And I am not a princess.'

'I have misjudged the situation. I am sorry. Your circumstances are still very satisfactory, though, don't you think?'

'In many ways, yes, but I still must answer to Sly. He hates me.'

'Forget about Sly. The world moves on. He cannot touch you here.'

'There is someone Sly can still hurt and who I care about.'

'You need not worry about Francis. He manages very well. He pines for you, but he will get over it.'

'It is not Francis I worry about.'

'Then who?'

'Jem Mason.'

'Mason? Be very careful.'

'You are changing your advice.'

'Harriet?'

'To follow the inclination of my heart. My heart is with Jem. That can't change.'

'I didn't know you still carried that with you. Is he not married now?'

'I don't blame him. I betrayed him.'

'Surely you saved him.'

'In one way, yes, but I didn't tell him the truth and I promised I always would. He was the person I trusted and he trusted me. I broke that trust.'

'You cannot punish yourself all your life.'

'Perhaps. I am surprised how easily the lies come now. Almost everything I say to Louis is a lie.'

'I think if we tell a man something he really wants to believe, then it doesn't count as a lie, even if it is.'

'You are very cynical.'

'I prefer to say that I am a pragmatist.'

'Do you know how many people say "You must trust me, Harriet"? Francis, Normanby, Louis, Strode. Who can I trust?'

'I cannot answer for all of them, but I think they all have your welfare in mind.'

Harriet gets up, walks to the window and opens a blind. She looks out at the street scene and the Tuileries Palace beyond, then turns, with the sunlight framing her silhouette, to face her guest.

'There is something I have been meaning to ask. Can I trust you, Margaret?'

'What has brought this on, Harriet? Are we not friends?'

'You said once that you saw me as an actress. Where was that?'

'At the Sadler's Wells. Opposite Samuel Phelps, in Romeo and Juliet. It was sublime. You were quite perfect.'

'Was that the only time?'

'Yes… yes, I am sure.'

'I am ashamed that women are so simple
To offer war where they should kneel for peace;
Or seek for rule, supremacy and sway,
When they are bound to serve, love and obey.
Why are our bodies soft and weak and smooth,
Unapt to toil and trouble in the world,
But that our soft conditions and our hearts
Should well agree with our external parts?'

'What are you talking about? Are you mad?'

'You never heard me say those lines? Tell me the truth.'

Lady Blessington looks down at the floor. She begins to weep, softly at first, but the tears flow and she bends forward, holding her face in her hands. Eventually, she recovers herself.

'I don't know what to say.'

'You were there, weren't you? At the audition for Taming of the Shrew. At Haymarket. I was to be Kate.'

'Can you ever forgive me?'

'You are forgiven. I know that Sly had some hold over you, as he does over me. And I know more than you think about what goes on behind closed doors. I am not stupid.'

'If there is anything I can do to make amends…'

'There is. I have been biding my time. Now, I need your help. Kate will have her revenge. She will not be tamed.'

Part Two

FIFTEEN
Putting the Pieces Together
Newmarket, England
1862

Martin was back in England and he sent word that he was on his way to see me again, at my racing yard in Newmarket. As I waited for him, there were snowflake clouds scudding fast across a blue sky. Swallows and swifts arced and dived high above me. The hay cutters were out and I saw the small conical hay ricks, characteristic of the area, scattered like scarecrow sentinels at the edges of the heath. The sweet smell of the hay mingled with the heady scent of the wild rosemary, thyme and mint, caught up by the scythes at the field headlands. On the horizon, a heat haze shimmered and the whole scene conspired to produce a positive feeling inside me. The last season with the steeplechasers proved successful and we continued our winning vein into the summer flat racing. I was suffused with a sense of goodwill. I thought to myself that days like this should be cherished and remembered because they can't always be like this. We shouldn't take them for granted. By the time Martin's brougham skittered into the yard, my heart jumped with anticipation.

He told me that more information was to hand. He was able to fill in more gaps in the story I outlined at our earlier meeting. He reminded me that, as I had recalled, Jem and Harriet, still called Eliza by her close friends and family, were the golden couple for a while. She went from strength to strength and made her name in the Shakespearean repertoire: The Tempest, Othello and Anthony and Cleopatra. Jem followed up his Grand National win in 1839 with several more big race wins and finished up champion jockey in 1840 and 1841. Lord Strathmore and Lord Beauclerk retained his services and he had the pick of the top horses.

It seemed, at the time, that they were leading a charmed life. Then, at some point in 1841, leading into 1842, things went wrong for them both. A few bad theatre reviews appeared, even though this was at odds with the sell-out houses. Whatever happened, Harriet went out of fashion and her roles dried up. I was sorry to hear that Harriet herself went into a decline. Martin didn't flinch when he told me what he found out from his latest detective work. Apparently, the rumour was that she, in her desperation to secure employment, gained the reputation of being free with her favours in return for acting roles.

This, unsurprisingly, put a strain on the relationship with Jem, who himself suffered some reverses during the same period. Lord Strathmore sacked him as first jockey, even though he rode a string of winners for him. *The Sporting Magazine* carried a story suggesting Jem had thrown a race at Northampton in return for a bribe, which I knew couldn't be true. I rode in the race and he was spitting teeth that I beat him a short head after his horse rooted the last fence and lost at least three lengths. Just after the 1842 Grand National, Jem had a bad fall that nearly killed him.

Of course, I knew many of these facts, but I couldn't put the pieces together in the way that Martin could. Hindsight, the distance of the years and some important new snippets of information combined to make some things clearer.

In the same year, Harriet disappeared from public view and wasn't heard of again in the theatre, apart from a brief, but ill-fated, attempt at a comeback a year later. Jem's career seemed to tread water. He was still highly regarded by the racing public, but the sporting press was cool on him. John Elmore and George Dockeray stood by him and made sure he rode plenty of winners. All the jockeys knew he was still the best.

Throughout this time, I remembered that Jem was tight-lipped about Harriet. He refused to answer questions about her and I gave up after a while. In late 1844, the news came that Jem would marry Emily, John Elmore's daughter. I attended the wedding and a pretty couple they made, but the faraway look in Jem's eyes gave me the feeling his thoughts were elsewhere.

I asked Martin if he was any nearer succeeding in his quest for the name of his father. I found some of the information he related quite upsetting. He found a story that Nicholas Sly had raped Harriet. He couldn't substantiate it, but he couldn't rule it out either. Sly's whereabouts were unknown. There was more information about Francis Mountjoy-Martin. It was confirmed that Harriet did meet him before his appointment as her guardian. Apparently, during one of the numerous tiffs between Jem and Harriet, she left a masked ball with a tall Guards officer. Martin had it on good authority, from a former Guards colleague, that it was Mountjoy-Martin. He was now rumoured to be in India.

Louis Napoleon continued as elusive as ever. He could be placed in London at Number One Carlton Gardens in 1838, but after a failed coup in France he found himself in prison. This didn't stop him fathering two children during that time – the mother, apparently, was Eleonore Vergeot, the laundry maid at the prison. Evidently being a Bonaparte brought with it certain concessions, even when incarcerated. Martin still couldn't rule him out. Some things were clearer, but some things were not.

'You know it is not me,' I said. I wanted this to be unambiguous this time round. I missed out the details of my relationship with his mother and I decided it would be unhelpful to add that the lack of any close engagement was not for want of trying on my part, at least in the early days of our acquaintance. Jem and I vied for her affections and he won fair and square. He was my best friend and I left it at that. Harriet became a good friend, too, but that was it.

'I believe that,' he said.

'So what is next?' I said. 'At least you have narrowed down the list, marginally.'

'That is what I thought, but there are new additions.'

'There are?'

'The Duke of Beaufort, Lord Normanby and Count D'Orsay.'

'That is extraordinary. You lose an old jockey, but gain a duke, a marquis and a count.'

'I am not taking the allegations about Beaufort and Normanby very seriously. They certainly showed a great interest in my mother, but I will have a very long list if that is the benchmark.'

'And it would not do to make those statements without firm proof.'

'Exactly. D'Orsay is an interesting one, though. I must find out more about him. The dates work out for him, as they do for Sly and Mountjoy-Martin and Mason, if my information is correct. I was born on 16th August, a few weeks prematurely, I believe.'

'Are there any other thoughts?'

'I will stay on my present course. I must resolve the question of the dates for Louis Napoleon. I need to find Nicholas Sly and Francis Mountjoy-Martin. I think this will not be easy. I need to talk to Jem Mason. I hoped you would help me meet him.'

I wanted to help, but my loyalties were torn. I was back in touch with Jem, who was now living at Clarendon Place in St John's Wood. We met infrequently and, although we spent time talking about the old days and going over the old stories, I felt the camaraderie, the closeness between us, was gone. Since my first meeting with Martin, I talked with Jem about him, but I didn't get very far. Jem wouldn't talk about Harriet and was vague about Martin. It was as if he wanted to shut that part of his life away forever. His health was fragile, it seemed to me. I wondered if Jem's personality was in some way shaped by all the injuries over the years. It can't be easy to live with that amount of pain. Even though he still rode out most days and even rode in the odd race, I began to doubt he would make old bones.

I asked Martin about Harriet.

'We are reconciled. Up to a point. We are talking, which is good, although not about anything I want to talk about.'

'How does she seem?'

'She is calmer, more settled.'

'Why do you say that?'

'She has finally rid herself of that mountebank Trelawney, for one thing. She seems resigned to living a simpler life. There are few visitors at the château. She tends the gardens, arranges the flowers in the chapel, visits the poor. The people in the village love her. I think she has found some contentment, perhaps. It is hard to know with her.'

It occurred to me, as he spoke, that the same could be said of Martin, compared to our first meeting. He was again calm, measured in his manner, but there was no added sense of urgency about him now. It was as if he knew that he was closing in on his goal and was happy to let things take their course. I watched him as he talked, rather in the way he had scrutinised me for clues when we first met. Six months ago, he seemed youthful, boyish, but now he was a man. His shoulders were broader, his handshake firmer, his jaw line more defined. His features seemed to have darkened, his eye sockets were more sunken and the black sideburns extended well below his ears. His demeanour, though, seemed lighter. He was no longer inclined to look at the floor or away, as he was prone to do before when talking. His habit of pinching his nose, between his eyes, had all but disappeared.

We talked all day and late into the night. I persuaded him to stay on, rather than rush back to London. We shared a bottle of port. He told me his plans. It was apparent that he was achieving notice as a promising rider. He enjoyed his time hunting the wild boar in the Fontaineblcau forests and he was winning races at the smaller steeplechase meetings, springing up around Paris at the time. He harboured thoughts of becoming a huntsman or perhaps a jockey. He asked me again about Jem and whether the stories about him were true.

I didn't know what he'd heard, but I told him one of my own.

'He was sharp as a hussar's sabre when it came to taking advantage of the rules. One new idea at the regulated tracks, in the early days, was the introduction of a flag man, who would stand halfway between the starting gate and the first fence. If the starter felt that there wasn't a fair, level break, he would signal to the flag man, who would wave a large white flag, indicating a false start, and the jockeys would return to the start and line up again. Failure to obey the flag man and the starter could incur a fine and repeat offenders faced suspension. One day, at Bedford, there had been false starts in the first two races, with some of the keener lads trying to steal a few lengths. All the jockeys were getting a bit jumpy at the gate, going into the third race. The starter was an irascible old sod and he warned them, in no uncertain terms, that if anyone tried it on again he would have them before the stewards for a hefty fine. This time, they jumped off level enough, but as the flag man ran back to the side he tripped in a divot and the flag shot up in the air. Jem, sensing indecision, shouted out: "False start, boys". The jockeys pulled their mounts up and turned back. In the meantime, the flag man had gathered up his flag and was back standing by the hedge. Jem gave his mount a kick and headed off towards the first fence, hell for leather. The remaining jockeys stood arguing with the starter, who shrugged his shoulders. "I didn't signal a false start", he said. By the time they realised they'd been tricked, Jem had jumped two fences and stayed that distance clear all the way to the finish, despite the best efforts of his rivals to reel him in. Later on, he sent a case of champagne into the weighing room for the jockeys, with a card saying: "Thank you for all your help. Jem".

The next morning I was able to see for myself what Martin was made of. It was a cruel trick when I thought about it later, but I couldn't resist it. Kingdom was a hard puller and he had a buck in him, too. All the lads avoided riding him out, but when they had to ride him, they put a variety of cross nosebands and curbs on him in an effort to anchor him. Even then, he had a habit of bolting and there were many times when he came careering back into the yard alone, stirrups flying and reins flapping, his rider deposited out on the heath somewhere. We persevered with him because he was a talented racehorse and won his share of races, but he needed a special kind of rider on him.

'You ride the bay horse, Martin,' I said. 'He's a bit of a quirk on him.'

I put him in a plain snaffle and crossed my fingers. I jumped up beside Martin on my grey, lead horse and we headed off to Long Hill. All the lads were craning their heads out of the boxes to get a look at what was going on. I knew there were wagers being laid about how long it would be before a riderless Kingdom was back in the yard.

It was another beautiful morning out on the heath and my positive mood continued as we reached the bottom of the gallops.

'Let's do a long, swinging canter up by the white posts and then we'll quicken up half speed over the last three furlongs and have a blow up to the top,' I said.

I needn't have been concerned. Kingdom was as quiet as an old hack. Martin had it all: the relaxed hands, the long rein, the easy elegance. He was a natural.

We walked back slowly across the heath. We let the girths out and allowed the horses to stretch their necks low on loose reins. We stopped on the knoll and jumped down to let them have a pick of grass. We lit up cheroots and sat on a fallen log, watching the long lines of second lots, snaking across the heath in the distance.

'If you decide to settle back in England, there is a job for you here.'

'I'll bear that in mind,' he said.

After breakfast, we said our goodbyes and Martin's brougham departed in a trail of dust down the lane. I realised how much I enjoyed his company and how much we shared in common. I was determined I would help him in his quest and I started racking my brains to see if I could find anything in my memories that might provide a missing clue.

SIXTEEN
Changing of the Guard
Paris, France
1849

Paris in springtime has a resonance through the ages, but Paris in early 1849 is a squalid affair. Everywhere there is disease and desolation. The French know what they don't want and the monarchy is swept away, but they seem unsure what they do want. Uneasy alliances ebb and flow, as Louis Napoleon marshals his supporters, but in the meantime Paris founders under a debilitating paralysis. The wealthy have left or are in hiding. The poor and the destitute fight among themselves for what little food is available. Sewage runs in rivulets in the streets and leaches into the Seine.

Harriet Howard can bear the uncertainty. After all, she is largely protected from it, now installed in her lavish apartments on the rue du Cirque. However, news of a different kind comes, which cannot be borne easily.

Lady Blessington is dead. The rumour buzzes around Paris and London for days, before the London newspapers confirm the facts. The facts, if they can be believed, are that Lady Blessington was found alone in her rooms at the Hotel Meurice, early in the morning of Monday the fourth of June.

A waiter, bringing a breakfast tray, could not gain access and the manager was alerted. He summoned a doctor, but nothing could be done. The cause of death was reported as heart failure.

∾

Lord Normanby hopes to be first with the news to Harriet, but he is already too late. He senses it as soon as he enters her drawing room.

'I'm very sorry. I know you were very close,' he says. 'She was a remarkable woman.'

'Indeed, she was – even more remarkable that she is dead. I was with her only a few days ago. She was in the best of health.'

'None of us can know when our time will come. She led a full life.'

'You are intent on seeing nothing suspicious in all of this?'

'I am guided by the information I have been given.'

'I see you are determined.'

'I see you are upset. Naturally. But nothing can be gained by subscribing to conspiracy theories. The dead cannot be brought back. I suggest you leave well alone. Mountjoy-Martin is on his way from London. I trust that will be some comfort to you.'

∾

Later that day, Francis Mountjoy-Martin arrives. Harriet

has had time to think things through. She tests her theory with him.

'This has Sly's hand on it. You know it as well as I do.'

'Sly is missing. He has not been seen since last Sunday.'

'How convenient.'

'I think you are on the wrong track this time. Sly has others do his work for him. He would not be implicated.'

He misses the opportunity for a flat denial and Harriet senses that he doesn't have his script fully rehearsed.

'I am sure, but I think you accept my doubts? This is not "natural causes".'

'I accept nothing of the sort,' he says, recovering. 'Normanby's advice is sound. If there is anything to be discovered, I will let you know.'

'Please do.'

'In the meantime, we must carry on with our task. I don't wish to be insensitive. Margaret was a friend to us both and I will miss her as you do. However, we must not forget our responsibility...'

'Our task. Our responsibility. I am the only active partner in this. Your role is to preen yourself, take credit for my sacrifices, and add ribbons and stars to your uniform. Congratulations are in order, I surmise.'

'As you observe, I am promoted. In the absence of Lady Blessington and the temporary unavailability of Sly, I will take full responsibility for looking after you.'

'How nice for you.'

'I had hoped you might find this satisfactory in the circumstances. I did not seek this. I will do my best for you, as I always do.'

'If you say so.'

'I have one more piece of news.'

'Please tell me.'

'My wife is dying. It will not be long now.'

Mountjoy-Martin gives her no opportunity to respond. He leaves the room before she can gather her thoughts.

∽

Harriet doesn't take in the implications of the new development with her sometime guardian. She is sorry for him, but her own grief blots it out for the moment. In any event, there are other appointments to be faced. She sends word to Louis Napoleon that she is indisposed and will not be available for her meeting with him, but he comes anyway. The president does as he wishes. Sensitivity is not his strong point and he provides her with a detailed description of his latest ailments, before her silence halts him.

'You seem distracted,' he says.

'I'm sorry. Margaret's death weighs on me. I wish more could have been done for her.'

'Such a vivacious person. We are all the poorer for her untimely death.'

'What a fine statement.'

'I don't follow you. You have something on your mind?'

'No, nothing. I don't expect you to understand.'

'Please, Harriet, if anything can be done, I will help as much as I can.'

'Very well. I am suspicious. This has the mark of murder on it.'

'You are one for melodrama. Lady Blessington lived hard. Anyone can see that. And I understand there were stresses behind the scenes. Please don't look for blame. It helps no one.'

'Someone is responsible.'

'In my experience, little can be gained from speculation. I share your sorrow, but nothing can be done.'

'Please leave me. I have nothing more to say to you.'

෴

Harriet hopes that Nathaniel Strode will be more forthcoming when he reaches her that evening. How refreshing, at least, to talk to someone without a motive. She values the businesslike nature of her relationship with Strode. He seems like a man who can be trusted, but she reminds herself that sometimes all is not as it seems. Nevertheless, she can have no argument with Strode's record in her dealings with him and she needs help.

'I was sorry to hear about Lady Blessington,' he says.

'Do you believe it?'

'I have no reason not to. I detect that, perhaps, you do?'

'In London, the cloak is drawn rather effectively, I hear. In Paris, there is talk.'

'That is not unusual.'

'Of course, but the sources I have here are reliable. Normanby was slow to be informed. The cover up was not immediately implemented.'

'Cover up?'

'Yes, Nathaniel. Margaret was not alone in the room as I understand it. Another body was found. A man. The room was covered in blood. Three maids had to be brought in from another hotel and it took them two days to clean it. Even now, the room is under guard. No one is allowed in.'

'How do you know this?'

'Let us just say I have my informants.'

'I see.'

'You are a resourceful man. Can you see what else you can find out?'

'My forte is money. I am not a detective.'

'I understand, but I would be most grateful if you could try.'

'I will see what I can do.'

'I am sorry to ask this of you. I am feeling exposed. She was a friend, a companion. I could not have survived without her and now she is gone.'

'I am sure your friends here will rally round.'

'Are you?'

'I see this has affected you greatly. Can I assure you that I will do whatever I can to support you? If there is anything else, please let me know.'

∽

Nearby, at the British Embassy on rue du Faubourg Saint-Honore, Lord Normanby and Francis Mountjoy-Martin are deep in conversation.

'So, you see, things have become rather complicated,' says Normanby. 'First, we hear that Louis may be thinking about marrying Miss Howard, then we have this business with Lady Blessington. It really is too much. Obviously, we need Miss Howard in place as a financial channel, but there are limits to what can be accepted.'

'What arrangements should I make?'

'I would only say that you may be here for some time. I would prefer to leave it at that for the moment.'

'As you wish, sir. I am happy to do what is necessary.'

'I am sure.'

As Mountjoy-Martin leaves, Jean Mocquard arrives. They acknowledge each other with a brief nod. Mocquard and Normanby know each other well. They are easy in each other's company. When they meet, there is no need for small talk and scene setting.

'Something very odd has gone on here with Lady Blessington, as I'm sure you may have heard. Do you know anything more about it?' says Normanby.

'I am afraid not.'

'Miss Howard makes a great show of mystified hurt. She is an accomplished actress.'

'Perhaps she is simply upset by the death of her friend.'

'Possibly. Find out what she knows. I think she knows a great deal more than she is letting on.'

'Of course, monsieur. It will be my pleasure to talk to her.'

'Yes. You are very taken with Miss Howard, I see. Don't be fooled by her. She likes to play the defenceless young lady, but she has steel in her. She is adept at having men in thrall to her charms.'

'That is evident.'

'Thank you, Mocquard. That will be all.'

∞

At the rue du Cirque, Harriet waits up late. Mocquard arrives, as he promised he would.

'I can't believe that Normanby doesn't know,' she says.

'He seems not to, at the moment at least.'

'What makes you say that?'

'He asks me to find out what you know. He suspects, but he is guessing.'

∞

In London, as the year wears on, the British Government breathes a collective sigh of relief that the revolutionary fervour in Europe seems not to have taken hold in Britain. The Chartists and the Irish nationalists gain support for demonstrations, but not direct action. Queen Victoria visits Ireland and the trip is hailed a success. Lord Palmerston, the foreign secretary, and Louis Napoleon enjoy several convivial lunches together, during which time Berrys' wine cellars in St James are seriously depleted. They each pronounce their great satisfaction with progress in Europe.

Lord Normanby travels back to London, for a briefing on Louis Napoleon, with Lord Palmerston and Lord Russell, the prime minister.

'Far too cocksure of himself for my liking,' says Palmerston, which is rather at odds with what he says to Louis Napoleon's face.

'That is the nature of the man,' says Normanby.

'True enough, but we need to stay the course with him.'

'We have no alternative. That much is plain.'

Russell stares at a spider's web in the corner of his window sill. A moth has just become entangled and the spider is inching towards it, as the moth jerks helplessly.

'What do you say on the matter, Prime Minister?' asks Palmerston.

'Oh yes, quite so, quite so. Yes, indeed. Mmm.'

Palmerston raises his eyes to the ceiling and then winks at Normanby.

'The prime minister wishes you to carry on as before. Keep us informed, won't you?'

∽

Back in Paris, October sees Louis Napoleon, tired of the squabbling among his supporters and the carping from his detractors, take matters into his own hands. He dismisses the puppet prime minister, Camille Odilon, saying that he proposes to take responsibility for government directly through his ministers, without the need of a prime minister. It is his clearest signal yet that he means to be Emperor. It can only be a matter of time.

Normanby calls Mountjoy-Martin to the embassy again. He feels the need to seek reassurance.

'Louis Napoleon is far from secure. He pushes his luck. Politically, he will probably pull it off, but as usual, he is running short of money. We will need Miss Howard's help again, I think.'

'She knows what is required. I will alert her.'

'Can we rely on her?'

'Events recently have unsettled her, but she will not let us down.'

SEVENTEEN
Everything Is Risked
London, England
Paris, France
1850

In the spring of 1850, Jem Mason and Tom Olliver are called to a meeting at Manchester House in Manchester Square, London. They arrive early and sit on a bench in the square to share cheroots. The plane trees are already in leaf and the lawns glisten under a light morning dew, as the sun rises over the rooftops. Thrushes pick at the moss and blackbirds rustle in the undergrowth of the ornamental bushes. As the air warms, the smell of jasmine mingles with the tarry tang of the cheroot smoke. Tom checks his watch and swings it into his waistcoat pocket.

At the appointed time, Lord Hertford receives them very warmly and they are ushered into an elegant drawing room at the back of the house, with wide doors opening out onto a courtyard, lush with greenery. His brother, Lord Henry Seymour-Conway, is in attendance and it is he who explains the purpose of the discussion. Jem reminds Tom later that it is not their first meeting with him. A few years earlier, Tom rode with Jem in an exhibition race at Croix de Berny, when jumping in France was barely heard of. Clearly, a seed was sown and it transpires that the French Jockey Club is keen to promote jump racing and a new course is almost complete, just outside Paris, beyond Ville d'Avray at La Marche. Lord Henry is a former president of the French Jockey Club and still an influential member. Lord Hertford is a great lover of all things French and spends a great deal of his time in Paris.

Paris is calmer after the disruption of the past two years and there is a sense of optimism again in some quarters. It is explained that a number of prominent owners, both French and English, are proposing to support the new venture by installing trainers at Chantilly and Saint Cloud and investing in bloodstock. They want the best jockeys available to ride them. This is where Tom and Jem come into the equation. Tom feels very flattered. Jem says, after the meeting, 'Who else would they ask?'

Things move on quickly and, within a few days, they are entertained at Lord Hertford's new Paris residence, Château de Bagatelle, in the Bois de Boulogne. They meet several members of the Jockey Club and are entertained at the Opera and the Café de Paris. Comte Achille Delamarre puts his entire staff at their disposal and they are given a tour of all that Paris has to offer. Paris has a lot to offer.

The detailed proposition is attractive and it is easy to accept. They can keep their best rides in England; the French racing will be scheduled to avoid the big meetings; they will earn twenty per cent of all prize money; and stakes are estimated to be twice the going rate in England. They will be on the best horses for the wealthiest owners. Apartments will be secured for them, but until that time the Hotel Saint James will be their home from home. Contracts are duly signed.

Looking back, Tom supposes it was obvious that Jem and Harriet were likely to meet again, but it wouldn't occur to him until later. Whether it was in Jem's mind, he didn't know. He didn't ask him.

❦

Paris in springtime, in 1850, is transformed. The change in a year is remarkable. Slums have been cleared and the green spaces in the parks and squares, especially around the Tuileries and the Élysée Palace, bristle with new planting. Cafés open up again on street corners and customers spill out onto the pavements. Music plays through open windows and the avenues echo with laughter. The Seine is free of sewer stench for the first time in many years and the booksellers return to their left bank pitches to ply their trade.

Events soon conspire to put Jem and Harriet in the same location. Harriet receives a visitor at rue du Cirque.

'Louis asks that I should entertain you today,' says Jean Mocquard.

'How thoughtful he is.'

'I am told there are races today at La Marche. Some of your countrymen and women will be there. I thought it might be an amusing diversion. Does it meet your approval?'

'It may do. Is there a programme for the day?'

'Indeed, there is. I have it here.'

She pores over the lists of owners, runners and riders. Her heart beats fast. She tries to stay calm, to regulate her breathing. She feels the colour rise from her neck to her face. Her hands begin to shake, but she manages to sit on them and attempts to project an outward display of nonchalance.

'I suppose it may fill a few hours. I see Lord Hertford has two horses entered. It would be quite interesting to see how they fare against the French horses, perhaps.'

'As you wish. I can make some other arrangements if you would prefer.'

'Let us proceed with your suggestion. Why not?'

'Perfect. I will have the carriage ready at eleven.'

'Thank you, Mocquard.'

༄

As soon as they cross the Seine at the Pont de Saint Cloud, the countryside seems to open out. May feels like an auspicious month; there is a fresh greenness to the boughs of the trees and there are primroses pricking the long grass of the roadside verges. The blossom on the hawthorn hedges hums with honeybees. When they make a brief stop for the coachman to adjust some harness, Harriet pulls down the carriage window and fills her lungs with the air. She spends too much time in town, she thinks. She enjoys the parks, but this is something else.

༄

At La Marche, Tom and Jem walk the course to familiarise

themselves with the layout of the track. The turf is a pristine, luxuriant green. Old turf. They find a figure-of-eight course, laid out on a broadly flat, meadowland site. The track goes right-handed, then left-handed, then right-handed again. The plain fences are tightly packed with birch. Unforgiving to a lazy jumper, thinks Tom. As well as the familiar fences found in England, there is a rail and ditch, a bullfinch, a bank, a water jump and a few sheep hurdles. Jem thinks it owes more to what might be encountered in a day's hunting in Ireland than an English steeplechase course. There is a complete absence of guide rails and only very occasional flags. It is a test of memory as well as bravery.

'Should be a craic,' says Tom.

'If we don't get dizzy first,' says Jem.

Harriet and Mocquard arrive at one o'clock. The newly painted grandstand shines white in the sunlight and multicoloured pennants flutter overhead in the breeze. On the first floor, an elegant dining room, fitted out with crystal and damask, greets the opulently dressed racegoers. French and English voices mingle. Waiters glide between the tables. In a far corner, a bearded student sits at a piano and makes a passable attempt at some Chopin sonatas. Harriet picks at her food and twists at the end of her napkin. When the horses come into the parade ring for the first race, the room empties as everyone makes their way to view the runners and riders. The scene never fails to excite Harriet, but there is an added frisson today. Standing across the paddock, she sees Jem Mason and Tom Olliver, smiling and joking together.

The afternoon passes in a blur of flashing jockey silks and the glint of gleaming thoroughbreds. Tom and Jem ride two winners each: Tom all power and strength and driving finishes, whip high, roaring, Jem almost lazy by comparison, long rein, squeezing the horses into the fences, his whip an ornament, patting the horses on the neck as they pass the winning post.

At the conclusion of the racing, Mocquard arranges an introduction to Lord Hertford in his private box. He, in turn, introduces his jockeys to Harriet.

'How lovely to see you again, Tom. You must tell me all the gossip from home,' she says.

'I see you know each other. Do you know Mason as well?'

'Hello, Jem.'

There are perhaps twenty-five people in the box, which has two balconies attached: one looking forward across the racecourse; one looking back at the stables and parade ring. Mocquard is adept at manoeuvring people around, making introductions here and there, turning this person to that; a deft pull at an elbow, a gentle hand in the small of the back. After a while, Jem and Harriet find themselves alone on the rear balcony. A door closes behind them.

'We may not have another chance, Jem,' she says. 'I don't want to live my life in complete regret. What do you want?'

'I wish I knew.'

'You wish you knew or you wish you could admit it?'

'You know what I think, but I don't, is that it?'

'No. I know what I think. I have no pride, but you are the mystery. Let me be clear. I would like us to be as we once were. I am prepared to risk a rebuttal, but I will have tried. Is it so hard to tell the truth? Walk towards me or walk away from me, but don't stand and look at me. What is it to be?'

When the carriages are called, Mocquard leaves without Harriet. She and Jem are nowhere to be seen.

∽

One morning, three weeks later, Harriet leaves her apartments, telling her maid that she is visiting her dressmaker and that she is not to be expected back until the evening. She wears a modest brown dress and a small, matching felt hat with a single feather, the like of which a milliner might wear on her day off. She turns left from the rue du Cirque onto the rue du Faubourg Saint-Honore. She passes the Hotel Saint James on her right. She gazes up at the windows. Perhaps Jem looks down at her from behind the curtains when he stays there. At the end of the road, she stops at the Eglise Saint-Philippe du Roule. She walks between the centre columns, flanking the entrance and adjusts her eyes to the semi-darkness. She looks up at the barrel-vaulted ceiling and moves to a corner of the church. She lights a candle. Back out into the sunlight, she tracks across to the rue de Courcelles. She passes the grand houses, then walks up through the southern entrance of the Parc Monceau, off the rue Rembrandt. Inside the park, there is a bench beneath a beech tree, behind the colonnade, looking across to the lake. This is where they agree to meet. Since their reconciliation at La Marche, messages have been exchanged. Tom Olliver is the go-between. Somehow it seems acceptable for Tom and Harriet to meet. Sometimes they will sit in one of the cafés, sometimes they will stroll in the squares. They are old friends and there is no suspicion that they might be romantically linked. Jem is a different matter. She knows there is talk. She knows she must be careful. It is only prudent to arrange to meet like this, away from prying eyes.

She sits on the bench and, a few minutes later, Jem joins her.

'I could not be sure you would come,' she says.

'I thought the same of you.'

'I will always come when you call.'

Harriet feels the tension rising up in her chest. She can hardly bear it. She has spent the last weeks thinking only of this day and what could go wrong. But he is here. They are talking. Something like the old flame is flickering again. He wants assurances she cannot give, but she senses a softening in tone.

'I am risking everything for you,' she says. 'Please don't press me.'

A nod from him accepts that the time for talking is over for now. They rise together and move towards the northern gate. He, walking tall, marking his halting gait with his silver-topped cane and she, leaning in, gripping his free arm in a double clasp and gazing up at him. Two lovers, taking a morning stroll in the park, with the promise of the day ahead spreading out before them.

EIGHTEEN
Power Behind the Throne
Paris, France
1851

The opposition to Louis Napoleon in the National Assembly secures a law limiting the voting suffrage in France, aimed at reducing Louis's appeal among the population. It does no more than irritate him. He is already elected president for four years until 1852, but he has ambition for something more. He is in no rush, but something will have to give. Harriet, though, feels the strain of her situation. She thinks she has more than delivered on her brief, as far as she can understand it. The requirement to provide regular updates for Lieutenant-Colonel Mountjoy-Martin has all but ceased. Louis seems preoccupied with matters of state and she has not spoken to him for several weeks. She and Jem meet when they can, but the need for secrecy weighs on them both.

When Mountjoy-Martin does call on her, at the rue du Cirque, she presses him.

'What more must I give? You have your man in place,' she says.

'I have asked Lord Normanby if you can be released from your duties. He says we are not quite there yet.'

'Who is driving this? Normanby? Sly? You?'

'As always, I am operating under instructions from Her Majesty's Government. It is not always easy to see from whence the orders originate.'

'And Sly?'

'Sly is in hospital, as I understand it. He has been very unwell for some time.'

'How unfortunate.'

'It remains unclear whether he will return to service. In the meantime, Normanby is conveying my orders and I am providing my reports on request. I doubt even he is any more than a messenger in the matter.'

'How mysterious.'

'That is in the nature of the roles we are performing. You understand that very well, of course. Nothing has changed in that respect.'

⁓

By the middle of the year, Harriet finds herself back in favour with Louis Napoleon. This either means that his other mistresses are failing to excite him or that he needs more money. In due course, it becomes evident that both are the case. Harriet is, as usual, able to accommodate him, but it feels as if she is acting out an old script. Nevertheless, the summer season is an enjoyable one. They attend Donizetti's *Nabucco* and Verdi's *Dom Sébastien* at the opera. New landscaping begins in the Bois de Boulogne, as Louis implements his plans to recreate an English garden in Paris and Harriet accompanies him on regular carriage tours to review progress. He is solicitous, but not demanding – save, of course, for the two hundred thousand francs routed into his account via Harriet.

At about the same time, Lord Normanby and Mountjoy-Martin meet at the British Embassy to discuss progress.

'Some sort of military coup seems inevitable,' says Mountjoy-Martin.

'This is very much in line with our thinking on the matter. Louis Napoleon's term as president ends next year. If we are to maintain his position, then steps must be taken. We are encouraging him to take the initiative. The French do so love an Emperor. Although much good it does them.'

'Will that not affect their thinking?'

'Probably not. The French are optimists where their leaders are concerned. And Louis has the popular touch. Although you would not know it to meet him. I can't think he would last five minutes at home.'

'But he remains our preferred candidate?'

'He does.'

∾

In October, Martin Harryet asks his mother about Louis Napoleon. Martin is nine. He has enjoyed, if that is the right word, a cloistered existence. Looked after by Harriet's parents in his young life, briefly playing happy families under Mountjoy-Martin's guardianship and hidden away at boarding school or with a private tutor, alongside Louis Napoleon's two sons, in London and now Paris, Harriet contents herself that, despite the challenges of her own life, Martin is protected. Indeed, he is largely immune from the gossip and the headlines, but he can no longer be protected from his own inquisitiveness. He has reached an age when questions are forming and he wants answers. He wants to know if Louis is his father. Like his mother, when she was a child, he is wont to stamp his feet and scream when things don't go his way, much to the astonishment of Louis Napoleon's sons, who are quiet and softly spoken by comparison. Harriet appeases him, but she knows that the questions will come back.

∞

Nathaniel Strode visits Harriet again after a long absence. She is pleased to see him. He provides a steadying influence. He has news.

'I am sorry it has taken me so long. The scent went cold for a long time. I wanted to check everything so that I was not merely peddling rumour. I am confident that what I have to tell you is true. It will not make for comfortable telling. Or for hearing. I have been surprised myself.'

'I have my own suspicions. I don't fear the truth.'

'You were right about Lady Blessington. She was murdered. The murderer was the man found in the room. She was stabbed through the heart. The man in the room suffered multiple stab wounds.'

'One of Sly's henchmen, perhaps? I fear Margaret was treading on some toes.'

'It is more complicated than that. Lady Blessington was in severe financial difficulty. She owed a lot of money. Count D'Orsay spent all of his money and then all of hers. Gore House is owned by the bank and the contents are to be auctioned to settle debts. Of course, her debtors will achieve only a small proportion of what they are owed. Some of those people are not to be crossed. There is a long list of suspects.'

'But the man in the room: was he dead? Has he been identified?'

'That is the odd thing. A male body was recovered from the same room. Of that there seems no doubt. But no death certificate exists. No paperwork of any kind. The body seems to have disappeared.'

'Do you have any more information?'

'That is as much as I can find for the moment. I will carry on my enquiries, if you wish.'

'Yes, please do. I will talk to Francis about what you have told me. He may know something more.'

'Might I counsel against that course of action? I think it would be best.'

'Why would you say that? I am sure Francis is as keen to discover Margaret's murderer as I am. She was a great friend to us both.'

'I warned you this would not be comfortable.'

'What are you saying?'

'The relationship between Lady Blessington and Francis was not as you understand it. They kept up appearances, but things had soured in recent years. He had been involved in litigation with D'Orsay over money for many years. Francis is one of the largest creditors of Lady Blessington's estate.'

'I cannot believe this.'

'It is true, I am afraid. I wish it was not. I count Francis Mountjoy-Martin a friend, as you do. He has generally been a force for good where you are concerned. Be assured of that. But he has other pressures. He has had to restore his family fortunes and his wife has been an emotional and financial strain for him. And Sly would not be an easy man to work for. We should not blame him if he strays from the truth occasionally. Sometimes it is necessary for his line of work. Don't judge him too harshly.'

'Thank you for your advice. I appreciate it. But why would he not help us with establishing the identity of Margaret's murderer?'

'Shall we just say that he has to support the official line and leave it at that? I can say no more.'

'Very well, Nathaniel. I think I understand. Can I talk to you on another subject?'

'Of course.'

'Can I rely on Lord Normanby?'

'I am not sure what you are asking.'

'I will clarify. Can I trust him?'

'Normanby plays a difficult game very well. He is a diplomat. He tries to keep everyone happy. With that in mind, I would say he sometimes does things he would prefer not to have to do. I know he likes you and he has tried to do his best for you.'

'You have not answered my question.'

'I am sorry. It is not my way to be evasive. As I have

said, I think you can trust him to try to do his best for you. Beyond that, I would be cautious.'

'I see. Is there anything more you can tell me?'

'I will tell you this in confidence: Normanby will not be in his present role forever. It would be as well to consider how things might change if he was not there. When I know more, I will tell you.'

'Thank you.'

'Is there anything else I can do?'

'Yes. Sly. Do you know the truth?'

'Honestly, I don't know.'

'Will you find out?'

'I will do what I can.'

༄

In December, Louis Napoleon seizes power as dictator. The coup lasts between the second and fourth of the month. With the military firmly on Louis's side, the outcome is inevitable. Opposition deputies are arrested and such rural rebellions as occur are ruthlessly put down. The newspapers, under Louis's control, call it a bloodless coup, but hundreds of lives are lost and thousands detained without trial or transported to the colonies.

Lord Normanby and Jean Mocquard meet for "a little chat", as Normanby calls them. After a brief discussion of Louis Napoleon's political ascendance, thoughts turn to other matters.

'The web is a mite tangled if you understand my meaning,' says Normanby.

'Of course, I understand perfectly. Things change quickly. Louis needed some time away from Harriet and Mason was a suitable diversion. But now you need a husband for Harriet and Mason is an unsuitable diversion. And Louis will need an empress, of course. And an heir.'

'You are a clever man, Jean. I should not have doubted you.'

'Did you?'

Mocquard has him on the back foot for a moment, but his poker face breaks into a smile and Normanby realises he is being mocked.

'I must admit I am a little puzzled by Miss Howard's apparent return to the fold. I understood Louis was making other arrangements,' he says.

'That is correct, but it is not easy for him to let her go. He has a real attachment to her. Nevertheless, I believe what we are seeing is in the nature of a swansong, as you say in England, I think. It is a matter of timing. And it does no harm to have the object of his attention kept on her toes.'

'Are we speaking of the Spanish Countess?'

'I cannot comment. I think all will be resolved in due course.'

'I hope you are right. In the interest of certainty, we will continue with our own strategy for Miss Howard.'

'As you wish, monsieur.'

∽

On Christmas Eve, Paris sees a light dusting of snow. A carriage sets Harriet down at the southern end of the five-arched Pont D'Austerlitz. Jem Mason arrives on foot at the quayside on the left bank of the Seine. They meet at the Jardin des Plantes; Jem entering by the top gate, between the Quai Saint-Bernard and rue Cuvier, and Harriet by the east gate on rue Buffon. Their circumspection is unnecessary today. Apart from them, the garden is empty.

Harriet would like to tell him everything, but something holds her back. She tells the truth, but not the whole truth. That will have to wait for another time. They give each other small presents. Harriet tears at the wrapping on hers. It is a tiny diamond brooch in the shape of a horseshoe. Jem slips his present, a silk stock and silver stock pin, into his pocket for later. The conversation is animated, but Harriet detects a vague reticence in Jem – something is on his mind. Eventually, it comes out.

'You are to be an empress?' he says.

'You must not believe what you read in the newspapers.'

'Then what should I believe?'

'Jem, I do believe you are jealous.'

They both laugh. It is a mark of how things have changed for the better between them that this exchange can happen without rancour.

'I don't say enough about my feelings for you,' he says.

'Men never say enough. Women sometimes say too much.'

'It is a strange thing. The words will hardly come out, even though I feel them so strongly.'

'Everything will be alright,' she says. She puts a finger to his lips.

Despite the clandestine nature of their meetings and

the pressure of the public relationship between Harriet and Louis, a more relaxed mood exists between them – an acceptance that each has another life. It is not as if Jem does not have other diversions. He has no expectation of monogamy – at least, that is what he tells himself.

NINETEEN

The English Empress
Paris, France
1852

2 Ferry Lane
Norwich

My dear Eliza
I do wonder what is going on when I read the newspapers these days. You know I do so love to hear from you, but it seems I find more about what you are doing from gossip and rumour than I do from you. I don't know what I should believe. Please do write and tell me the truth, as it worries your father and me to think about it all. Your dear father has enough to contend with, what with his gout playing up so.

They say that you are not going to marry Francis at all and that you will marry the French Prince. I suppose that is an achievement, even if he is a foreigner and perhaps you cannot wait forever for Francis, as his wife does hang on to life so, despite her illnesses.

It seems we never see you now and if that isn't enough we never see dear little Martin and I worry that he won't even recognise us if we ever do see him. Are you so ashamed of your poor dear parents that we are never to see you both again? I am sorry if I speak plainly, but that is how it seems and I don't think it is fair. I really don't think we should be punished in this way.

Please write as soon as you can.
Send Martin my love.
Mama

༄

Rue du Cirque
Paris

Dearest Mama

I am so sorry I have not written before, but everything is so upside down here and I scarcely have a moment to myself. I was much grieved by your letter. I beg you not to feel cross with me and to berate me for my inattention. I cannot say how much I reproach myself for making you feel this way and I promise to make things right as soon as I can.

I really must urge you to pay no attention to the scurrilous talk in the newspapers. As you know, I am attached to the embassy here in Paris and, as such, I am obliged to be in the company of Prince Louis Napoleon and his entourage from time to time. Lord and Lady Normanby have been most kind and adorable in looking after me and I am, of course, still under the guardianship of Francis, even though he has so many other duties here and in London. Please don't concern yourself with my marriage prospects. I have no plans at present, but you will be the first to know if I do.

Martin does very well and is uncommonly pleasing in his look and manner. He is taught alongside the Prince's own sons, so you can be assured he is receiving the best possible education and is growing up quite the young gentleman.

I think of you and Papa all the time and, much as Paris is all gaiety and animation, I pine for the simple life of old England and the sea air and the Norfolk skies. As soon as the weather improves, I will make arrangements for Martin and me to come and see you both.

God bless you
Your loving daughter
Eliza

✑

In March, Lord Normanby invites Harriet to a ball at the embassy. Louis Napoleon is otherwise detained, as seems so often the case these days, and Normanby finds her an alternative dancing partner.

'May I introduce Captain Trelawney?' he says.

'Good evening, Captain. How lovely to meet you.'

'And for me to meet you. I have been most anxious to make your acquaintance.'

Clarence Trelawney is tall, angular, with curly black hair over a close-shaven, high-cheeked, blue-eyed face. He wears a beautifully tailored Austrian hussar's uniform. Harriet guesses she might give him a few years in age. She thinks he has a rather weak mouth, but there is no doubting the general view that he is a dashing sort of fellow. He is attentive throughout the evening and as carriages arrive, he asks if he might call on her. He expects he will be in Paris more often in the future, he says.

∽

Louis Napoleon receives a visitor in his new apartments in the rue de Duras, in touching distance of the Élysée Palace. Mocquard assures Princess Mathilde that her cousin is not available for visitors, but she ignores him and bursts into the inner room. Louis is in front of a long mirror attending to his hair with one hand and adjusting his sash with the other.

'Every inch the Emperor,' she says.

'If it is the will of the people,' he says.

'The people. Of course, the people. If they clamour for you, you will not deny them. It is your duty.'

'It is my destiny.'

Louis Napoleon appears master of all he surveys, but he is not immune to advice and his cousin, Princess Mathilde, is never short of an opinion.

'You are not serious about this woman?' she says. 'You cannot be Emperor and marry a common prostitute.'

'I will not have you speak about Miss Howard in that way. In any event, I have made no decision on the matter. I can see there would be complications, but I owe her a great deal. I have all but made promises.'

'Then you must break them.'

'It is not so simple.'

'The future of France is at stake here. The second empire is within your grasp. History will judge you harshly if you falter when the prize is so close.'

'I thank you for your interest.'

∽

As Nathaniel Strode hinted, Lord Cowley takes over from Lord Normanby as the British ambassador in France by mid-year. Normanby is taking a break before heading south to take up a similar post in Italy. Cowley is returning to the post he held previously when the monarchy still ruled.

'I must brief you on Harriet Howard,' says Normanby.

'Ah yes. The English Empress,' says Cowley.

'By God, not you as well.'

'I'm sorry. It is all the talk in London.'

'That is as may be. It won't happen, I can assure you. Despite what you might think, that would not suit us at all. Fortunately, Louis Napoleon has other plans.'

∽

Before he departs Paris, Lord Normanby decides he should show his hand with Harriet – up to a point, of course.

'We have worked well together, wouldn't you say?'

'You have been kind beyond measure.'

'I thought I might take this opportunity to mark your card, as it were. Politics are in a most awkward state at the moment in England. We have had a good run of stability. Change is the order of the day now, though.'

'What are the consequences for me?'

'It is hard to predict. Cowley is a sensible enough chap and he knows the ropes here in Paris. I have hopes he will leave things as they are. It would not do to make waves. Louis Napoleon is proving an honest ally and we have reasonable expectations this will continue, provided he doesn't overreach himself.'

'And my role?'

'I think you should let things take their course. You are under no specific obligation any longer. Francis looks after you very well, I believe. Mr Strode manages the finances most adroitly and Louis is paying his debts.'

'Are you saying I am free to do as I wish now?'

'That would be too simple, I'm afraid. We would have to admit that you have not been free, which, of course, we could not do. It is better if you let things emerge. Events are running your way. All I would say is that, if you were to be married, I think that would finally sever the link with your role here. The uncertainty in England is in your favour.'

'May I press you for some more advice?'

'Yes, of course.'

'I believe I must make some decisions, from what you say. There are suitors, as I'm sure you know.'

'I do.'

'Would I be right in thinking that a marriage to Louis would not be looked on favourably?'

'You would be correct. That would be a step too far. My own feeling is that he will be guided by ambition and you will be guided by emotion. I don't think it would be good for either of you.'

'How would you advise me on Francis?'

'Francis? Well, I think that would also be a mistake. He is rather besotted with you, but his prospects are limited. He has been too long out of the mainstream of the military. He will need to buy any further promotion and his finances are in a parlous state. I say this as a friend. I like Francis, but he is not for you. There is also the small matter of him already having a wife, although the poor soul doesn't even know him now.'

'And Captain Trelawney?'

'I don't know enough about his situation to pronounce upon it. He comes from a very good family, I understand.'

'But you would not be against it?'

'No.'

'And a marriage would be advisable?'

'Yes.'

She plays along with this. She knows something is going on, but she cannot quite put her finger on it. She is being pushed towards Trelawney and away from Louis. She is used to being manipulated, but usually the pretext is clear. Here, it is not. She tries to get something out of Mocquard, but he will not be drawn. She prays that her trysts with Jem are undiscovered, but she cannot be sure. Her occasional, and more public, appointments with Clarence Trelawney, will, she hopes, put any interested watchers off the scent. Something tells her that she has not heard the last of Nicholas Sly and she knows she must stay on her guard. Strode has promised he will find out what he can and she awaits the news with a sense of foreboding.

∽

As the year draws to a close, France sees the long-expected official crowning of Louis Napoleon as Emperor Napoleon III. Lord Palmerston sends him a telegram, congratulating him. Not everyone shares the enthusiasm.

The Spectator, Friday 3rd December 1852

FRANCE AND EMPIRE

On the 2nd December, Louis Napoleon "accepted" the Empire of France, as on the day of which Thursday was the anniversary at which he laid violent hands on the capital and assumed unlawful power. From this time, therefore, the conspirator and usurper is wrapped in the imperial purple; and deference will be claimed to the "majesty" of France, self-intruded among the Sovereigns of Europe. History will never forget, indeed, that on the 2nd December 1851 Louis Napoleon subverted that constitution which he had sworn to maintain; that against the capital of his own country, which had readmitted him from exile, he secretly arrayed a traitor army, and that the hand which snatched arbitrary power was reddened with the blood of French citizens, of the unoffending and the gentle as well as the strong and the resisting. But France is destined to undergo a second subjugation by Corsica and in "accepting" the Empire, Louis Napoleon, with matchless countenance, declares that it is conferred on him by the "logic of the people".

The Times announces that the Allied Powers have so far yielded to Louis Napoleon, that they will recognise him as Emperor de facto if he will accept the treaty obligations of 1815 and, in his speech on assuming the diadem, he formally declares that he accepts the liabilities of past governments, condescending not to date his reign from 1815 but from 1852. The Allied Powers, however, refuse to recognise him as "Napoleon the Third". He has nonetheless assumed the title. In this inflexibility, he does not depart from his usual line of action. In his short but full career, inflexible tenacity of purpose is his chief characteristic. He may have seemed to yield, but only in semblance, to the necessity of the hour. He consented to be a private citizen, asseverated that he wanted no more; he consented to be president for four years, swore to it; he consented again to be president for ten years; in one year he consents to be Emperor; realising that which before the beginning he sketched in his "Idees Napoleoniennes" and which has never been absent from his mind, never abandoned, never yielded through all those oaths and protestations. He only bides his time. Meanwhile, the other powers wait and watch – they cannot trust.

TWENTY
For Services Rendered
Paris, France
1853

As the new year begins, President Louis Napoleon Bonaparte is safely confirmed as Emperor Napoleon III of the second French Empire. The so-called referendum of December 1852 gives him virtually unlimited executive power and elects him for a minimum period of a further ten years. The year is also an auspicious one for Harriet Howard. She begins her thirtieth year, having experienced more in those years than many would achieve in a long lifetime. Relations with Louis Napoleon have reached a sort of equilibrium. They still enjoy each other's company on an occasional basis, but talk of marriage promises has ebbed and Harriet already knows that it will not happen. She is relieved, in part, but also piqued at the thought of someone else taking her place on Louis's arm. Martin seems settled at boarding school alongside Louis's sons, Eugene and Louis Alexandre. Harriet has the three children at home at the rue du Cirque with her every other weekend. They all call her Mama. Awkward questions from Martin have abated, for the time being. Jem Mason and Tom Olliver are installed in comfortable apartments on the rue de Lutece for their French forays and Harriet is a frequent visitor there, although she still takes care about when she visits and she never follows the same route twice.

༄

When news comes, via Jean Mocquard, that Louis wishes Harriet to undertake a mission on his behalf back in England, she happily accepts. It seems that there is some blackmail afoot, aimed at the Emperor, and she is asked to use her contacts in London to ascertain the source and arrange for reparations, such that the threat will go away. It is suggested that Nathaniel Strode might be a useful ally in England and that Mocquard can help her and act as a travelling companion. Plans are made and Harriet looks forward to seeing London again and, perhaps, finding time to visit her parents in Norfolk.

There is frost overnight and a sparkling clear sky as the carriage and four rattles to a halt in front of the apartments on rue du Cirque. Harriet peers down from her window to see the blurred shapes of Mocquard and the coachman stamping their feet and flapping their arms. She clears a hole in the condensation on the window glass and sees the breath of the horses, billowing up like small clouds. A brazier glows dull beside them. She is soon installed in the carriage, wreathed in blankets and furs. Mocquard taps his cane on the seat panel behind him and they are away.

They make good progress in the first part of the journey. The roads are quiet and the mist along the Seine gives way to bright sunlight. By the time the towers of the cathedral at Rouen come into view, the weather turns and grey skies roll in. The cathedral is visible from many miles away to the east, but it is only when Harriet steps down from the carriage and looks up at the west front from the Place de la Cathedrale that the full majesty of the towers strikes her. She stands and stares, unable to take in the sheer, glorious intricacy of the gables, windows, statues, turrets, screens and soaring spires. Mocquard gives her all the time he dares, but there is a ship to board and they still have a distance to travel. He steps in and whispers at her side. She hurries into the cathedral, lights a candle and soon rejoins him.

'Will we have time on our way back?' she says.

'Of course.'

The second part of the journey proves uneventful and Le Havre is reached in good time. At the port, the weather sets in. A light drizzle gives way to heavy rain and by mid-afternoon, the sky is alive with lightning. Mocquard makes enquiries and, as the rain blows in sideways, it becomes clear that their ship is most unlikely to sail. Ever resourceful, he books rooms at the Lion d'Or.

'It is as well to be prepared,' he says.

'Was this forecast?' she says.

'I am not sure.'

'No.'

As dusk falls, they accept the inevitable.

'The captain tells me we should be able to sail tomorrow,' he says.

'Then we should rest. Until tomorrow.'

'Goodnight.'

Harriet spends a restless night. She dreams. Recently, she is in the habit of dreaming about falling. She stands at the top of a tall tower; a man comes towards her; she is pushed over the edge of a crumbling parapet. Her mouth opens in a scream, but no sound emerges. In the morning, she wakes early. There is no one around in the hotel, so she walks down to a café, frequented by fishermen, near the quay. A post-chaise clatters past and the coachman throws out a bundle of newspapers. Glancing down, she catches sight of a headline on the front page.

La Presse, Friday 21st January 1853

LOUIS NAPOLEON ENGAGED TO COUNTESS OF TEBA

We are pleased to announce the engagement of Louis Napoleon Bonaparte, Emperor Napoleon III of France, to Maria Eugenie Ignacia Agustina de Palafox y Kirkpatrick, Countess de Teba of Spain, the daughter of Don Cipriano de Palafox y Portocarrero and Maria Manuela Kirkpatrick de Closbourn y de Grevigne. Don Cipriano is Count of Teba and Montijo, Marquis of Algava and Duke of Pearanda, and fought with distinction alongside Emperor Napoleon I in the Peninsular Wars. It is expected that the marriage will take place in Paris within the month.

❧

When she returns to the hotel, she enters the breakfast room.

Mocquard looks up. She tosses the paper onto the table in front of him, sending his coffee cup spilling towards him.

'That was an unnecessary adventure, was it not?' she says.

'I must admit it. I am sorry.'

'I know you must do your master's bidding. Let us say no more about it, Jean. There is nothing holding us here now. Shall we go back to Paris?'

'Certainly.'

They take the return to Paris in silence. Harriet is lost in her thoughts and Mocquard knows that nothing he can say will help. The truth, however, is that Harriet is finally free of a relationship she never sought and never relished. She is annoyed because she has been deceived. The more she thinks about it, the more she realises she should be relieved. They drive through Rouen without stopping. When she reaches the rue du Cirque, it is soon clear that her apartments have been, albeit discreetly, ransacked. Every drawer has been opened, every wardrobe inspected. Everything has been restored after a fashion, although some important letters will never be seen again. It is a clumsy artifice. She knows exactly what has happened.

∽

Of course, the great British public loves a royal wedding, even if it is between a Frenchman and a Spaniard. The *Illustrated London News* produces an "Imperial Marriage Supplement" to their latest edition, complete with a full-length image of the Empress in a wedding gown. Some unkind commentators say it looks more like a wedding cake than a wedding dress, tiered as it is, and there can be no mistaking the resemblance to a meringue. On the inside pages, the reader is treated to the sight of head-and-shoulders images of the esteemed couple. Louis Napoleon wears the laurel crown of Caesar, without a trace of irony, and Countess Eugenie, it must be said, looks like a lady who would brook no nonsense in an argument. Everyone hopes they will have a long and harmonious relationship.

∽

On his return from honeymoon, the Emperor Napoleon calls on Harriet in her apartments.

'I wish you great happiness,' she says.

'I would like to explain...'

'That may be so, but I am going to deny you that opportunity. I will not listen. If there was explanation to be made, you have had ample time.'

'I don't want us to be on bad terms with each other...'

'Then we shall not. I beg you not to speak of the matter again.'

'As you wish. I am, of course, greatly in your debt and I wish to make some amends.'

'As you wish, sir. I ask for nothing.'

'That is understood. You have always been most gracious. I will come to the point. You will be the Comtesse de Beauregard with immediate effect. There is a château and land at La Celle-Saint-Cloud, which goes with the title. It will need some work to bring it up to the standard you deserve. Funds will be made available. Mocquard will see to everything.'

'So I am to be bought off.'

'I hope you will not see it that way.'

'I flatter myself that I am always able to see things clearly, for what they are and for what they are not.'

'I cannot answer to that. There is one more thing. Martin will become the Comte de Béchevêt in due course. I will help him in his life if he ever needs it.'

'I understand.'

'If there is ever anything I can do for you, I hope you will let me know.'

'You will not hear from me on that subject.'

'I hope we shall still be friends.'

'Friends? How will this work out exactly? You have a new wife with a reputation for jealousy. Your cousin, Princess Mathilde, briefs against me at every opportunity and makes her dislike for me plain. There is a campaign in the newspapers to erase me from history.'

'I am sorry if I have caused you any distress. The situation was impossible. I have to put France first. I can explain everything.'

Yet he cannot find the words. He is at the end of his prepared speech and he can see that Harriet is in no mood for forgiveness.

'I am waiting,' she says.

'Let us leave it there for now, Harriet. You are angry with me. I understand that.'

When Nathaniel Strode calls, he tells her to see the positive side of things. It could be worse.

'You should see it as a long-term project, but it is fundamentally a sound property. It will be a solid addition to your portfolio.'

'That is something, I suppose. Is there any update on Sly?'

'Not yet.'

Harriet does not have long to wait, though. Francis Mountjoy-Martin visits after a long absence.

'You have been neglecting me,' she says.

'You seem to be managing well enough without me, Harriet. Or, should I say, Countess.'

'I am guessing you have not come merely to flatter me. Do you have news?'

'Indeed, yes. I have been in London. While I was there, I saw Sly.'

'And?'

'Sly is a cripple. He walks with two sticks and then not easily.'

'I wonder he has not summoned me.'

'You should not. He would not have you see him like that. He is broken, but do not underestimate him. He still has some power and influence. And he hates you with a vengeance.'

'I have only ever done his bidding. He should have no quarrel with me.'

'Harriet, he knows. And I know, too. Do not take us for fools. Be careful.'

∽

Back in England, Jem has a fall in a steeplechase at Dunchurch and it reaches the front pages of *Bell's Life*. Of course, falls don't make the headlines often. It is in the nature of the jump jockey's existence. Jem is not seriously hurt, but it is the circumstances that create the news story. The theory is that the horse in question has been doped. In other words, a drug has been administered that effectively stops the horse running on its merits. In this case, the doping is so severe that the horse ploughs straight through a fence, appearing not to see it. There is no suggestion that Jem has been targeted. The conclusion is that someone wanted the horse stopped, presumably to win a bet, and Jem was the unfortunate jockey. When Harriet hears the news, she reaches a different conclusion.

✍

The year ends with a disagreement between Jem and Harriet. Harriet is more paranoid than ever about secrecy. She refuses to meet at a hotel or at his apartments and insists they go back to outdoor meetings. It annoys him, but he goes along with it. He can deal with the arrangement with Louis. He has pieced together the truth of it, but the rumours reaching his ears about Captain Trelawney cannot be brushed aside so readily. He is not entirely convinced by Harriet's explanation of Trelawney as a helpful smokescreen for their own relationship.

TWENTY-ONE
House of Cards
Paris, France
1854

Clarence Trelawney makes some rather half-hearted attempts, Harriet thinks, to advance their friendship. He sends flowers, but no message. She gives him scant encouragement. He remains a helpful diversion, but she senses Jem's latent jealousy and doesn't want to do anything more to damage their already-fragile progress together. The news from Francis Mountjoy-Martin about Nicholas Sly plays on her nerves. She imagines Sly back in his offices in London, dreaming up new ways to inflict misery on her. Of course, she has always known that it was Nicholas Sly in Lady Blessington's room. Poor Margaret paid the price for her haste. If only she had waited, as they agreed. Harriet would like some confirmation about Sly's state of health. Her normal sources draw a blank. Strode says he is still making enquiries, while Lord Cowley, who would be no help anyway, seems to be avoiding her.

In March, the British and French Governments announce that they are at war with Russia.

Louis Napoleon feels the need to flex his muscles, as far as foreign policy is concerned. The Emperor needs a military success to complete his list of achievements. Taking on the Russians, alongside the British and the Ottomans on the Crimean peninsula, looks like a fight readily won. He places Armand-Jacques Leroy de Saint-Arnaud in charge of the French troops and waits for news of victory. It will all be over within the year, he thinks.

There are other items on Louis's list. Driven on by the success of the 1851 Great Exhibition in Britain, he announces plans for the Exposition Universelle to take place in Paris in the next year. It will be a celebration of all things French and, more especially, a celebration of France and the empire and, perhaps even more especially, the Emperor himself. This is no time for modesty. As part of the grand design, he sponsors the development of a Bordeaux wine classification; this will secure France's reputation as the premier wine producer. He knows there are pretenders in Spain and Italy. They need to be put in their place. At the same time, it will promote Louis's château and vineyard-owning friends to the top of the pyramid. No doubt they will show their appreciation in the usual way. Lord Palmerston is unimpressed.

'Most Frenchmen are happy just to drink it,' he says. 'Louis Napoleon wants to categorise it. No one will take any notice. Mark my words.'

∞

On the first day of August, the wealthy Parisians leave the town. Those lesser mortals left behind are the beneficiaries. In the early morning, a calm serenity pervades the parks and open spaces. By mid-morning, gypsy children in ragged clothes sail makeshift, wooden boats across the lake in the Jardins du Luxembourg. The park-keepers are taking their annual holidays and there is no one to chase the children away. The new "pelouse interdite" signs, so widely hated and thus ignored, are completely unenforced and impromptu picnics spring up here and there as lunchtime approaches. Small groups grow to larger assemblies and the wine flagons are passed around. A crackle of activity creeps across the park. Just after one o'clock, with the sun's rays scorching the grass, the noise subsides. Solace is sought from the heat and the shady bases of the horse chestnut trees are encircled by reclining figures, sleeping off the effects of the food and alcohol. The occasional lurcher lies sprawled, legs twitching at the thought of a dream rabbit. Only the whispering whirr of the hummingbird hawk moths, flitting between the verbenas, seeps into the slumbering silence.

Harriet enters the gardens by the top gate on the rue de Vaugirard. She looks left and right. She is well practised. Her hair is pulled back into a black bonnet and her plain clothes give her the look of a teacher, or perhaps a lady's companion. No one gives her a second glance. She walks diagonally south and then turns east along the southern face of the Palais to the eastern end of the gardens, breathing in the scent of the musk roses as she goes.

Jem enters by the lower gate, at the meeting of the rue d'Assas and the rue Auguste Comte. His stride is long but halting, as if he carries a weight in one shoe. He looks straight ahead. When he reaches the Medici fountain, he sits down on a bench and lights up a cheroot. He leans back, one arm resting along the back of the bench. He crosses his legs and blows out a series of smoke rings. Presently, one of the gypsy children scampers towards him and sits beside him, swinging his legs. They exchange a few words and Jem presses a coin into the boy's hand. The boy looks at the coin and a beam breaks out across his face. A few more words pass between them and the boy skips away again. Jem finishes his cheroot and stamps it into the dust. He is on the move again.

At the far end of the garden, below the fountain, is an orchard. A wooden building in a beamed, Normandy style, festooned in wisteria, sits almost hidden. There are a few garden tools scattered about and a wheelbarrow stacked against a wall. A pool of water, from a leaking water butt, spills along the edge of the path and a robin dots down and takes a long drink, ignoring Jem's approach. Jem pushes at the door of the building and goes in. Harriet is already inside.

They meet like this often. It is not ideal, but it is a relationship of sorts. Sometimes she flies at him, ripping at his clothes, like an animal tearing at flesh. At other times, she sits, looking down, waiting for him to come to her. He never knows what he will find. A lot goes unsaid. There is an unspoken rule between them that the lives they live when they are apart are not talked about. They live in the moment. Today, however, there is a different charge in the air. Harriet senses it as soon as he comes in.

'We cannot carry on like this,' he says.

'Like what?'

'I cannot bear the dishonesty. I don't want to be slinking about in the shadows.'

'You know my situation very well. It is difficult. I am hopeful that things will resolve themselves soon. I don't want to put you in danger. That is my first concern.'

'I can look after myself.'

'That is pride talking. I don't doubt your bravery, but this danger cannot always be seen. It comes out of nowhere. It is driven by spite and fuelled by hatred.'

'You are talking in riddles.'

'I am sorry. Please trust me that we must remain covert for the time being. Nothing would please me more than to be open.'

'I think we need some time to think things through. I don't know where we are going. Do you?'

'I am trying to hold us together in difficult circumstances, but I can't do it on my own. Will you not meet me halfway?'

The question hangs unanswered between them. Jem stares at her. He looks as if he might speak, but in the end he kicks the door open and walks out, without a backward glance.

∽

Even weeks later, Harriet still blames herself for the disagreement, going over the conversation, wondering how she could have managed things differently. Her thoughts go around in circles. At least Nathaniel Strode is right about the Château de Beauregard. It is a sound property and potentially a very beautiful home. He arranges builders on Harriet's behalf and by the middle of September she is able to move into the west wing. She retains her apartments in the rue du Cirque.

One of the first visitors to the château is Harriet's old adversary, Princess Mathilde Laetitia Wilhelmine Bonaparte, Louis's cousin. Mathilde has a surprise in store.

'I owe you an apology,' she says.

'I am not often lost for words. You have me.'

'I thought you a schemer. An opportunist. I believed you sought advantage from your relationship with Louis. I find I was wrong on all counts.'

'That is gracious of you to say so. Your apology is, of course, accepted.'

'Thank you.'

'May I ask what has changed your mind?'

'I find that it is our Spanish friends who I should have been concerned with. And Monsieur Mocquard has been most helpful in explaining things to me.'

❧

Lord Cowley also visits. Harriet is not quite sure why he is there. It is soon apparent that he doesn't really know why he is there either. Lord Palmerston has asked about her, it seems, and since Cowley has had nothing to do with her for the best part of a year and Lieutenant-Colonel Mountjoy-Martin is carrying out other duties in England he decides he better see for himself. After the usual polite exchanges, it is inevitable that the conversation turns towards the Crimean War.

'Was this why you wanted Louis at the head of the French Government?' she says.

'We don't interfere in French matters of state. We are nevertheless pleased that the French share our views about Russian aggression.'

'Sir, have you come here to insult my intelligence or do you have some other purpose?'

Cowley makes his excuses and leaves before she can get into her stride.

The Battle of Alma seems like a positive turning point in Crimea, but in the weeks that follow the war swings this way and that without any clear direction emerging. Despite being outnumbered by the French and the British, the Russians prove resilient. When Harriet reads the *London Gazette* account of the Charge of the Light Brigade in October, she is shocked by the loss of life. How many dead? Two hundred and fifty men killed and many more wounded. Four hundred and seventy-five horses killed or maimed. Was this what her support for Louis Napoleon was all leading to? She feels ashamed. No, more than that. She feels angry.

∽

When the war continues to go badly, Louis Napoleon decides he must intervene himself. He will lead the troops at the front, just as his uncle, Emperor Napoleon Bonaparte, did. When Lord Cowley hears this, he is horrified. He rushes back to London with the news and explains the problem to Lord Clarendon, the foreign secretary.

'The damn fool will get himself killed and our investment with it,' he says.

'That would not do at all.'

Clarendon charges Cowley with persuading Louis that it might not be a sensible course of action. He is not easily persuaded, but Lord Palmerston knows the way to bring him to heel.

'Tell him he and the Empress are invited to Britain for a state visit.'

It is the breakthrough Louis has been seeking. The royal houses of Europe are cool towards the upstart Emperor, as they see him, but approval from Queen Victoria and Prince Albert will, he is sure, bring them all round. Thoughts of military adventure are set aside and plans put in place to secure the grand alliance.

◦∕◦

Just before Christmas, Captain Trelawney makes an unexpected visit to Harriet at the Château de Beauregard. He explains that he is planning to come to live near Paris. His family has settled a generous allowance on him and he has wealthy associates who wish him to set up a stud, to breed racehorses on their behalf. He is thinking of setting up at Chantilly or, possibly, Saint Cloud.

'Perhaps we will be neighbours,' he says.

'The grass is very good here. The foals and yearlings seem to grow well on it.'

'Or perhaps we could even form an association. Your mares and my stallions. That would be a match, would it not?'

He is an adept, if not very subtle, flirt. She realises that this visit is in the nature of a formal courtship. There is no doubting he is a handsome man. And Harriet knows she is at risk of doing what she always does when she quarrels with Jem. She punishes him.

TWENTY-TWO
Cavalry to the Rescue
Paris and Nice, France
1855

Large parts of Paris have the look of a building site. The Emperor has ambition. His architect, Georges-Eugene Haussmann, is brought in to give substance to the great man's vision. Paris will be a modern city, full of wide boulevards and elegant buildings. A city to be envied, a city appropriate for the capital of a grand empire. Construction work springs up all along the north banks of the Seine and as far west as the Pont de Saint Cloud.

Harriet and Jem don't meet again after their argument in the Jardins du Luxembourg. Jem and Tom Olliver continue with their contracts, riding at the Paris tracks, but Jem doesn't stay, preferring to travel in and out. Railway building also gathers pace and the Compagnie de l'Ouest links all the lines between Le Havre and Paris. Tom and Harriet still meet occasionally, but it seems clear from what little indication Tom gives that Jem is not in any mood for reconciliation.

'Is it over, Tom?' she says.

'I can't say. I never guess what Jem will do. I have known him a long time. I sometimes think life would be much simpler for Jem if he could spend it on a horse. At least there he knows what to do. He doesn't have to think about it. Intuition takes over. Back on the ground, everything is more difficult.'

'I have tried to make things work, but there is too much against us, isn't there?'

'You never really know a man like him. He is not easy. Be patient.'

'Will patience be enough?'

'You are your own worst enemies. You both blame your circumstances for your inability to sustain your relationship.'

'You are the expert now, are you?'

'I'm sorry. I don't mean to offend you or to criticise Jem, but to say nothing is to deny my responsibility as a friend to try to help you. Everyone who cares about you sees it.'

৩৯

Louis Napoleon no longer visits. Harriet thinks it is probably for the best. Jean Mocquard occasionally calls, with a thinly disguised offer from Louis, but when she refuses Mocquard shrugs. His heart is not in it and neither, she thinks, is Louis's. A rumour circulates that all is not well "dans la chambre" with Eugenie. When Harriet tests this with Mocquard, he shrugs again and smiles. Mocquard can say a lot without speaking. Inevitably, they discuss the newspaper stories of how well Queen Victoria and Prince Albert have got on with Louis and Empress Eugenie at the reciprocal state visits.

'A great success by all accounts,' she says.

'By all accounts.'

'Then there may be more you can tell me, I surmise.'

'Newspapers, here and in England, have a habit of giving us the news that our lords and masters want us to hear. It is the way things will go now. We should not imagine that we are hearing anything in the order of truth.'

'Then it was not a success?'

'You might think that. What is important is that the Russians think that the relationship between our countries continues all sweetness and harmony. The Tsar thinks an alliance between us cannot hold and he is relying on it. Anything that dents his confidence serves our joint interests. The war in Crimea depends as much upon attitudes as military strength.'

Mocquard turns the conversation towards Harriet's own situation. He is concerned about her. She seems distracted, not quite herself.

'I feel I am in a sort of limbo,' she says. 'As if I am waiting for something to happen.'

'Do you know what you want to happen?'

'You always ask the obvious question.'

'In my experience, the obvious question is never so obvious. I have built a career on it. Shall I ask it again?'

'No. I used to be a great planner. The truth is that I have been buffeted through my life by chance events and inescapable decisions made by others.'

'It may seem like that, but you have navigated your way through them admirably, if I may say so. I have observed you. To my mind, you have never lost sight of your intentions. Your parents are well cared for, because of you. Martin is a promising young man, because of you. I might even say that Europe is a more stable place, because of you. Don't underestimate your achievements.'

'You flatter me.'

'I only say things as I see them. I hate to see you dragged down by self doubt. You deserve better. Don't give up on what you still want to achieve. It is never too late.'

'If only that was true.'

He leaves some letters from Louis. 'Nothing important,' he says. 'Just some financial detail, I think.'

∽

Francis Mountjoy-Martin is an infrequent visitor and Lord Cowley is invisible. No further news on Nicholas Sly emerges and Harriet doesn't ask. Martin is doing well at his schooling. He continues to thrive, alongside Louis Napoleon's sons, Eugene and Louis Alexandre. She supposes she should welcome the calmness of her situation. She wakes one morning after a restless night. She dreams about being pursued again. The dream always ends with her falling and waking with a silent scream.

Nathaniel Strode arrives unexpectedly at mid-morning. Harriet receives him in the small drawing room.

'Your assets and accounts have been locked,' he says.

'What does that mean exactly?'

'It is complex. I need hardly say that. Your parents' arrangements are intact. I must say that first. The property is on a long-term, paid-up lease and their income secured with an annuity. I took that precaution in case of just such an event.'

'That is something, at least.'

'Your situation appears less satisfactory. We had no warning of this and I was unable to liquidate anything before the injunction came into force. The Treasury and the Revenue seem to be a law unto themselves these days.'

'Can you spell it out? What are the implications?'

'Apart from the Italian current accounts, there is no further income with immediate effect. The good news is that you still have your repayments from the Emperor.'

'Yes, I was meaning to mention that. Mocquard left me some correspondence, indicating that Louis is obliged to suspend those payments for the moment. There is some financial awkwardness, I understand.'

'Did he say when the payments will be restored?'

'No. The letter indicates it might be some time.'

'In that case, we are in the embarrassing situation of having outgoings significantly in excess of incomings. The château is a financial drain, not to put too fine a point on it.'

'What do you propose?'

'I will need time. Loans can be raised, but it is unfortunate that the income streams from both France and England have ended at the same time.'

'More than unfortunate.'

'I will see what can be done. Leave it with me.'

'One more thing: perhaps you could advise me on Captain Trelawney?'

'I think I understand the question. Captain Trelawney could be a solution of sorts. I will say that. As to the relationship between you, that must be entirely a matter for you. I cannot guide you.'

'Nor am I asking you.'

'Of course.'

She sends Francis Mountjoy-Martin a message, asking him to call. When he does, she asks him the same question about Captain Trelawney.

'Are you insane?' he says.

'I am not. An answer needs to be found. Trelawney could provide that answer. He is rather dashing in any event and tolerably handsome. We share a great number of interests and I cannot say that there are other possibilities in view. I have hardly been in hiding these last few years and he knows my history. Do you have a better suggestion?'

Mountjoy-Martin can barely contain his anger. He has offered Harriet an alternative suggestion many times, but she has always turned him down. Now she wants advice on a rival. He leaves without another word.

∽

Strode returns a few days later. Harriet rushes to meet him, hoping for good news. There is none. Instead, he suggests a trip away. He is looking for a way to make the best of a bad situation. Of course, Normanby and Cowley are under instruction not to intervene. They know their first duty is to Her Majesty's Government. They are, after all, career politicians. Strode is similarly instructed, but he is not so easily controlled. He ploughs his own furrow. He feels it unnecessary to tell Harriet he is disobeying orders, but, of course, she suspects it.

'At the moment, we cannot access the money you are receiving in rent from your property in Nice, so no benefit accrues,' he says. 'The current lease has just expired. The property is furnished; there is staff in attendance, who have been paid for the season; and the weather looks set fair. It might be interesting for you to actually visit one of your investments. In any event, I think it would be wise if you kept a low profile for the moment. May I make the arrangements?'

'I cannot travel alone. It would be intolerable.'

'I understand that. I have made arrangements for Miss Findon to accompany you.'

'Melliora? How did you find her? I have not heard from her in years.'

'It was not easy at first. Eventually, I contacted Miss Lampard. As luck would have it, she was recently in receipt of a letter from Melliora after a long lapse. Melliora would be delighted to travel with you.'

'You make a very persuasive case.'

'Then it is done.'

⁕

In June, Harriet and Mellie Findon set out on the long journey south by train. The Compagnie des Chemins de Fer de Paris à Lyon et à la Méditerranée incorporates all the smaller railways south of Paris and, for the first time, provides a main line connecting Paris to the Côte d'Azur by way of Dijon, Lyon and Marseille. It is a time for reflection. There are no distractions, save the rattle and hum of the carriages and the trees and fields rushing by the window. Mellie proves the perfect companion: silent when Harriet is thinking and a willing respondent when she needs conversation. They are old friends and they reminisce about their time at school on the Isle of Wight and their days hunting with the Grafton and the Pytchley.

Harriet feels she should use the time to think about the future – perhaps that is what Strode intends. No doubt he will ask her on her return. By Montbard, Harriet resolves to sell up in France, when circumstances allow, and go back to England; by Dijon, she determines that she will live quietly in Norfolk, perhaps, or Northamptonshire; by Chalon, she decides that Martin will go to boarding school in England and that she will visit her parents often. Nicholas Sly can do his worst. She will go to see Jem and tell him everything. Then, it will be up to him. Jem can look after himself. He says as much.

∽

They break their journey at Lyon, the halfway point. Here, they stretch their legs in the labyrinth of lanes and visit the Cathedral of St Jean Baptiste. They stay at a comfortable lodging house on the rue du Boeuf. They dine at the Auberge de L'Ile Barbe, on a tiny island at the confluence of the two great rivers: the Saône and the Rhône. They eat duck pâté, roast pork and local cheeses, washed down with a fine Morgon. Harriet feels a fleeting sense of well-being. Late into the evening, Mellie and Harriet talk about their lives. Mellie is reticent. Things have not gone well for her and, without going into detail, it seems that the offer to accompany Harriet is a welcome escape. She proves better at asking questions than answering them.

Mellie asks about the visit to the cathedral.

'Do you take comfort from your religion?' she says.

'I love the hymns, the buildings, the rituals. I am happy to light a candle or say a prayer. I agree with some of the values: honesty, truth, kindness. But I am not driven by religion. God has never come to call. But then, why would he? The priests will say I have sold my soul to the devil.'

'What about the Ten Commandments? Do you remember Bible classes at Carisbrooke?'

'I do. I was not a very good pupil. I will tell you about it one day. It goes back to my childhood.'

Mellie turns the conversation to Harriet's financial situation. It cannot be avoided.

'Will Strode resolve things?' she says.

'I hope so, but I fear the future,' says Harriet.

'What do you fear?'

"There are three things that are important: my parents' happiness and security, Martin's education and prospects, and Jem's love. Strode may be able to rescue something for the first two, but I think I have missed my chance with Jem. I have been a terrible daughter to my parents. The only way I know how to respond to them is to look after them. I think if I saw them no good could come of it. We maintain the pretence of planning to visit each other, but I think they feel the same. They disapprove of me. My father, especially. I always wanted them to be proud of me. I have tried to be a good mother to Martin. I don't know whether I have succeeded. It is not for me to say. He will judge me one day. Jem is almost lost to me.

'Will Jem not see reason?'

'Yes, I think he would see reason, but that is not the issue. The issue is my inconstancy. I tell myself that my acting career ended, but that is not true. I have been acting these last ten years. In the part I play, I set my feelings aside. I build an armour around myself. I have lost the ability to tell Jem how I feel about him. He is better than me at expressing emotion, but that does not say much. Ours is the great romance that won't speak up for itself. I am almost resigned to it.'

'Will you try again with Jem?'

'If the opportunity comes, but it may not – although I never give up hope. What about you, Mellie? You are very quiet about your own romances.'

There is a pause while Mellie chooses her words carefully.

'I have not enjoyed the convivial society of men.'

'I see. I hope you will find what you enjoy one day.'

'Perhaps. Like you, I never give up on the idea. It just hasn't happened yet.'

'Then we must make a toast. Here's to never giving up.'

༄

At Marseille, the rail part of their journey ends. Strode arranges for them to take the late mail coach for the last leg of their trip into Nice. Much as they have benefited from the speed of the railway, they enjoy the comforting rhythm and sway of the carriage and they sleep soundly through the night. At dawn, when she sees the sun rise over the sea, Harriet reconsiders her resolutions. She would be mad to go back to England now. There is nothing for her there. And Sly cannot be trusted. Jem would never be safe. Martin would never be safe. Perhaps she would never be safe. What was she thinking?

In Nice, Mellie and Harriet settle into the Villa Danetti. The house is delightful. Strode is a good judge of property. The villa sits high on the hillside and looks down into the bay at Villefranche. It is a white, beautifully symmetrical, four-storey building with bay windows and pilastered balconies. Inside, the rooms are large and elegantly appointed, with panelled walls, marble fittings and mosaic floors. The aroma of lemons, oranges and cloves pervades the air. The lush green cypress trees seem to cling onto the very edges of the terraced grounds. Beyond Villefranche, further views look across the bay, over the wild olive and carob trees on Mount Boron to Nice in the west, towards Cap Ferrat in the south, and east beyond Beaulieu to Monte Carlo. It is easy to feel settled and comfortable here. Harriet breathes deeply.

'I was thinking to myself that this is a place where I could be happy,' she says. 'Or am I deluding myself?'

'It is a charming town. There is no denying that,' says Mellie.

'I feel there is a "but" hanging unsaid.'

'I have listened to you talk about things all the way down from Paris...'

'I am sorry to burden you.'

'I didn't mean that as a criticism. I have enjoyed getting

to know you again. It has been a delight to spend so much time together, just the two of us.'

'But?'

'I think your happiness cannot be determined by your location. It is beautiful here, but so is La Celle. As you say, you will only relax when Martin is happy and when Jem is happy and when you are no longer threatened. Then, you will be happy also. I am sorry if you think me forward. That is what I think.'

'Thank you, Mellie. You understand me very well. Better than I understand myself, perhaps.'

∽

Next morning, they set out to wander the streets and explore the Old Town. They buy new clothes. There is an account set up for the villa and the credit seems to hold. Harriet enjoys the sense of freedom. No one knows them here. They are just two women on a holiday together. They take coffee in a small café on the seafront. Harriet is struck by the vivid colours: the bougainvillaea, a deeper purple; the plumbago, a paler blue; and the hibiscus, a brighter pink. The colours are unlike anything in England or Northern France. She sits and stares, mesmerised by the shimmering azure blue of the Mediterranean in front of them and the blind whiteness of the snow-capped Alps behind them in the distance. A note arrives, back at the villa. The tide may be turning, says Strode. He hopes he will have good news for her shortly.

༄

A few days later, they sit at a bar in the early evening, in one of the cobbled, narrow lanes. Even the jasmine smells different here: more pungent, more alive somehow. Nice is not Paris and no one judges them. Besides, their attire looks too restrained for anyone to infer the wrong idea. Presently, two naval officers in British uniform sit at a table beside them. They are agreeable company: witty without being flirtatious and attentive without being intrusive. Harriet realises she is enjoying herself. After a while, one of the men begins to stare at her.

'I am sorry,' he says. 'Your face seems familiar. I am trying to place you.'

In the street behind them, whistles blow. In the port, a ship's bell chimes out. The crew is being called back and the two men stand up and straighten their uniforms.

'It has been a great pleasure to make your acquaintance,' says the other man. 'We must leave, I am afraid. We sail at first light. May we have the honour of knowing your names?'

'Elizabeth and Ann,' says Mellie. 'We are sisters.'

'It really has been lovely to meet you,' says Harriet.

At the villa the next morning, Harriet makes plans to cut short their visit and return to Paris.

'It was a mistake,' she tells Mellie. 'I thought that the distance would help, but I can never escape my circumstances. There is no more a solution here than at home.'

It feels like a long journey back. There is ample time to reconsider all of the resolutions she made on the way down. By the time she reaches Paris, she has resolved nothing.

∽

There is no good news when Harriet returns to the château. Another letter from Strode awaits, this time explaining the severity of her situation. Debt accumulates and there is no solution in sight. He will do what he can, but if she can see a way forward from her own resources, he says, then she would be well advised to take it. She understands him perfectly.

Mocquard visits. He has bad news, he says. He very much regrets that Louis Napoleon has decided to take back his two sons and place them under the care of their birth mother, Eleonore Vergeot, now Madam Bure following her marriage to Pierre Bure. It feels like one further body blow.

∽

As the year draws to a close, Harriet considers the many pressures on her. She needs money. She needs a new tutor for Martin. Martin needs some discipline in his life. He is fourteen and asking questions again. While she considers what she must do, a messenger arrives. The note asks if Harriet would be happy to receive a visit from Captain Clarence Trelawney, who is most desirous of a meeting with her.

TWENTY-THREE
Ends and Beginnings
Paris and La Celle-Saint-Cloud, France
London, England
1856

2 Ferry Lane
Norwich

My dear Eliza

Really, I don't know where I should start. Your dear father and I are quite distraught. It seems you are married to Captain Trelawney and not a word to your poor dear parents. It is not for us to guide you these days, of course, but a captain? What are we to think? One minute you are going to be an Empress, then by all accounts you reject Francis, who is, after all, a lieutenant-colonel, even if he is still married.

I really think you might furnish us with an explanation.

Please send Martin my love.

Mama

Château de Beauregard
La Celle-Saint-Cloud

Dearest Mama

I am so sorry that you and Papa are upset. All I can say is that I acted for the best and my first concern was for you both and for Martin. I cannot tell you all that has happened here, but it has been a most stressful time. I am hopeful that the worst is behind me now and that Clarence and I can have a happy marriage, and that your future and Martin's future will be secure.

I am making plans to visit England as soon as I can and Clarence, Martin and I will come to see you, of course. There is much news, but it is better I leave it until we meet than try to explain it in a letter.

God bless you.

Your loving daughter.

Eliza

∽

Harriet is still invited to the British Embassy from time to time. She thinks it is probably when they are short of numbers. At least it saves Lord Cowley a trip to La Celle when Lord Palmerston asks about her. Cowley is sociable enough, but she does not have the same relationship with him as she did with Lord Normanby. They meet infrequently and it is more or less understood between them that her role is redundant. As Normanby advised, she lets things take their course. When news comes, during dinner, that the Crimean War is at an end, it seems a cause for celebration, but an inner anger still simmers in Harriet. Cowley bears the brunt of it.

'The killing is over,' she says. 'For the moment. No doubt you will have other plans.'

'We have no plans. War is not sought. We engage with great reluctance.'

'So you say. Have you not been spoiling for a fight with the Russians for some time? You just wanted the odds stacked in your favour. Even then, you managed to demonstrate some spectacular incompetence. It is hardly a glorious victory.'

'We do not seek glory. We seek to protect our interests and to bring peace in Europe.'

'How grand and worthy that sounds.'

'I will not apologise for stating Her Majesty's Government's objectives.'

'Of course not.'

Cowley turns away towards the guest on his other side and the discussion ends. He makes a mental note not to invite Harriet again.

'You were a bit harsh on old Cowley, weren't you?' says Trelawney.

'Perhaps.'

∾

Within a few days, the Treaty of Paris is signed and Russia is defeated. Emperor Napoleon III acts as if he achieved the victory on his own and his soldiers march up and down the streets of Paris for weeks on end. The Emperor is often at their head, astride one of his famous black stallions. "Vive la France" and "Vive L'Empereur" shout the crowds, at least for the first few days. Louis Napoleon is finally established. France has her conquering hero: an Emperor and a Bonaparte.

In the same month, despite the rumours, Eugenie gives birth to Louis Napoleon's son, to be called the Prince Imperial. It is another excuse for celebration across the nation and enormous numbers of cannon salvos are fired off to mark the occasion. In a few days, however, there is rather less cause for celebration for Louis. Another rumour has it that the Empress, having donated a successor and fulfilled her obligations, feels it will be unnecessary for Louis to visit her again in her bedchamber.

∽

Later in the year, Britain celebrates peace in Europe by announcing that the country is at war with Persia over Afghanistan. The Persians try to take the southern town of Herat, but the British side with Afghanistan and send troops to the Gulf. Lord Palmerston can usually be relied upon to keep the forces busy. He doesn't disappoint.

∽

Jean Mocquard has no particular reason to visit Harriet, but he comes often. She is always pleased to see him. He is, as ever, a terrible gossip and provides all sorts of stories about Louis Napoleon and his entourage that he should not. One such story concerns the conception of the Prince Imperial. It seems that Louis was in the habit of entertaining the Comtesse de Castiglione in his apartments with Eugenie nearby. In this way, Louis could ensure that he was in a suitable state of excitement before adjourning to his wife. Apparently, there were a number of accidents before the desired end result was achieved. It earns the Comtesse the nickname "the Teaser" – the name given to the stallion employed to ready the mare for impregnation before the arrival of the real stallion. It enables an expensive stallion to be saved the time-consuming task of foreplay and only appear for the main event, so to speak. Mocquard, perhaps demonstrating a certain lack of tact, tells Harriet that Eugenie was only third choice as Empress. Princess Carola of Vasa, the granddaughter of King Gustav IV Adolf of Sweden, was first. German Princess Adelheid Hohenlohe-Langenburg, a niece of Queen Victoria, was second. Both families said no. Harriet wonders where she stood in the pecking order.

It is a bonus that Martin and Mocquard get on well. He has been a constant in Martin's life since Harriet arrived in France and Martin calls him "Oncle". Mocquard is a fine advisor to Martin on dress code and etiquette, and a good tutor on the finer points of horse conformation. He also teaches him to swear in French.

'Fils de pute,' says Martin, when he breaks a shoelace.

❧

In England, Jem marries again, quietly, away from publicity. What did Harriet expect? Jem does what he always does when they quarrel. He punishes her. And, of course, she was the one who started it. This time. Jem retires from race riding. The falls take their toll and the travelling to France loses its fascination. He tells Tom that he is going to settle down, buy and sell a few horses, enjoy some days hunting. His wife is the daughter of a well-known Oxfordshire horse dealer and there are opportunities for a man with Jem's gifts on a horse.

'Will you never learn?' says Tom.

'What have I to learn?'

'I am talking about both of you. You and Harriet should be together.'

'Unless it has escaped your notice, she is married to someone else.'

'It wouldn't have happened if you had persevered. She thought it was over between you. She was in deep financial trouble. She needed a way out.'

'We both have a capacity for making bad decisions. It is almost a habit nowadays. I wish we could escape it.'

'You could, but you are both too stubborn.'

'I think it is more than that. Harriet is closed off. There is something she keeps from me. It is a barrier between us. I think that without being honest about everything it is hard to rebuild the trust we once had. I'm sorry. I'm not being very clear.'

'It is clear. I think there is something that weighs on her. I don't fully understand it, but I know there is a man in London who she answers to. Something to do with the government. Mountjoy-Martin is involved. There is a mystery about Harriet that I have not fathomed.'

'I think you are right. I have asked her about it, but she

won't say anything. She is afraid of something. If you ever find out what it is, will you let me know?'

'I will, but would it change anything?'

'I don't know. It might. I am sorry about the way things have turned out for us. I hope she will find happiness one day, but I don't think it can be with me. I think this is our fate. I will do whatever I can to help her achieve her freedom, but I need to start a new life. The past cannot be recaptured.'

✑

Louis sends a belated note, via Mocquard, congratulating Harriet on her marriage to Clarence Trelawney. It is curt and rather pointed. It signals an end of sorts, but Mocquard lets her know that Louis would be most happy to call on her at any time if she wishes it. She lets Mocquard know that she does not.

At Beauregard, Harriet does her best to be happy with her new life. The house is comfortable and the stables are buzzing with her husband's burgeoning string of horses.

Nathaniel Strode visits. Money flows through the accounts again, although it is erratic. Strode tells her she should exercise restraint until he can audit the books.

'Should I be worried?' she says.

'Let me do that for you.'

'Very well. Please keep me informed. There is one more thing: Mocquard. What should I make of him?'

'You understand him very well, I think.'

'He has become a good friend over the years. But he serves many masters, does he not?'

'You are asking me for confirmation of what you already know. Jean is possibly the worst double agent in existence. He cannot keep a secret. If you want the other side to be fed a story, it is only necessary to tell Jean something in strictest confidence. Next day, they will know it. And yet, he is well regarded by all those who come into contact with him, here and in England. That is his genius.'

'You are right, of course. I knew it.'

'He is a great supporter of you, though. Don't doubt that.'

∽

Trelawney spends a great deal of time at the races and viewing horses. Research is an important part of his stud ambitions, but Harriet does sometimes wonder whether this warrants his spending so much time away on long trips. Perhaps he suffers under the delusion, as many have before him, that the right horse will eventually be found if only the searcher travels far enough from home. When he is at the château, he is a very occasional visitor to her rooms. It is not long before doubts spring up in Harriet's mind and Strode rather fuels them, but she pushes negative thoughts away. Trelawney takes Martin with him sometimes. Martin is only too happy to swap a day with his books and his tutor for a day at the races, or a day hunting boar at Fontainebleau. Harriet is pleased, of course, that he spends time with his new stepfather. He needs an authority figure in his life – someone to respect. After one such foray, though, Martin returns subdued. He refuses to talk about what has happened. Eventually, he relents.

'There is something not right about that man,' he says. 'I don't like him.'

∽

Back in England, Nathaniel Strode witnesses an odd occurrence in Threadneedle Street one day, while he is on his way to a meeting in Aldgate. He cannot quite make sense of it until he reads the newspaper the following day.

Morning Chronicle, Thursday 4th September 1856

THE ROYAL BRITISH BANK –
GREAT EXCITEMENT

Yesterday forenoon, about eleven o'clock, the passengers passing along Threadneedle Street were attracted by a placard placed upon the doors of the Royal British Bank, which is located in the premises of the site of the old South Sea House, of unfortunate memory. The placard announced that "The business of this bank is suspended pending negotiations." It would appear that there has been a considerable run upon the bank for the past few days, but, notwithstanding, it opened for business at the usual hour in the morning, when, from some sudden cause which has not been ascertained, the doors were closed at the time above mentioned and the placards posted upon the doors. From that period until a late hour in the afternoon, that part of the street became near impassable, during which time several parties arrived at the bank, evidently, from their blank countenances, disappointed at not being able to draw cash from their cheques, many of them driving off in frantic haste by means of cabs, which were continuously arriving at the spot with a view to obtain fares. Several parties rang violently at the door bell, trying to gain information, but, receiving no answer, left in apparent discomfiture. The police endeavoured, but with little effect, to keep the thoroughfare clear and, notwithstanding, groups assembled near the bank discussing the affair, some loudly complaining of the bank having opened in the morning for the receipt of money and others, who had arrived with cheques, evincing great agitation; many were greeted by individuals having no interest but that of curiosity, with unseemly and not very feeling jokes as to how much they expected to receive in the pound. Some went as far as to offer 10s in the pound while others offered 1s 6d. For some time past, the affairs of this bank have been in a very doubtful state. The actual amount of liabilities due by the bank has not yet transpired.

TWENTY-FOUR
What Have We Done?
La Celle-Saint-Cloud and Paris, France
1857

At the Château de Beauregard, there is a continuous hum of activity. New horses arrive and temporary structures are erected to accommodate them. More paddock fencing is put in and extra stable grooms are taken on. Martin is much happier working in the stables and schooling the youngstock than attending his lessons. Rather than argue the point, Harriet lets his tuition lapse. Everything seems set fair with her husband's venture, although Harriet does wonder whether, at some point, any of these new horses will actually be sold. She is not a businesswoman, but she is fairly sure that the essence of a successful enterprise requires that there has to be money coming in, as well as going out.

Clarence Trelawney announces that he is going to England for a few weeks. He has important business meetings, he says. He needs more funding for his plans for the stud. He promises he will send regular messages and keep Harriet informed of progress. After a week, she hears nothing. When news does come, Nathaniel Strode provides it.

'Trelawney doesn't have a centime to his name. That is the plain truth of it. He has run up debt in his own accounts and in yours. What money he did have went down with the Royal British Bank.'

Harriet listens intently, as Strode catalogues the full extent of his discoveries. He thinks Trelawney may be in Italy and, given the circumstances, unlikely to return in the foreseeable future.

'I have been foolish. The man is a fraud,' she says.

'I think there was, perhaps, error on both sides.'

'I can always trust your honesty.'

'There is no point pretending.'

'No, but where does that leave us? Or, should I say, me?'

'I have hope of a settlement.'

'And in the meantime?'

'I won't let you down. Have I ever?'

'No, indeed. You have been consistent throughout. I am forever grateful. What will the arrangements be?'

'If it comes to it, I will act as guarantor myself.'

'I cannot ask you to do that.'

'I think you will have no other option. If there was someone else, I would let them, believe me.'

∽

In England, Tom Olliver decides that he will retire from race riding. He is older than Jem Mason, but he has been luckier with injuries and, apart from the occasional broken collar bone, he retires intact. Like his friend, he thinks about dealing in horses, but an offer comes to train horses for Lord Chesterfield at Newmarket and he doesn't turn it down. Tom and Harriet still correspond and it is he who alerts her to a change in Jem's circumstances. Although the former jockeys no longer race ride in France, Harriet persuades Tom to find some way to place Jem in Paris again. He is happy to oblige. He asks Jem to travel a horse to Saint Cloud for him and then bring another horse back. Jem stays over at Saint-Germain-en-Laye at the Hotel Pavillon Henry IV. It is a small, elegant two-storey building set in an elevated park with views to the east across the Seine and towards Paris in the distance. Harriet tells the concierge she is expected and he directs her via the balustraded staircase to Jem's rooms on the first floor.

Jem greets her cordially, but, she thinks, a little stiffly and they sit at two matching leather wing chairs, looking out through the open windows and over the wrought iron railings of the balcony. Harriet wears a fitted blue-grey tunic dress, demure yet still alluring, and a narrow-brimmed bonnet with a single feather. Jem is still in riding breeches and top boots, having ridden out at Maisons-Laffitte that morning. Somewhere outside, a chaffinch sings and the musk roses below send their heady scent into the room as the sun warms them. As ever, she favours the direct route.

'Why do we always choose the wrong course?' she says. 'It seems we have a talent for it.'

'Are you speaking for us both?'

'This is not the time for scoring points. I am seeking to make amends.'

'Amends?'

'Why so infuriating? I think I have made a gross error of judgement. I am prepared to admit that. Do you have the gumption to admit your own error?'

'I married someone for whom I had a great fondness. Sadly, she decided she did not share that feeling. It can happen, I believe. You, on the other hand, married someone who you thought had money to bail you out from your financial situation, only to find he was broke. You are seeking to equate these two examples as comparable errors of judgement. Am I correct?'

'I hate it when we bicker like this. I'm happy to be the bigger fool if that pleases you. I want us to be talking again, at least. We are both estranged from our erstwhile partners. We could be friends again, couldn't we?'

'I think this time it is too late.'

The discussion meanders. Jem offers no hope of reconciliation. In the end, Harriet leaves with no progress made. She wonders how many more "last chance" meetings with Jem she can bear.

The outcome puzzles them both. It is not that they don't arrive at their meetings with positive intentions. They do. Harriet's careful planning of exactly what she will say and how she will say it and Jem's intuitive belief that the right words will come to him when required both prove unequal to the task. Harriet can never sustain her script and Jem always manages to say the exact opposite of what he intends. When they part, Harriet goes over the conversation endlessly, to no purpose, and Jem gets no further than scratching his sideburns and rubbing his eyes.

❦

Harriet is invited to dine with Princess Mathilde at her mansion on the rue de Courcelles in Paris. Mathilde is in buoyant mood and clearly unaware of the latest developments.

'Louis wants to have his cake and eat it, as you say in England,' she says. 'Is that not so?'

'You have a great command of the English idiom. You are correct. But he will have to be satisfied with what he has. The menu has changed.'

'I hoped you would say that. I am sorry that my dear cousin is such a weak man.'

'But an Emperor nonetheless.'

'As you say. He has given the French what they wanted.'

'And he has the Empress he wanted.'

'Then he has made his bed and he must lie in it. Is that not so also?'

'I could not have put it better myself.'

'Monsieur Mocquard has taught me well.'

Her time with Mathilde reminds Harriet of her friendship with Lady Blessington. Like Margaret, Mathilde is witty and charming, although that would not be immediately apparent from her outward demeanour. But Harriet does not know Mathilde well enough to confide in her. She wants someone to whom she can tell everything. She wants to tell the truth: about Sly, scheming in his office in London; about Trelawney, hiding from his creditors in exile in Italy; and about Jem Mason, prevaricating as only he can. She decides that, for the moment at least, she must keep up appearances.

'And you, Harriet. How is Beauregard?'

'Beauregard is a fine property. There is much to do there.'

'And your handsome husband, Trelawney?'

'He has gone to Italy on business. I expect he will be back soon.'

'And your son, Martin. What will he do? He must be almost grown up now.'

'He continues with his education,' she says, aware that the conversation, at least on her side, is sagging under the weight of half truths. 'He enjoys his work with horses. He has a talent with them. But I think it really too soon to say. Young people can change so much at that age. He is quite a strong-willed character. They say he takes after me.'

It is a stilted conversation and Mathilde is sensitive enough to read the signs and change tack. She relates the story going around, that Lord Hertford has paid the Comtesse de Castiglione one million francs to spend the night with him. Harriet wonders what Louis will think of this when he hears it.

'They say he got his money's worth,' says Mathilde. 'She was in bed for a week, recovering.'

Harriet laughs politely. She finds that she cannot find too much amusement in such tales, given her own experience. The conversation drifts and eventually stutters to a halt. Harriet says her goodbyes and returns to La Celle.

When she reaches there, another message arrives, from Louis Napoleon. His latest tone is pleading. She deduces that his other mistresses are not pleasing him and that

Eugenie continues to refuse him access to her bedchamber. He may be the conquering hero in public, but in private he is not. Harriet sends her usual reply.

❧

Lord Cowley and Francis Mountjoy-Martin meet at the British Embassy on the rue Faubourg Saint-Honore for an update on events. Harriet is first on the agenda.

'Well, I didn't see that coming. Did you?' says Cowley.

'I am afraid Trelawney has form. It is not the first time, it seems. Harriet has been hoodwinked. Of course, hindsight is a wonderful thing.'

'Unfortunate. Hope you weren't involved with that business at the bank. Very bad show all round.'

'Thankfully, no. I gather Lord Palmerston says he will bring in new laws to make sure this can't happen again. Banks will not be allowed to fail.'

'He is rather prone to the grand statement.'

'Is there any help we can give Harriet? I understand her circumstances are much reduced.'

'I am sorry, but Miss Howard will need to make her own way now. She is no longer our responsibility.'

The conversation moves to Louis Napoleon. Cowley has news of a change of heart in London.

'The Emperor is on borrowed time now, I think. Palmerston believes he will go the way of King Louis Philippe and become unstable. The talk of assassination plots has rattled him; there is no doubt of that. He wants to appease the Italians, but the price may be war with Austria.

We could not support that. News reaches us, from the usual sources, that Empress Eugenie is making her presence felt and becoming involved in politics. An unexpected development.'

'Will a point come when we can no longer support him at all?'

'It may. At the moment, he is the least worst candidate rather than the best candidate. What happens next is in the balance.'

Finally, they discuss the new Treaty of Paris, signalling the end of Britain's war with the Persians.

'Let's hope we will finally realise that meddling in the affairs of countries where we are not welcome is a recipe for disaster,' says Cowley.

'Indeed.'

'Too many lives have been lost.'

'And for little gain. At least we will always have India.'

∽

Strode sends word that he has secured a credit arrangement, which tides Harriet over until the end of the year, but he warns that this will be finite and that something more substantial and long term must be put in place. Economies will be required, he says, but that alone will not be enough. Jean Mocquard arranges a place for Martin at a boarding school, near his family home, where he can keep an eye on him. Leave the details to me, he tells Harriet. We can discuss it later. She is grateful for some respite at least, but she cannot but recognise that she has brought this situation on herself. Trelawney, far from being a solution, has made things a lot worse. How could she have been so foolish?

∽

Tom Olliver brings horses over for the races at Longchamp, the new racecourse in the Bois de Boulogne, and calls on Harriet at La Celle, where he stables the horses to break their journey. There is plenty of room. Most of the horses acquired by Trelawney are reclaimed by their former owners, due to non-payment. The rest go to a dispersal sale, where they make a fraction of their value. Tom is making a great success of his training career and the contrast with Harriet's own situation is stark. They talk about hunting and racing gossip and mutual friends, although Jem Mason is not mentioned.

'Things have gone badly, Tom,' she says.

'So I hear. I am sorry for it. Can I do anything?'

'I don't think so. Strode will be my saviour if anyone can.'

'If it is a question of money, I will see...'

'No, Tom. I must see this through myself, whatever the cost.'

When Tom leaves, he goes over his conversation with Harriet. It is clear that while she puts a brave face on things, the outlook is bleak. Surely something can be done. There must be someone, somewhere who can help. He arrives back in England determined to come up with a plan, but rather unclear about what it might be.

TWENTY-FIVE
Retribution
London, England
La Celle-Saint-Cloud, France
1858

Morning Chronicle, Thursday 18th February 1858

THE ATTEMPT TO ASSASSINATE NAPOLEON
THE THIRD

Indictment against the prisoners Orsini, Rudio, Gomez, Pieri and Bernard.

The trial of the prisoners charged with the attempt to assassinate the Emperor of the French stands fixed to commence today before the Assize Court of the Seine. We place before our readers a translation excerpt of the important document:

Act d'Accusation

The Procureur-General declares that the following facts appear from the documents in the instruction: A new attempt has been made on the life of the Emperor. His Majesty was not injured, but many victims were struck down around him; no consideration restrains the fury of demagogic passion.

The pistol and the poniard no longer suffice for them; these instruments of murder have been succeeded by machines designed and prepared with infernal skill. A band of foreign assassins, coming in the last instance from England, whose generous hospitality is used in furtherance of the most execrable designs, undertook the task of throwing at the Emperor these new instruments of destruction. To attack his sacred person, the assassins did not shrink from devoting to death an august princess, known to us by the good she does, nor from scattering death at random amid a crowd of spectators. But Providence watched over the country. Providence has preserved the precious life of the Emperor, as also that of the noble companion associated with his dangers and has permitted that the direct authors of the attempt should be immediately arrested and brought to justice, to answer for a crime directed not less against the greatness and prosperity of France than the life of the sovereign, whom France has chosen.

On Thursday January 14th, their Majesties were to be present at the Opera. The cortege arrived at about half past eight. The first carriage, occupied by officers of the Emperor's household had passed the peristyle of the theatre; it was followed by an escort of Lancers of the Imperial Guard; which preceded the carriage in which were their Majesties and General Roguet. At this moment, three successive explosions, like the report of cannon, were heard at intervals of a few seconds. The first in front of the imperial carriage and in the second rank of the escort of Lancers; the second nearer to the carriage and a little to *the left; and the third under the carriage itself. Amid the general confusion, the first thought of all those present, who had not been too cruelly struck, was to proclaim by their unanimous acclamations that the Emperor and Empress had been preserved. Heaven had, indeed, most visibly extended its protection to them, for the danger from which they had escaped was frightfully proved by the scene around them. On a pavement inundated with blood, there lay a large number of wounded people, of whom several were so mortally. It has been judicially ascertained that 156 persons were struck and the number of wounds according to medical reports amounted to 511. In this long list of victims were comprised 21 women, 11 children, 13 Lancers, 11 Gardes de Paris and 31 police agents.*

❧

Lord Palmerston summons Lord Cowley to London at short notice. They meet at Number 10 Downing Street in the small dining room. Palmerston has already resigned as prime minister, but Lord Derby graciously allows him to continue with his meetings.

'This is a fine mess,' says Palmerston. 'Louis Napoleon nearly manages to get himself killed and we get the blame for harbouring the assassins. Trust the damned French to come up with that one. What is going on?'

'I am afraid relations with the Emperor are at a low ebb. The Empress is no friend to Britain, according to Mocquard. I hesitate to say this, but one might think we backed the wrong horse after all. Without Miss Howard's sage presence, we struggle for influence.'

'How very helpful of you to point that out.'

∽

Spring finds the Château de Beauregard and the whole estate at La Celle-Saint-Cloud in a dilapidated condition. Weeds and brambles flourish unrestricted in the paddocks, rabbits multiply in the overgrown ditches and hedgerows, and moss grows between the cobbles in the yards. Ivy is rampant and walls crumble, roofs rot and fences fall under its insidious progress. It is astonishing how quickly nature reclaims wildness from order. A passer-by would probably pronounce the château derelict. Inside the main house, rooms are closed off, mildew forms and dust gathers. Martin arrives back at La Celle, having been expelled from boarding school. He grows wild with his surroundings. He is just fifteen. Harriet tries teaching him herself, but it makes things worse: his behaviour is unruly and they argue. He is more and more unhappy with her evasion. Why won't she say who his father is? Why is it so difficult?

'Were you so much of a whore you couldn't tell?' he says.

For the first time in his life, Martin feels the force of a blow to the head from Harriet, who launches at him with all her strength. He is dumbstruck. For the second time in her life, Harriet feels her anger completely out of control. She rushes to her bedchamber in tears. She shakes so much she grips the bedpost to steady herself.

⁓

By the time Francis Mountjoy-Martin comes to the Château de Beauregard for a rare visit, Harriet is not in the best mood.

'More ribbon, Francis. How nice,' she says.

'You are a horror to me, Harriet. I do not deserve it.'

'You are a colonel now. The world is yours to command. Will you go abroad and make your fortune?'

'If you will come with me.'

'I am a married woman. I have responsibilities.'

'Do not play games with me, Harriet. Your marriage is a sham and a disaster. You are in grave financial difficulty. You forget that I know your situation as well as anyone. And I have eyes to see what is happening here. I have come with a very good offer. You should not dismiss me lightly.'

'I am listening.'

'I am to sail for India. There have been some difficulties with the locals and we are technically at war with the Chinese over the supply of opium. The government will take over the East India Company and I will play a significant role in the transfer of our armed forces. There will be commercial opportunities at the same time. It is a chance for me to start again. It could be a chance for you.'

'Only you could describe the Indian rebellion as "difficulties with the locals".'

'It is in the nature of our newspapers to exaggerate things. It will all blow over.'

'You will forgive me if I don't take your word for it?'

'Please think about it. You will never be free, here or in England. Sly does not threaten you physically, but he has a grudge. He means to take you down financially. Even Strode cannot save you.'

'You are right about one thing. I will never be free while Sly lives, wherever I am in the world. And neither will those who are dearest to me. Running away to India is not the answer for me, Francis.'

'Very well. I will not ask again. I will say goodbye.'

∽

Nathaniel Strode visits La Celle again. Harriet's money problems escalate and Strode's tables, columns and diagrams only magnify the scale of the disaster.

'I need your help and advice,' she says. 'Is Francis right?'

'Francis is, unfortunately, right that your finances remain unresolved, with no solution in sight. I cannot trace the problems directly to Sly, but I think it is a reasonable assumption that he is behind it. He is a bitter man, from what I can deduce. He is not acting for Her Majesty's Government now. That I do know. But he does have a grudge against you. Francis is quite correct about that.'

'Is there news of Trelawney? Can anything be salvaged there?'

'I am afraid not. There is no news and his family is proving unhelpful.'

'I am feeling as if everything is against me.'

'You must not lose heart. The tide will turn in time.'

'Then I must place my faith in you.'

∽

She thinks things cannot get any worse, but they do. Martin reaches his sixteenth birthday in August and disappears. All the rooms and outbuildings are searched, but there is no trace. She convinces herself that he has been abducted. What other explanation could there be? Weeks go by without news. She imagines him lying in a ditch somewhere. Eventually, he is found at Dieppe, trying to stow away on a ship to Dover. It is Mocquard who goes to him and brings him back.

'What did you hope to achieve?' asks Mocquard.

'I just wanted to get as far away from my mother as I could.'

⁓

An unexpected piece of information brings Nathaniel Strode back to Harriet sooner than planned.

'I have news about Nicholas Sly. He is dead. There is no mistake. Someone has exacted retribution.'

'Why do you say that? What were the circumstances?' she says.

'He was found with his throat cut in an alleyway in Cheapside.'

'Perhaps he strayed into the wrong place at the wrong time.'

'That is possible, of course, but he was not robbed. The police found money in his pockets and rings on his fingers.'

'I have wished for this, but it is strange. I don't know how I should feel.'

'Emotion is complicated, I have no doubt, although I try to avoid it myself. But there are practical implications. We can begin the process of unravelling the financial restrictions. If we are right that Sly was behind them, the doors should begin to swing open again.'

'Is there any clue to the killer's identity?'

'No. There was no weapon and no sign of a struggle. In short, no clues. A professional job. Apparently, one policeman described the cut as having "military precision". A single cut with a sharp blade, rather than a jagged knife.'

'No clues. Really?'

'I am sure the police will do their work diligently.'

'Of course.'

'There will not be any official record of the death, as I understand it. Mr Sly will be recorded as "missing".'

'But you are sure there can be no doubt?'

'None.'

'Thank you.'

'If you will excuse me, I will start work on your behalf.'

∽

The year ends in confusion. The doors don't swing open as Strode hopes. At the château, almost all the rooms are closed up. Frost etches the windows in the few habitable spaces and a blanket of snow covers the estate. There are two servants left. Furniture and stable partitions are chopped up for firewood. Strode sends money when he can, but no news, and Mocquard arrives with parcels of provisions. One morning, Harriet finds a food basket at the gatehouse, left by someone from the village. She and Martin don't speak to each other for weeks at a time. At least she begins to sleep better. The dreams stop. In the week before Christmas, a letter arrives.

The Bell Inn
Horndon-on-the-Hill

Dearest Harriet
By the time you read this, I will be on a ship bound for the East Indies. I very much regret that you are not with me. I wanted you to know that I always loved you. I was foolish on occasions and was not always honest, but your welfare was ever my concern. I think it likely our paths will not cross again. I trust you will find happiness, as you deserve. I hope, in a small way, that I have been able to pave the way for you to be free. I am only sorry now that I did not act sooner.
Your faithful servant
Francis

TWENTY-SIX

The New Politics
Towcester and Chislehurst, England
Chantilly, France
1859

Henry Fitzroy, the fifth Duke of Grafton, is at home at Wakefield Lodge, his hunting estate near Towcester, some forty miles north of London. His arthritis troubles him and he is unable to travel. Like his father before him, he has a tidy mind and he has a list of issues and questions he wants resolved. His physician assures him he is generally in good health, but he knows better. He asks Lord Normanby, now retired from diplomatic service, and Sir George Lewis MP if they will call on him. The old families still have some clout in England. Normanby travels up from London and Sir George breaks his journey from his country seat at Radnor, on his way back to town.

The two men arrive at about the same time, turning in off Watling Street at the turnpike, and several footmen and stable hands are waiting to take over the horses and carriages.

'Any idea what this is all about?' says Normanby. Sir George shrugs.

The enthusiastic under-butler greets them and they make their way along the north face of the house. The visitors ask polite questions about the architecture and they learn rather more about Venetian windows, flattened arches and semi-elliptical lunettes than is strictly necessary. Nevertheless, it cannot be denied that the overall appearance and style of the place is attractive.

Fitzroy meets them in the main hall. It is a room designed to impress: from the elegant, balustraded, wooden gallery and the beamed, ornamental, plaster ceiling to the magnificent stone chimneypiece, adorned with carved trophies of the hunt: a fox's head on the left and a badger's head on the right, undercut with bows and spears. A log fire roars in the grate and a rather splendid oil painting of a mare and foal, by Mr Herring senior, sits above. Candles are alight all around the room and the soft glow bounces off the mirrors and the silverware, set for tea. It has all the appearance of a cosy fireside chat, but that is not at all what the Duke has in mind. He is in no mood for small talk. An apparently chance meeting with Tom Olliver at the Cesarewitch meeting at Newmarket last year has alerted him to the situation Harriet Howard finds herself in. He wants action.

'Enough is enough,' he says. 'She has endured a great deal. I feel an enormous guilt that we did not do more when we had the chance.'

'It was a matter of national security. We had to do the right thing for the country,' says Normanby.

'I am weary of this. I am an old man now. I made a promise on my father's memory. I will not go to the grave having failed. Let us do the right thing for Miss Howard. Call off the hounds once and for all. I insist upon it.'

'I am sure you realise that these things take time...' says Sir George.

'I don't have time. And I will not be patronised. Between you two, you have the means to resolve this. Please get it done. Let me know when you have. I won't hear another word. Do I make myself clear?'

When they are gone, he sends them each a letter, confirming the agreements between them. A month passes without any sign of action, so he copies the letters to Lord Palmerston, now prime minister again following the collapse of Lord Derby's minority government. Henry Fitzroy and Palmerston are old adversaries in the hunting field. The Duke makes it clear that he holds the prime minister personally responsible for ensuring that the agreements are implemented. He mentions that he is still keeping the matter of Palmerston's liaison, with the unnamed governess, strictly between themselves. He hopes to keep it that way, he says.

♊

South of London, Nathaniel Strode has a property at Camden Place, near Chislehurst in Kent, acquired at the beginning of the year. Harriet is Strode's guest. He is insistent that she come there, despite her protestations. Château de Beauregard is shuttered up and the doors boarded. She has nowhere else to go and no access to any funds. Strode has other properties and his family does not live here. He assures her that she can stay as long as is necessary. He hopes that he will have better news soon.

Strode tells her, one day in June, that Lord Palmerston himself is calling on them and that he wishes to speak to her. Obviously, Palmerston has decided that he doesn't want anything left to chance. On the appointed day, Harriet spends the morning in Strode's well-stocked library.

Strode finds it difficult to reconcile the appearance up close of the prime minister with his great reputation as a hard rider to hounds and serial ladies' man. Now in his mid-seventies and a man who would long ago have succumbed to grey hair, he sports an auburn pate and whistles through ill-fitting teeth as he speaks. His purple cravat is adorned with the remains of his breakfast. Strode shows him into the drawing room and leaves him with Harriet. Palmerston waits for her to say something, but she stays silent. Eventually, he clears his throat.

'I am pleased to have this opportunity to set the record straight,' he says.

Harriet thinks he looks anything but pleased and she has no intention of making things any easier for him. She is prepared.

'And what record would that be?' she says.

'I see you intend to punish me for what has gone before. I understand and I sympathise. I am here to apologise and to let you know the steps I am taking to ensure this sort of thing does not happen again. The government is keen to learn from the mistakes that have been made. I propose a new politics in which we are all directly accountable to the electorate. There will be no more cloak and dagger. I can assure you of that.'

'How exactly do you propose to ensure this? Your own record lacks some credibility, wouldn't you say?'

'As I say, we have learned our lessons. I have instructed the new home secretary, Sir George Lewis, that we must have absolute clarity on the role of State Services...'

'Some might say you are a very slow learner. By my reckoning, since 1836 you have been foreign secretary for a total of ten years, home secretary for two years and prime minister for three years. You have spent your career at the very highest levels of government and yet you have only now discovered the truth of what has been going on. Either you have been extremely unobservant, which I know you are not, or you have been complicit in allowing your secret service – let us not shirk from the truth with euphemistic titles – to get away, quite literally, with murder.'

'I was warned that you are inclined to believe all the conspiracy theories. I cannot stop you. I am not here to apologise for things we did not do. On the other hand, I don't pretend that mistakes were not made. Indeed, they were. You have been poorly treated. I am fully persuaded of that by the account Lord Normanby has provided.'

'Thank you, but, apart from platitudes and promises, what else are you here to say?'

'I offer a full apology for our role in any unpleasantness. I offer a guarantee that we are taking steps to avoid this sort of thing happening in future. There will be a financial settlement, of course, subject only to your acceptance that all of this will remain confidential.'

'What a way with words you have, sir: "unpleasantness", "this sort of thing", "settlement". How prettily they trip off the tongue. Let us call it what it is, sir. You are offering me a bonus payment for whoring for the government, topped up with a bribe to shut me up.'

'I don't blame you for having your day. Berate me if you must. Beat me if you wish. Here.'

Palmerston pulls the coat aside from his waistcoat and makes a rather theatrical show of prostrating himself before her. It stops her in her tracks.

'I really am sorry,' he continues. 'I comfort myself with the fact that Europe is a safer place with Napoleon III as our ally. This could not have been achieved without you. But that doesn't make what we did right. Mr Strode will take care of things. I bid you good day.'

'There is one more thing.'

'If I can do something else, I will.'

'I would like an audience with Queen Victoria.'

'Really, Miss Howard, you go too far.'

She turns on her heels and, with a swish of her skirts, exits the room. Palmerston slumps back in his chair and blows out his cheeks.

∽

Harriet is rather pleased with her day's work. When she relates the conversation to Strode, he can barely contain himself. She hardly remembers him even smiling before – perhaps an occasional smirk – but here she has him holding his sides, the tears streaming down his face. She has not forgotten her acting skills.

'Bravo,' says Strode. 'If Mr Boucicault was here, he would cast you on the spot.'

'I am not familiar with him.'

'You have been too long in France. I shall take you to see *London Assurance* in Covent Garden by way of a celebration. There is a character called Lady Gay Spanker. You will see what I mean.'

'I am intrigued.'

The conversation marks a change in her relationship with Strode. He is always strictly businesslike; always very serious. He never mentions anything personal, certainly not his private life. Whatever he has in mind, it is clear she has much to thank him for. She says as much.

'You are an important client. I will always do my best for you,' he says. 'But it is Tom Olliver you really must thank.'

She looks puzzled for a moment, but slowly the pieces fit into place.

༄

Back in France, Jean Mocquard finds Martin a job at a racing yard in Chantilly. Martin rides out his three lots every morning and mucks out until lunchtime. He has his first ride in an amateur race and gets up in the last stride to win by a head. His formal education is further interrupted, but he is an avid reader and Mocquard provides him with a steady supply of English and French novels. Martin devours Dickens, Thackeray, Balzac and Dumas, but it is Robert Smith Surtees's tales of hunting that really capture his imagination.

'Perhaps I shall be an "untsman",' he says, in a letter to Mocquard.

'I think you can be whatever you wish,' comes the reply. 'Let me know how I can help.'

❧

Politics in France goes from bad to worse, at least from a British perspective. Lord Palmerston seems intent on replacing his reputation as a warmonger with that of Europe's peacemaker and he makes a great show of disapproval of Louis Napoleon's foreign ambitions. How times change. In March, Sardinia announces itself at war with Austria and by June Louis Napoleon supports Sardinia to defeat Emperor Franz Joseph at Solferino.

Lord Cowley tells Palmerston what is becoming a familiar story.

'I think the Emperor has really lost any sense of perspective. He has taken command of the troops himself. He is determined to have his day. He is happy to leave Empress Eugenie in charge of affairs at home. He is taking risks.'

❧

Despite British reservations, by November the Treaty of Zurich confirms the Treaty of Villafranca and brings the Austro-Sardinian War to a close.

'He is making enemies wherever he goes,' says Cowley. 'He has no strategy. The Germans are against him and the Sardinians don't trust him. But he will take Savoy and Nice before he has finished.'

'Not completely without a strategy then, I suppose,' says Palmerston.

❧

Later in the year, buoyed by her success with Palmerston and the news from Strode that her bank accounts are freed up, Harriet turns her mind to Jem again. Strode finds himself operating well outside his brief as Harriet's financial advisor. Naturally enough, they have become closer over the years, despite Strode's cool exterior, and he is asked for advice on all manner of things. It is Strode himself, though, who volunteers to speak to Jem Mason and see if the deadlock between Harriet and Jem can be broken. Strode judges that his calm detachment and common sense might have some currency with Jem. He doesn't know Jem well, but he feels he shares some of Jem's personality: a man of few words and diligent in his work. Jem is reluctant, but Harriet perseveres and eventually, with Strode's help as intermediary, he arrives at Camden Place. This time, she will be conciliatory, she tells herself. She will not argue and she will not lose her temper. Tom tells her, in a letter, that Jem's separation from his wife has come at a cost.

When they eventually sit down for tea in the drawing room, they are awkward together, as if everything that has gone between them never happened. The conversation is stilted. He asks about her parents. They talk about Tom and his latest training successes. There is a long silence. She senses he is about to leave. She feels a tightness in her chest and cannot contain her thoughts.

'Are you determined that we should never be reconciled?'

He looks down. He adjusts a buckle on his boots.

'We are both married to someone else.'

'That is detail. It can be overcome.'

'It is not so easily achieved as you seem to think.'

Another long silence ensues. They both look as if they may speak at any moment, but they hesitate. Jem pinches his nose between the thumb and forefinger of his left hand. He looks down again and shakes his head slowly.

'What is stopping us?' she says.

'I won't do it now. It must be on equal terms. I will not be beholden. It would be the same if the shoe was on the other foot.'

'I am not familiar with your financial arrangements. You are implying that my wealth exceeds yours, I think. Why is that important?'

'It was important to you once.'

'By heaven, what an irritating man you can be. If I have too much, I'll give it away. If you need more, then I'm sure you and Tom Olliver can devise a way to find it. Please don't put excuses in the way.'

'I must think about it.'

'Please at least do that. Life is short. We have wasted too much time apart as it is.'

The meeting ends without resolution. She hopes something can be rescued in their relationship, but the more she thinks about it the more she convinces herself that this may really have been her last chance. She berates herself for her lack of patience. Despite what she promised herself, she could not hold her tongue. She thinks she will probably never see Jem again.

By contrast, Jem feels the meeting a positive one. After all, has he not said he will think about things? What more could he say?

TWENTY-SEVEN
A Royal Appointment
London and Chislehurst, England
Paris and La Celle-Saint-Cloud, France
1860

At Buckingham Palace, Harriet waits for her appointment with Her Majesty The Queen. A court official looks her up and down and sniffs.

'You will be required to curtsey to the floor and remain there for ten seconds or until Her Majesty indicates you may rise. Her Majesty may be addressed on introduction as Your Majesty and then as Ma'am, rhymes with jam. On no account use any other form of address. You may not ask a direct question. You may respond to a topic Her Majesty raises and you may respond directly to a question she poses. You must not attempt to change the topic of conversation. This is for Her Majesty to decide. Her Majesty will indicate when the conversation is at an end. You must not extend the conversation beyond this point. You must not turn your back on Her Majesty, but wait until she has turned away. Are there any questions?'

'No, thank you.'

'Then please wait. You will be called forward in due course.'

Harriet is eventually ushered into a library. It is an intimate room. There are family photographs on an ornate mahogany desk, official papers neatly piled on a side table and a log fire blazing in a polished, register grate. When Queen Victoria appears, she strikes Harriet as younger than she expected. She is slim, almost petite. There is a vivacity and alertness about her that does not come through in her photographs.

Of course, no such meeting takes place officially. It does not appear in any diary and no one is party to the discussion. It would be inappropriate to guess at the ground that was covered.

After the meeting, travelling back to Camden Place again, Harriet reflects. Of course, she did not expect an audience. She wanted to make Palmerston uncomfortable and she certainly achieved that much. Queen Victoria proves a willing ally in discomfiting Palmerston. Compared to her other prime ministers, she finds Palmerston a tiresome old man. He has none of Melbourne's style and sagacity or Peel's courage and common sense. The Queen impresses Harriet with her keen intellect and adept management of her politicians, but underneath it all Harriet's lasting impression is of a modest, family-minded woman, who married the love of her life and is happy. Harriet wonders if it is too late for her.

∽

The Emperor and Jean Mocquard meet at the Élysée Palace. Louis Napoleon wears the uniform of general, as has become his custom. The tunic rather pulls at the seams and the buttons strain across his stomach. His face is pale and deep lines stretch out from the corners of his eyes. He chews at his nails, biting them down to the quick.

'Will Harriet not see me?' he says.

'She will not.'

'And is this her final word?'

'Yes.'

'I think she may have been more grateful.'

'Perhaps.'

'You doubt it?'

'It is not for me to say.'

'I am asking you to say what is on your mind.'

'I am your loyal servant. I do your bidding. Do you press me?'

'I do.'

'Miss Howard has supported you from the very beginning. From what I gather, she has asked for nothing in return. I believe it is you who should be grateful. Indeed, all France should be grateful to Miss Howard. That is my honest opinion. I am sorry if I speak out of turn.'

Louis twirls at the ends of his waxed moustache and strokes at his beard. He considers for a moment.

'You are right, Jean.'

∽

Lord Palmerston makes a rare visit to France to meet the Emperor. Relations between them have dipped over the assassination attempt, now known as the "Orsini affair", but it is nothing that a bottle of Krug and two bottles of Château Latour cannot put right. When he discusses the meeting the next day with Lord Cowley – at least what he can remember of it – he reluctantly admits that Emperor Napoleon is becoming a liability.

'Not content with fighting the Austrians, he wants to invade Mexico. This will end badly,' he says.

'There is even talk that war is possible in America. Mocquard says Louis would intercede there, if only he could make up his mind which side he supports.'

'God spare us.'

'Even Fialin begins to despair. If anyone is a Bonapartist, it is he.'

'Fialin has been a sound adviser from the early days and a trustworthy ambassador, even if he is a rather strange fellow. We have much to be grateful for, where he is concerned. The Empress has taken against him, though, and his days of influence are numbered. Who will replace him?'

'He must be a bold man who speculates on the Emperor's intentions. I must doubt whether he knows them himself.'

'Indeed. I think Her Majesty sums him up very well. He has charm, she says, but he is untrustworthy and unreliable.'

'Quite so.'

∽

At the Château de Beauregard, the restoration is in full flow. Weeds and brambles are grubbed out. Paddocks are reseeded and post and rail fencing is restored. Hedges are cut and laid throughout the estate. The stables thump and scrape with the sound of carpenters' tools. In the house, plasterers and painters press on with the renovation of the rooms. Harriet stays in Paris at the Hotel Bristol while the work continues at La Celle and Princess Mathilde visits regularly. She seems to have taken Harriet under her wing.

'Can I advise you?' she says.

'I would welcome it.'

'Look after your own interests. Louis is resigned to his fate now. He need not concern you. Martin will make his own way. He has every advantage. It is not too late for you to be happy. Jean tells me there is someone.'

'Jean is a gossip.'

'He is a friend. He has a great affection for you.'

'We have come to know each other well.'

'You should know that you have friends here and in England. They will help if you need them. Do not be afraid to ask.'

Later, Harriet thinks over Mathilde's advice. She senses a change in momentum and her thoughts turn to the future. What does she really want? If she could have the life she wanted, how would it be? It is not so easily answered. She decides she will write it all down. She settles down at a desk, overlooking the Place Vendôme. She takes a piece of paper and draws a line down the middle. At the top of the left-hand column, she writes "wants". At the top of the right-hand column, she writes "doesn't want". She sits, gazing out of the window. She doodles on the blotter. She leans forward and rests her head in the crook of her arm. She sleeps. When she wakes, the room is dark. She lights a lamp and looks down at the page she has prepared. Both columns are empty. She looks up. She crumples the page tightly in her hands. What has she ever wanted? She begins to compose a letter to Jem, but the words won't come. Eventually, she gives up and writes a different letter.

Le Hotel Bristol
Place Vendôme

Dearest Mama

I hope you and Papa continue well and that everything in England is as I remember it. There is a little of England that still calls out, but I have been here in France for so long now that I think of it as home. I don't think I shall ever come back now.

As you may know, there have been some small financial details to organise recently, but I am happy to say that all is now settled. Captain Trelawney and I have decided to separate, most amicably, and I will live at the château with my staff and Martin. My work with the embassy is now complete and so I shall throw myself into my gardening and my charitable work. Martin is grown into a fine young man and is about to fly the nest for good. Nathaniel Strode is helping me with my finances and I am determined all my affairs will be in order by the end of the year.

I have been thinking about the best arrangements for you and Papa and I would like you to come and live here in France, at the château, with me. You would have your own apartments and servants and would live a most comfortable life. Please let me know when you would like to join me here and I will make all the arrangements.

God bless you.

Your loving daughter.

Eliza

❧

2 Ferry Lane
Norwich

Dear Eliza

It was lovely to hear from you and to hear that things are settling down. I told your father that I never did have a good feeling about Trelawney and I'm pleased you are rid of him. I hope you won't mind me saying that, although you seem to have done well enough for yourself, you have always been a very poor judge of men. There, I've said it. I'm afraid your dear old mother has to say what is on her mind these days.

I am pleased that Martin has grown up so well. It is only a shame that we didn't see more of him. Of course, the same could be said of you, but I suppose you will say that you were very busy with your important job at the embassy and that your poor dear parents had to be sacrificed to matters of state.

Thank you very much for your offer to come and live in France, but I hope you won't mind if we decline. We are old and settled in our ways now and couldn't cope with uprooting ourselves and living among a lot of foreigners. I wonder that you have managed it when you are always telling us how you pine for old England. Please don't think we are ungrateful for what you have done for us, but I think it best we stay as we are now.

Is it too much if we ask that you might come and visit us here and bring Martin with you? Even a short visit would be appreciated. I wouldn't want to keep you long from your gardening and your charitable work. I am sure it will keep you very busy.

Please write again soon.

Mama

TWENTY-EIGHT
A Quiet Life
La Celle-Saint-Cloud, France
1861

Harriet takes stock of her life. She is in her thirty-eighth year. She has a grand château, a title and an estate of one hundred and eighty-four hectares, three kilometres north of Versailles. Relations with her son are improving, slowly. Her parents are looked after and in good health. She knows her mother is right about staying in England. It could never have worked and Harriet has to admit to herself that it was only out of selfishness that she asked anyway.

Nathaniel Strode tells her, in a note, that her financial situation is becoming ever more favourable. She is free, whatever that means. Certainly, she is free from any obligation to the British Government and free of her nemesis, Nicholas Sly. She is in radiant health and still turns heads wherever she goes. She thinks that she should be happy. Indeed, some things do make her happy.

There are plans to remodel the north face of the three-storey château into a more classical style. She pores over the designs and allows herself a smile. The tree men have been in, to open up the view towards Le Chesnay and eastwards to Paris. She finds the prospects pleasing. On the south face of the château, two large wings extend outwards to make a courtyard. There is a fountain in a large ornamental pond, cleared of weed and restocked with fish. The terrace overlooks a new parterre garden, alive with butterflies. On sunny days, she sits here and takes tea in the afternoon. She finds pleasure in the shadows cast by the mansard roofs on the coach house beyond and the bobbing of the wagtails across the fish-scale tiles. The stable yard echoes again with the chiming of the farrier's hammer, the clink of harness and the ring of metalled hooves on cobbles. At feed times, she finds herself listening out for the comforting sound of whickering horses. She tells herself she should be grateful for her situation. Yet, for all this, something nags at her. She resists the plain truth, but, finally, she admits it. She feels alone.

∽

In late June, Strode comes to visit Harriet. She always looks forward to seeing him. He has a way of simplifying things when they seem complex. He speaks directly and concisely.

'As I mentioned, all is restored. Your financial concerns are resolved.'

'Thank you, Nathaniel. I am grateful to you as ever.'

'Inflows comfortably exceed expenditure and I have taken the liberty of adding some new options to your Italian portfolio. I think they will do well.'

'Thank you. And Trelawney? Is there news?'

'Indeed, yes. I have spoken to the family and they are minded to agree to the legal separation, with no strings attached on either side. It is a good agreement. I will have the papers drawn up.'

'Please do. It will be a great relief to have this settled.'

'I believe we can safely say that your situation is looking very positive on all fronts. Lord Palmerston has delivered on his promises, at least as far as the finances are concerned. I understand, though – this must remain between us – that Her Majesty was unhappy with the initial proposal and told him to double it.'

'It seems we have friends in high places in England now.'

'So it does. May I ask if you have given any thought to your future plans? If there is anything I can help with, you only have to say.'

'I am not sure yet. It has been a long time since I have been able to consider my own interests freely. I need to think about Martin's future. He is almost a man now. He must make decisions about his career.'

'I have heard good things about Martin. They say he has your spirit. But from what you have told me it has not always been easy between you.'

'He has my temperament. That much is true. He must not be told anything. He has to discover it for himself. I was the same. If I was told a thing, I would never believe it. How little trust I had. I always blamed it on circumstances, but it was deep within me. His circumstances have been unsettling as he grew up, but that is not why he is as he is. It is because of me.'

'At least he has not wanted for education and you are now in a position to give him a good start in his adult life.'

'He won't take anything directly from me.'

'That is not a bad thing. He should make his own way. He will inherit eventually, but that is a long way off. You could make some investments on his behalf to pay out in stages, say at age twenty-five, thirty and so on. It would be up to him to take the proceeds, draw an income or leave it invested. Shall I put some proposals together? I can act for him, as I have for you, when he reaches twenty-one, if you both wished it.'

'I am fortunate to have someone so level-headed when it comes to money. Please do.'

'And I saved a snippet until the last. There is a full and final debt repayment from the office of Emperor Napoleon III.'

∽

At the end of the summer, Melliora Findon comes to live with Harriet in the main house. A lady companion is not Harriet's first choice, but it is something at least and Mellie is a great friend. Days are spent in the drawing room, where they read novels and sew a little. They read out stories from newspapers and magazines to each other. Mellie is an accomplished pianist and the sounds of Chopin and Saint-Saëns tinkle and trill around the music room and out into the hall. Harriet wonders if this is how her life will be now. It is a pleasant enough existence, but not what she hoped for.

Martin has his own cottage in the grounds, although he is rarely there. He spends time with Mocquard, who, apart from the appalling words and phrases he teaches him, is a positive influence. He is enthusiastic about meeting Strode, to put his own finances on a sound footing and to plan for the future. He has friends in the racing world and he is already an accomplished amateur jockey. Harriet thinks of writing to Tom to ask him if he will consider giving Martin some rides, but she abandons this approach in favour of a more ambitious plan. When she discusses it with Jean Mocquard, he is only too happy to help.

∽

Behind the scenes, Nathaniel Strode takes the initiative with Jem Mason. It is true that Strode has a business motive for talking to Jem. He has a client with a genuine interest in bloodstock investment in France and Jem's knowledge and contacts there make him the ideal intermediary. And, of course, where better to view horses than the Château de Beauregard. But there is another motive. Princess Mathilde is right. Harriet has friends who will help her.

While Strode works on Jem Mason, Mellie takes up the challenge of guiding Harriet. One might almost think it is being coordinated. One day, at the end of a long conversation over lunch, Mellie, usually so restrained but occasionally capable of striking right to the core of the matter, takes Harriet by surprise.

'You tell me what you think, but not what you feel,' she says. 'It is just an observation.'

'I prefer to keep my own counsel.'

'I doubt that is the reason. You are afraid of feelings. It is deep in you. I see it.'

'When you are haunted by your past, as I am, it doesn't do to examine your feelings too closely. If you had led my life, you would know that. Don't judge me, Mellie.'

'I don't judge you. I sympathise with you. I understand you a little, I think. Shall I go on?

'Please do.'

'From what you tell me, you plan your meetings with Jem; what you will say and how you will say it. You employ logic. You create a compelling argument about the case for reconciliation, which he will not be able to counter.'

'And?'

'It doesn't work. That is what you have told me.'

'So what do you suggest?'

'A different approach, perhaps.'

The simplicity of the advice disarms her: the source so unexpected; the truth so clear. Harriet feels as if a curtain has been drawn back.

∽

In December, news reaches La Celle that Prince Albert has died. He was forty-two years old. It seems that a sudden mysterious illness afflicted the Prince Consort and ten days later he was dead. All Britain is in shock.

London Evening Standard,
Tuesday 17th December 1861

THE NATION MOURNS

The nation now mourns one of the heaviest losses that has happened to the present generation of Englishmen. To slightly vary Southey's eloquent words, 'the death of the Prince was felt in England as something more than a public calamity; men started at the intelligence and turned pale, as if they had heard of the loss of a dear friend. An object of our admiration and affection, of our pride and of our hopes, was suddenly taken from us, and it seemed as if we had never till then known how deeply we loved and reverenced him.'

The whole country yearns to condole with the gracious Queen in her bereavement. The sobered tone of talk in every man's mouth, the arrest of public amusements, the outward symbol of mourning that everyone adopts as the readiest earnest of the great affliction which has visited us all are the outward visible evidence that a nation mourns. In its sorrow, the pulse of the nation beats as one man.

So ably wisely and unostentatiously did this lamented personage take his part in the progress of England – in the decrees of its councils, the public education morally and socially, the advance of his adopted countrymen to the highest intellectual achievements, the liberal arts which raise men from the selfishness of society, the avarice of trade, or the mere indulgence of the senses – that his death for a while checks, confuses or even stops the development and completion of various measures that were adding to the greatness or honour of the country. Wherever he held office, the Prince did fit service; for each distinction, he sought to render the duty attached to it; and with a discretion, tact and calm intelligence he shed around the performance with which he was entrusted, the light of an example for all in high place, or with large responsibility, to admire and imitate.

∽

Harriet remembers her meeting with Queen Victoria and how happy she was. She recalls how she envied the Queen her settled life with the man she loved. She finds herself weeping, quietly at first, but then uncontrollably, unable to fight back great sobs of grief. She cries for a life cut short in its prime. She cries for Queen Victoria, who has been so kind to her. She cries for the children, who will grow up without a father. But in the end she realises she is crying for herself. She is crying for the life she could have had.

∽

As the year draws to a close, Jem goes to see Harriet at the Château de Beauregard. Nathaniel Strode is nothing if not persuasive. His straight-talking, man-to-man approach helps Jem to understand some home truths. Strode's parting words ring in Jem's ears.

'Remember, Jem, don't put obstacles in the way. This is your time. Seize the day.'

The château is empty. The staff is stood down for the day and Mellie goes to Versailles at Strode's suggestion. A mist still hangs in the meadows below the château, as the La Celle church tower chimes out the midday bells. When Jem arrives, Harriet has no time to prepare. The fact that he is here on his own account must be a good sign, she thinks. She knows she has to cut through the layers of defence they have both built over the years. She must take things back to the basic truth: talk from the heart. The ostensible motive for Jem's visit, to view horses, is ignored.

'We could have a life here,' she says. 'The stables, the paddocks, the long rides. It would be a quiet life, but at least we would be together.'

'It is a beautiful place. I don't know how to answer you.'

'What is the real reason you cannot answer? Is it that you no longer love me? It would be as well to admit it. We can get on with our lives.'

The dart hits.

'I will never be able to say that of you,' he says.

'Nor I of you, but do you know what love is? It is holding someone in your soul every second of every day and thinking of them always, no matter which way life takes you. Can you say that, Jem? If you can't, you are not in love. Remember when we first lived in London. I said I wanted us to build a dream together. I still want that, Jem. More than ever. What do you want?'

'You shame me. You did then and you do now. I want the same, but I don't have the words. If you can be patient with me, I will try…'

She doesn't let him finish. She moves towards him and places a finger on his lips. She slides her hand around the back of his neck and pulls him to her. The passion of the embrace unsteadies them both and they crumple to the floor. The sound of their quiet murmurings drifts into the slow rhythm of the afternoon and finally the resistances melt away.

∽

When Mellie's carriage returns much later, Jem's horse still stands and fidgets in the stable. She waits in the harness room until she hears Jem and Harriet saying their lingering farewells at the terrace gate.

'I will come again soon,' he says. 'Strode is keeping me busy here.'

'Don't keep me waiting too long,' she says.

It is a breakthrough. They both sense it. Maybe, this time, things will be different.

Part Three

TWENTY-NINE
Resolution
Newmarket, England
1862

I could hardly wait for Martin's return. There was a chill in the air as he arrived early one morning and I ushered him into the kitchen to warm himself in front of the range. I wasted no time in idle chatter. The young man's story captured my imagination and I had more questions. The list of names puzzled me.

'It was Mocquard who gave me the list, but it was Mama who supplied it,' said Martin.

'I am being slow. Why would she put my name on the list, knowing it was impossible?' I said.

'She wanted me to meet you.'

'And it pleases me greatly. But what was she hoping to achieve?'

'Well… would you say we are friends?'

'Indeed, yes.'

'Then you have your answer.'

'I think I am clearer, but not completely.'

'My mother is a clever woman. I think many things about her, not all positive, but I do not deny her that. The truth is that the list was all part of an elaborate plan. She has watched me grow up, with all my faults. She knows me well. I share many of her character defects. The one we share to the greatest extent is that neither of us can ever be told anything. We must discover things for ourselves. Our distrust is so inbuilt that if anyone tells us a fact we immediately disbelieve it. It makes for a difficult life and it makes us awkward to deal with. Relationships are always strained. It is no surprise that we fight.'

'And the elaborate plan?'

'We don't trust the truth, Mama and I, but we seek it. And growing up I was full of questions, like any child. Why are we in St John's Wood? Is Francis my father? Why are we living in Paris? Is Louis Napoleon my father? Are Eugene and Louis Alexandre my brothers? She was always evasive, which, of course, made things worse. As I grew older, the questions settled into one big mystery. Who is my father? It gnawed away at me. Of course, once I was old enough, I read the newspapers and listened to the gossip. I started making guesses about things. Mama was famous, perhaps even infamous. She seemed to live a glamorous life, but she was never happy. There was the speculation about her marrying Louis: the "English Empress". Then, there was the news about the Spanish Countess. Put yourself in my shoes, Tom. What was I to think?'

'I see it was difficult for you. I sympathise. But the plan: what was your mother's plan?'

'I am coming to it, Tom. I never gave up hope. I thought that one day Mama would sit me down and say, "Martin, now it can be told. I am going to tell you the truth". But it never happened. And now I know why.'

'Why?'

'Think about it, Tom. Suppose she sat me down and told me everything: about Sly; about the Duke of Grafton; about Lord Normanby; about Lady Blessington; about Count D'Orsay. What would I have done?'

'Of course, I see now. You would not have believed her.'

'Exactly. I would have railed at her. I would have called her a fantasist and a liar. No good could have come of it.'

'So she set you the task of solving the mystery for yourself. And the list of the names was the starter's flag.'

'You have it. She laid the trail and slipped the hounds loose. And I'm nothing if I can't hunt hounds. We are mixing our metaphors rather, Tom, but you see the nub of it.'

'I do. My role was to guide you. I'm flattered. I hope I have performed the task well.'

'You have. Mama judged that, because she liked you and trusted you, I might do the same. She wanted a positive example for me. Someone who would not judge, but would ask questions.'

'It has been a pleasure meeting you, but is the mystery solved?'

'There are some things I can be more sure about – that much I can say. We already know it is not you. It is not Louis Napoleon. Mama could well have met him in the years between 1838 and 1840, but I think she did not. Although her appearance was much changed when she met "Prince Louis Napoleon" in the summer of 1846, it is hard to imagine he would not have had some recollection of her. I think it was their first meeting and it takes place around four years after my birth. There is no record of him escaping the Château de Ham prison in the intervening years.'

'That seems clear-cut. And the others?'

'It is not Nicholas Sly. I think it is not Count D'Orsay, a late addition to the list, as we discussed last time I was here.'

'I see. What has led you to these latest conclusions, may I ask?

'Mama's friend and companion, Mellie Findon, is the main source. Mellie has been in my life for many years now. She is an old school friend of Mama's. I call her Aunt Mellie, although, of course, she is nothing of the kind – any more than Jean Mocquard is my uncle, I suppose.'

'Harriet mentions them both in her letters. I think it marks a pattern of trying to surround you with people she trusts and who share her concern for your well-being. What did Mellie tell you?'

'She said that Mama confided in her about Nicholas Sly. I am sure Mellie was only passing on this information because Mama gave her permission. Apparently, Sly made two attempts on Mama. He failed, not because he couldn't overpower her, but because he couldn't, as Mellie delicately put it, "perform".'

'Did you ever solve the enigma of Nicholas Sly?'

'Up to a point. I'm not entirely sure what he did, but he was linked to the government in some way, as you thought.'

'Did you find out how he died?'

'He was murdered. That much is sure. Strode is always careful in his language, but I think the finger points at Francis Mountjoy-Martin. What is more interesting is that it wasn't the first attempt on Sly's life. Lady Blessington tried to kill him. Mellie says that Mama still feels guilty about that. Lady Blessington was acting on Mama's behalf, apparently. The plan was for the two women to act together, but Lady Blessington took the initiative herself. It proved a fatal mistake.'

'And D'Orsay?'

'Count D'Orsay died in August 1852, but Mellie seemed confident that he could also be ruled out. She said that, although she understood "activity of an intimate nature" took place and further promises were made, D'Orsay couldn't collect on them before his Scottish play ended its run and Harriet escaped any further attention. The other rumours of dukes and marquises were just tittle-tattle – which leaves Francis Mountjoy-Martin and Jem Mason.'

'But still a mystery?'

'I have to face two possibilities. One is that Mama does not know who my father is. In that case, as you once said, this has been an elaborate charade, but arguably an educational one for me. If she does know, then the truth cannot come soon enough. Maybe there never was a mystery, but without the mystery to solve I would not have come to you. How would I have found out about Sly? How would I have learned about the friendship with Lady Blessington? The names on the list gave me the whole story, not just the piece I wanted to know. And it bought time. Time was important because Mama was protecting someone. Someone who led another separate life. Someone for whom an illegitimate son might be a distraction or an embarrassment even. And time was important because Mama never found the moment to tell my father that I was his son.'

'And it is time for the truth now?'

'Let us just say the process of resolution is playing itself out. She promised me last time we spoke that she would answer the propositions I put to her. I think she has some unfinished matters to deal with before we can speak openly about the facts, as I now understand them.'

'And you, Martin. What is left for you now? How will you feel if your quest is over?'

'I don't know yet. I don't know what to feel. Perhaps even because I don't know how to feel. I have built a wall around me.'

'Do you know what you want?'

'What does any of us want? To be happy? To feel worthwhile? To do something good?'

'It could be any of those. Or all of them. The thing is to try and work it out It is a help if you know where you are going; where you should put your energies.'

'I see that. I have not thought much about it. I have been too busy blaming Mama for everything. I have been a spoilt brat.'

'But you can change. You have a good brain. You have shown you can be diligent and hardworking when you have a clear aim in sight. You have a great natural talent with horses. You have the benefit of a fine education. You can be witty and charming when you choose. You are a fluent linguist. The world at your feet, if you wish it.'

'Now it is you who flatters me.'

'I am just telling you the truth as I see it. Don't waste your talents and don't look back. That is my only advice.'

'Tell me another story about Jem,' he said. I was happy to oblige.

'One time, at Dunchurch, he walked the course the

night before racing and saw there was a shorter route, saving about fifteen lengths, going to the last furlong, but you had to jump a huge rail the size of a dogcart over a furze hedge. Only a madman would try and jump that, but Jem got the idea to have one of his associates saw through the rail in the early morning, so that when he jumped it and hit the rail in a race, the rail would break. Unfortunately, the man tasked with the sawing got drunk the night before and failed to turn up. Lucky for Jem, his mount in the first race was withdrawn and he didn't have to test his man's handiwork or lack of it. Doubly unlucky for Will Pope, though, who got wind of the plan through some loose talk in the Red Lion and decided to try it for himself. He was just behind the leading group in the first race and while they all took the longer route, with a wicker hurdle to negotiate, Pope dug his spurs in and had at the big rail for all he was worth. His horse had no chance, hit it halfway up and put Pope over the top. He flew through the air like a trapeze artist, but, with no net to save him, he hit the ground headfirst and broke both collarbones. He didn't speak to Jem for a while. You could never be angry with Jem for long, though. I never heard him speak ill of anyone and there wasn't a jockey who didn't respect him – even Pope. Everyone knew he would try anything to win a race and the owners always wanted him. When the big races came up, they competed for his services.'

'I can see you have a great admiration for him, despite his sometimes unconventional approach.'

'He earned my admiration. He was often getting me out of scrapes. I had a way of letting money through my fingers when I was younger and I could never pay my debts at the month end. There were many times when Jem would arrive in the nick of time and pay off the bailiffs before they started carting off my possessions. I never paid him back, even though I always meant to. He would say, "It's your comradeship I value, Tom. And having to ride against a man like you makes me concentrate. I can't let up with you at my quarters. If I ever need your help, I'll ask you and I know you'll give it without question. We are gentlemen, Tom. Don't forget it". And in my mind, there is no one like Jem Mason. He is a rare man. There is no truer friend a man could have and no finer horseman.'

'What is his situation now?'

'I'm afraid the tables are turned these days. He has suffered some financial setbacks and he is not in the best of health. He is not very good at asking for help. I do what I can.'

We talked on through the day. We covered a lot of ground, but his thoughts kept coming back to Jem.

'What would you say is the nature of their relationship: my mother and Jem Mason?'

'Then or now?'

'Both.'

'When they first met, I think it was just an adventure for them. Harriet, or Eliza as she was then, had men falling at her feet. She was quite mesmerising. I think she enjoyed the excitement. There was a rebellious streak in her and I think she liked to shock. Of course, Jem had a way with the ladies, as he did with the horses. He was not what you might call "a ladies' man". He didn't go out of his way to charm them with clever lines. That was more my line of attack. I gave them the full blarney and Jem always said they let me take them to bed just to shut me up. Jem was different. As brash and arrogant as he could be in male company, with a girl he was diffident – almost shy. Jem and Harriet were a love match, no doubt. They both played the field, but they were always doing it to make the other jealous, as it seemed to me. I knew how he felt about her. I think she felt the same.'

'And now?'

'As you might expect, it is more complicated now. From what she says in her letters, Harriet has tried her best. I really believe she has tried to make it work. But they are both contrary. When one is inclined towards compromise, the other is not. In many ways, any obstacles to them being reconciled have been removed. I think it is just a question of pride.'

Martin sat back in his chair. I sensed he was raking over our discussions; looking for a conclusion, a way forward.

'I think we are in danger of coming up with the answer we would both wish for,' I said.

'You are right, of course. I want it to be Jem. I feel as if I know him well, with his many accomplishments and faults. Like us all, he is flawed. Taciturn, moody, proud, awkward – these accusations can all be levelled at him, from what you say. But he is a good man: loyal to his friends and serious about his craft. And while he frustrates and annoys my mother, he is the one person she could be happy with. If only they could see it.'

'But how will you feel if it is Francis? It could still be him.'

'Indeed, it could. It is as likely to be Francis, from what I can glean from Mellie. He was always kind to me when we lived together, but I was too young to really take in the relationship. He also has his strengths and weaknesses. Essentially, though, I think he tried his best.'

'You seem to be rather relaxed about the answer to your quest. Does it not still gnaw away at you?'

'I did say that, didn't I? Strange as it may seem, no. I surprise myself to say that. If it is Francis, well and good. He is in India now and unlikely to return, as far as I can tell. He has never done me any harm and I understand now the many pressures he endured. If it is Jem, that shapes everything. He is here and I can still get to know him properly. It is an opportunity. Whatever the truth, there is a bigger truth that exercises me now. Mama and Jem must be reconciled. That is the greater prize. Mellie says Mama worries she has been an awful mother to me, but, frankly, I have been a worse son to her. I feel I owe it to her to do something.'

Our conversation seemed to run its course and I suggested we canter a couple of the younger horses that were in light work before he left for his return to London. He accepted readily.

'No games today,' I said, conscious of the trick I played last time he was here.

I led out a wiry grey colt, about sixteen hands tall, for Martin. He was a straightforward enough ride, but he had a habit of wrenching at the bit and throwing his head around. Once settled he was fine, but he was far from a novice ride. I mentioned this to Martin, as I legged him up. I used the mounting block to get astride my horse, an uncomplicated bay colt – smaller than the other horse, but also very athletic. They were evenly matched as we breezed four furlongs. I watched Martin closely. With jockeys, it is all about balance and good hands. Martin's hands were light as a song thrush. The colt didn't throw his head once. That is a gift. You can't teach it. During the ride, Martin was quiet – preoccupied, I thought. When we got back, we unsaddled the horses, rubbed them down and put day rugs on them.

Martin eventually spoke, as he emerged from his thoughts.

'I am formulating an idea in my mind. Will you help me?'

'Of course,' I said.

THIRTY
Last Chance
Wroughton, England
Paris and La Celle-Saint-Cloud, France

1863

Fairwater Stables
Wroughton

Dear Martin
Great news to tell. I've secured a move back to Marlborough and I have taken over the old Fairwater yard at Wroughton. I've had a wonderful time at Newmarket, but the chance to move back to Wiltshire is too good to miss. William Cartwright will put up half the money and I will have more boxes and my own old turf gallop up on the downs. All the team is moving with me and I know we can train a lot of winners here. I can't wait to show you around when you come over. You will love it here. William has a new horse I want to show you as well. I think he could be the horse we have been looking for. Please

*write and tell me when you can come. Don't leave it
too long.*
    Your loyal friend
        Tom

⌒∽

        Château de Beauregard
        La Celle-Saint-Cloud

Dear Tom
    *I'm excited about your news. I may even be with
you before you receive this letter. Much to relate and I'm
feeling optimistic about the future.*
        Yours ever
            Martin

⌒∽

At the Élysée Palace, Jean Mocquard is called into Emperor
Napoleon's office. Each elevation of Emperor Napoleon III,
real or imagined, brings with it the need for a larger office
with more ornate fittings. The new office is resplendent
with gilt trimmings on all the surfaces, fine Belgian wall
tapestries and grand Italian oil paintings. On this day, the
sun bursts through the long windows and scatters shards
of light into every angle of the room. A new portrait of
Louis Napoleon hangs behind him, replacing the earlier
portrait of his illustrious forbear Napoleon I. The whole
ensemble is designed to project power and virility, but the

attempt at aggrandisement, surely the intention, fails. If anything, the figure of Louis Napoleon is diminished. His uniform hangs limply about him, the epaulettes droop and slide forward from his shoulders and he seems even shorter than when Mocquard last saw him, only a few weeks ago. As Mocquard enters and looks across the wide expanse to Louis's desk, his impression is of a small, sickly child, lost in a giant's lair.

Mocquard has no expectation that the call is particularly of note, but he senses that there are other voices in Louis's ears these days. He still has influence, but he is consulted less often; the Empress is a contrary force and there are those in Louis' circle with different motives to him. Unusually, he has not heard the latest rumours and he is unprepared.

'The new chief of police says that Harriet is a spy,' says Louis. 'He believes she is in the pay of the British Government, that this was the original source of her wealth. He plans to have her arrested.'

'Could I suggest we don't act too hastily. Perhaps I could look into the evidence myself and see if there is any substance to his suspicions?'

'Very well. I would hate to judge Miss Howard unfairly, but it does rather explain some things I was uneasy about.'

'I think Monsieur Toulon wishes to make a name for himself.'

'You don't think there is any truth in it?'

'I think I would know about it.'

'What do you advise?'

'I think he should concentrate on your security arrangements. There are still those who wish you ill. You and the Empress cannot risk anything less than his full attention.'

'You have a point, I suppose.'

'Even if it was true, which I am sure it is not, it would be hard to say that we had come to any harm by it. Imagine if the British Government had funded our campaign. That would be a cause for amusement rather than retribution, I think.'

'You are right, of course, as ever. Nevertheless, I would be grateful if you would review the case with Toulon for me.'

'Of course, leave it with me.'

Mocquard wastes no time in dealing with his task. It is an important reminder that nothing can be taken for granted. Harriet continues to live in danger, despite the fair wind blowing at her back recently. She cannot entirely shake off history.

cs

It is a bright, cloudless morning on the gallops above Wroughton and two men on grey hacks survey the scene in front of them. In the far distance, three horses and riders appear through a white, painted gate and begin to canter towards them. As the horses pass a stone marker, they switch to a gallop and quicken their pace.

'Don't say anything, just watch,' says Tom. 'He is the chestnut horse with the white star on his forehead. Freddie Adams rides him. The other two are my best sprinters. They are going to work upsides in front and the chestnut horse in behind. Freddie will see if he can get to them going up the hill in the final furlong. We will know more then.'

As the horses come by the watchers, the trailing horse latches on to the pacemakers and, in a matter of strides, powers three lengths clear. Martin says he has never seen anything like it. Tom smiles.

Back at the yard, Martin can barely contain his excitement.

'Right, we know we have the horse. I'm a novice in race planning. How do we pick the race? And how do we get the odds? And how do we get the money on?'

'Patience,' says Tom. 'I'll give him a quiet run somewhere early in the year. Freddie will ride him. He'll do what he's told. In any case, the distance will be too short and I'll leave him short of work. He won't win. Maybe fifth or sixth. Enough for us to know he can translate his ability from the gallops to the track, but not enough to attract attention. Then we'll keep him ticking over, getting him in peak condition. When the longer races come into the calendar in September, we'll find a seven-furlong race with some fancied horses that have already won. We'll be one of the outsiders. I'll get one of the top men to ride. Someone who can be trusted. We'll place the commissions late, so there can be no chance for the bookmakers to know what is going on. We'll try for some match bets with the owners of the favourites in the race.'

'It sounds easy, but what if something goes wrong?'

'It won't. This is the best horse I've ever trained. He could even be a Derby horse, but that is for another day.'

'By the way, what is he called?'

'Ely. Like the cathedral.'

Martin goes on to talk about his mother. He and Harriet are on better terms. Jem is discussed openly between them. She calls Jem "my dear friend", but Martin knows he is more than that.

✑

In the week that follows, Tom invites Jem to Wroughton and arranges a repeat performance up on the gallops. Jem is impressed. Anyone would be. While he takes it in, Tom moves the conversation in another direction.

'It is none of my business, but what are your intentions regarding Harriet?' he says.

'There is something afoot here. This is not a casual enquiry, is it?'

'We have known each other a long time. We shouldn't need to dance around the subject. This horse will win, probably at Doncaster, later in the year. There is a great deal of money to be made. I want you to be a part of it. I would want you in anyway, as a friend, but there is a motive.'

'Go on.'

'Harriet thinks you still love her. Is it true?'

'Are you my keeper now?'

'No games, Jem. Just tell me.'

'It is true, but …'

'But nothing, Jem. Don't be a fool. You think she is too good for you?'

'I know she is.'

'Well, we are both agreed on that much, at least.'

'Where is this leading?'

'She thinks you have some idea, that because she is wealthy and you are not, your pride does not allow you to go to her. She is free and she wants you with her. Is that hard to understand?'

'It is not hard to understand, but it is complicated.'

'No. It is simple. You are the only complication.'

'I have been a fool. You are right. I married twice, but I managed to make the same mistake twice. I ended up being married to the boss's daughter. It never works. I know the woman I love has been in front of me all the time, but we always managed to argue. It has been my loss.'

'Listen to me, Jem. When we win at Doncaster, we will all be rich. What stands in your way, then?'

'Nothing, I suppose.'

'What a romantic you are. I know things have not gone well for you with women. And I know there have been problems with money, but it doesn't have to be like that. I was always the one in debt. You were the one who baled me out, time and again. Now it is my turn to help you. Think of it as paying you back for all those times before.'

Tom tells Jem the plan, just as he outlined it to Martin. Jem lights a cigar and takes a long pull on it.

'Alright, I'm in,' he says. 'Thank you. I am fortunate to have a friend like you. By the way, I'm sorry to be so secretive. Things have moved on, even since you heard from Harriet last. Harriet and I are on good terms again. We are seeing each other. We are taking it slowly.'

∽

All is calm at the Château de Beauregard. Harriet and Mellie are settled into a routine of elegant domesticity. However, it is a long time since they ventured into Paris and, Harriet's trysts with Jem apart, they both feel a certain lack of excitement in their comfortable existence. Lavinia Lampard brings tidings that spark them into life, although it is news of a death that prompts the change. Their old accomplice at Carisbrooke School flits into their consciousness only occasionally. They know most of the story already, but not how it ends. After leaving school on the Isle of Wight, Lavinia and Harriet enjoyed London society and Lavinia formed a close friendship with Tom Olliver. Her father, however, was unimpressed with her London friends and sent her to Dublin in search of a husband. She soon found a wealthy Irish landowner, some twenty years her senior, who took her off to his country estate in Waterford. In Lavinia's eyes, the lack of London entertainment was more than compensated by her own stable of hunters and racehorses and a seemingly unlimited budget for clothes and house parties. Raymond Fitzgerald may not have been everyone's idea of a love match, but he suited Lavinia well enough and their long marriage lasted where others failed. And when Raymond was carried into the Manor House on a makeshift stretcher one afternoon, having suffered a crashing fall at a black ditch, while out with Lord Waterford's hounds near Tramore, she was genuinely moved to sorrow. She nursed him for three days and nights, but the injuries proved fatal and by the time the priest arrived Lavinia, who thought a good deal during her time at the bedside, already knew how she would spend her enforced widowhood.

Leaving matters with her lawyer and her estate manager, she travels first to London, then to Paris, where she installs herself at the Hotel Windsor, overlooking the Jardins des Tuileries, and sends word to Harriet and Mellie that she would be delighted if they could meet again to talk over old times and tour the sights.

At about the same time, Harriet receives news that Princess Mathilde is also back in Paris. Relations with her lover, Count Alfred van Nieuwerkerke, ebb and flow and, from what Mathilde says, things are at a very low ebb.

∽

And so it is that at noon, on Friday 5th June 1863, Harriet Howard, Melliora Findon, Lavinia Lampard and Princess Mathilde present themselves at Vefour restaurant on the rue de Beaujolais, beside the Palais Royal in Paris, and order a jeroboam of champagne. They are all attractive women, around their fortieth year, but there the similarity ends. Mathilde wears the most extraordinary purple and white striped, half-domed, crinoline dress, with a French lace shawl. It is an awkward construction and it takes the assistance of two waiters to arrange her at the table. Beside her, Lavinia's black mourning dress in the style of Queen Victoria and Mellie's beige, tunic dress merge quietly into the plum-velvet banquette. Harriet's fuchsia-pink, crinoline dress, in other circumstances strikingly bright, looks a model of restraint beside Mathilde. Suffice to say that the four women make an impression. Even Vefour, all gilded mirrors, chandeliers, inlaid carvings, gold ceilings and painted neo-classical panels seems muted in comparison. The afternoon goes downhill rather swiftly and four hours and two more jeroboams later, the ladies, now the only diners – if that is the right word – left in the restaurant, are in a philosophical mood.

The conversation moves through various subjects, but the condition of the male of the human species is the one to which they return. Mathilde, who betrays a certain disdain for the men in her life, of which there have been many, is moved to announce that "men can never be trusted".

'I think that may be too sweeping,' says Lavinia. 'My dear husband was always as good as his word. He possessed many positive qualities.'

'I am happy to hear it. What would you say was his best quality?'

'He was a very kind man. I think that is a characteristic often overlooked.'

'Indeed, but what about passion? Surely a relationship cannot survive on kindness.'

'I think it survives very well. Passion is fleeting and capricious. I would never trust passion if that was all there was between a man and a woman.'

'Perhaps that is where I am going wrong. What about you, Harriet? Kindness or passion? What would you have?'

'I aspire to both.'

'Nicely said. And you, Mellie? You are quiet on the matter.'

'I speak little because I know so little. Men are not my specialist subject. I am happy to listen and learn.'

Melliora's reply slows Mathilde for a while. She is not

sure what to make of it. However, she is soon back on track.

'Harriet, let us not skirt around the subject any longer. Is it true you will be reconciled with Jem Mason at last?'

Lavinia and Mellie sit forward and rest their chins on their forearms as if choreographed by an unseen director, their eyes fixed on Harriet.

'And what does Jem Mason have to commend him, after all these years?' adds Mathilde.

'He was the first man I cared about and that emotion never left me. He was always his own man. I admired his independence. He put into words what I felt, about making my own way in life, when I was a young girl. That stayed with me.'

'When will the great romance be reinstated?'

'There are some small obstacles to be overcome. I will tell you all about it when I can. I think it really will be our last chance, but we are determined not to fail this time.'

'How marvellous. I can hardly wait.'

⟆⟆

Nearby, Jean Mocquard and Martin sit at a café on the rue de la Paix. Mocquard knows about the plot for Ely.

'I think about what could still go wrong,' says Martin.

'But Monsieur Olliver remains very confident, does he not?'

'I am sure of Tom. That is not my concern. I worry that Louis may come back into Harriet's life somehow and ruin everything.'

'I am pleased to say there are no difficulties there. I would not have been able to say that a few months ago, but an awkward situation has been resolved.'

'You didn't mention it.'

'I didn't want to worry you without reason.'

He relates the story about Toulon and his supposed evidence.

'I was able to intervene to some effect. My influence is not entirely faded.' He smiles. 'I also took the precaution of briefing Princess Mathilde,' he adds. 'She applied her own special means of persuasion to Monsieur Toulon. He saw the wisdom of dropping his interest in Harriet.'

'Can we be sure?'

'Louis will not trouble her. He has a new fascination: her name is Marguerite Bellanger. She is an actress, but that will not surprise you. He and Eugenie are hardly on speaking terms. I can only think it will end badly, but he heeds my advice only infrequently these days. You need not concern yourself with him now. Nor should Harriet. The chapter on that part of her life is closed. She must only look forward.'

'Thank you.'

'By the way, we should probably keep this between us and Mathilde.'

THIRTY-ONE
Landing the Odds
Wroughton and Doncaster, England
Paris and La Celle-Saint-Cloud, France
1863

Martin and Tom meet again at Wroughton. Tom is all smiles again. The horses are fit and healthy and seem to be running well. Even at this early stage in the season, Tom sits at the top of the trainers' table. Martin has news of Harriet and Nathaniel Strode.

'She told me there are only two people in the world that she trusts implicitly. One is Nathaniel Strode and the other is you.'

'That is an onerous responsibility. I hope I will not let her down.'

'Strode is to help me with my financial affairs. He seems a clever man. He is rather unenthusiastic about putting stake money up for our scheme, but Mama has insisted upon it. He says it is the only time she has ever gone against his recommendation.'

'We are playing for high stakes. It is not just the craic and giving the bookmakers a bloody nose. If we pull this off, Jem will be financially secure and on equal terms again with Harriet. It is all that stands between them.'

'No doubt they will find other barriers.'

'I think they are finding their way, from what I understand. Maybe they don't need our help, but it is too good a plan not to see it through and it will do no harm. The rest is up to them.'

'I won't ask. I will just thank you for your help.'

'Thank me when we win.'

At the mid-year, Tom finds a nice quiet race for Ely, first time up and all goes to plan. The horse finishes fifth.

∽

In July, news comes that Lord Normanby is dead. It is a sign that the old order is changing. Harriet's perception of Normanby troubles her. Of course, he and Lady Normanby were always very kind to her, but there are nagging doubts now about his role in the wider politics. Could he have done more to protect her from Sly? Could he have stopped things altogether? She doesn't dwell on it, though. It is all in the past and it is too late now.

∽

In August, Martin's twenty-first birthday begins quietly, with Harriet and Aunt Mellie at Beauregard, but a carriage arrives mid-afternoon and by five o'clock Martin walks into Chez Brébant on the boulevard Poissonnière in Paris.

Seated around a table are Jean Mocquard, Tom Olliver, Nathaniel Strode and Jem Mason. It is a pleasant surprise. He takes them in. Jean looks much as he has always done, although a walking stick assists his stiffening movement. Tom is wiry and youthful still, only slightly round-shouldered and stooped. Nathaniel oozes a languid, effortless charm, sinking back into his seat, with an arm draped along the back of the seat beside him. Jem has the upright swagger, but, facially, he looks drawn, with exaggerated crow's feet at the corners of his eyes and sunken cheeks. Martin regards "Oncle" Jean and Tom as his most trusted friends. Strode is a new acquaintance, but they have already shared several agreeable lunches and Martin is drawn to Strode's sharp brain and ready wit. Of course, he knows that Jem's attendance forms part of the grand plan to bring Jem and Harriet back together.

The way Tom and Martin have it, by the time the plan is achieved Jem and Martin will also be friends. After that, well, they will just have to see how matters unfold. In the meantime, here sit the two men, linked to the same woman, who may or may not be father and son and who have ploughed separate furrows throughout their lives, Harriet making such a fine job of protecting her son from the outside world and such a success of keeping her relationship with Jem a secret that they barely knew of each other's existence until Martin came looking. If Jem thought of Martin at all, it was as Francis Mountjoy-Martin's son. It never crossed his mind to question it. Now, brought together as co-conspirators, they enjoy each other's company. They discuss horses, hunting, books (both share a love of Smith

Surtees), theatre, music and tailors – the similarities of view are uncanny. And when Jem looks at himself in the large wall mirror as he crosses the restaurant and thirty minutes later watches Martin do the same, even he cannot miss what everyone else sees.

❧

At the beginning of September, Tom invites Martin to call at Wroughton to finalise the details of the race they are aiming at for Ely. Tom has news to impart.

'Count Frederic Lagrange has let it be known that his filly, Fille de l'Air, is unbeatable at Doncaster for the Champagne Stakes.'

'Best avoided then. Do we have an alternative?'

'On the contrary. Ely is flying. The Count will accommodate any match bet we care to propose and lay us generous odds. The bet will be struck in Paris with his agent. Jem's man there will look after the commission. We can take our profit without even troubling the bookmakers here – though, of course, we'll do that as well.'

'You are confident?'

'Never more.'

❧

The day dawns at Doncaster. The racecourse is just outside the town on the old Town Moor. The race is over seven furlongs; the going is good but not firm and there are only four runners. The weather looks set fair and Tommy

Aldcroft is booked to ride. Ely's work before the race, on the gallops above Wroughton, is nothing short of sparkling and the commissions are in place. Tom travels Ely to Doncaster the day before, with his head lad, Harry O'Brien. He tells Harry to sleep in the box with Ely and to let no one else near him.

∽

In the morning, at breakfast, Martin meets Tom at the Mount Pleasant hotel for a briefing on the day ahead.

'We'll walk the course before racing,' says Tom. 'Whatever happens, we'll track the French filly. I am sure she'll come up the stand rails. She slightly favours her off fore lead and if she comes off a straight line she'll move right-handed. We'll come on her near side.'

Martin is impressed. It is the attention to detail that makes Tom the trainer he is. Nothing is left to chance. By the time the horses line up at the start, Martin is bursting with confidence. There is confidence, though, in another quarter and the buzz around the track all day is that Count Lagrange's Fille de l'Air has been "catching pigeons" on the gallops. At the off, Lagrange's filly is made evens favourite; Linda, ridden by Tom Chaloner and coming off a brilliant win at York last time, is 5/4; and Ely, despite the commissions, still trades at 10/1. Rouge Crosse is any price.

When the flag falls, all the horses break evenly. Fille de l'Air makes the early running, with Linda just behind. Ely and Rouge Crosse sit at the back of the field. They go a steady pace and none of the jockeys shows their hand.

At the four-furlong marker, Martin looks across to Tom, seeking encouragement, but Tom's face is impassive. All the jockeys hold position until Chaloner, on Linda, decides to kick for home with two furlongs to go. Rouge Crosse drops away quickly and Fille de l'Air and Ely move readily in behind Linda. The winner can only come from these three horses as they go clear. Entering the final furlong, Fille de l'Air breezes past and her jockey, Watkins, moves his mount onto the rails, takes a look over his shoulder and sees Ely three lengths down and making no impression. The crowd roars as the favourite quickens away.

'We're beat,' says Martin.

∽

At Beauregard next day, Harriet waits at the window of the small drawing room, doodling on a notepad and jumping each time she hears the sound of wheels on gravel, hoping the afternoon mail carriage will bring a copy of *The Sporting Life* with the vital result. Tom offers a private messenger or a telegraph, but she refuses.

'I will only believe it when I see it in print,' she says.

The Sporting Life, Wednesday 17th September 1863

ELY TAKES THE AIR
A shock result at Doncaster in the Champagne Stakes yesterday, when the colt, Ely, in only his second racecourse appearance, floored the well-backed favourite Fille de l'Air by a comfortable two lengths under a

confident Thomas Aldcroft. The favourite looked sure to win, when sent clear entering the final furlong, but Ely showed a remarkable turn of foot to collar the leader with one hundred yards to run and win going away. Fille de l'Air was widely touted as the best two-year-old of the year and already supported for the Guineas and the Oaks next year. Her owner, Count Frederic Lagrange, would not hear of defeat before the race. If reports are to be believed, Ely landed somewhere in the order of thirty thousand pounds in bets here and in France, with a large part arising from a direct match wager between the Count and Ely's owner, William Cartwright. It is thought to be one of the biggest gambles ever landed. It was Tom Olliver's greatest success since relocating from Newmarket to Wroughton and it looks like he will be as good a trainer as he was a jockey, having won the Grand National three times in his riding days.

⧼⧽

That is not the half of it. Jean Mocquard finds himself the owner of a splendid townhouse, near the beach, in the new resort of Deauville. Princess Mathilde displays an ostentatious, diamond brooch, styled in the shape of a rose, on her décolletage. Matters of taste are, of course, in the eye of the beholder. Even Nathaniel Strode, not best known for taking risks, buys his fiancée an unexpected gift: a five-carat, yellow diamond, gold ring.

A celebration seems in order. Of course, William Cartwright organises a party at Wroughton for Tom and all the stable staff and jockeys involved, but Tom and Martin have another, more intimate soiree in mind and arrangements are made to hold the event at the Château de Beauregard a few days later. Jean Mocquard and his wife, Marie-Anne, Nathaniel Strode and his fiancée, Eleanor, Lavinia, Mellie, Tom, Martin, Jem and Harriet are all in attendance. Only Princess Mathilde and guest are absent. The Princess does, however, send a rather large quantity of champagne by way of an apology. It is a relaxed affair. Tom admits he is more relieved than anything. Anyone in racing knows that it is one thing to plan a coup like theirs, but quite another to pull it off. However confident Tom was, beforehand, he admits only now that his nerves were shot by the day of the race.

'You did a good job of covering that up,' says Martin.

'Never in doubt,' says Jem. 'Tommy Aldcroft told me he always knew he was going to win.'

The champagne and canapés are served in the dining room at midday, but the weather proves unseasonably warm and a last-minute decision is made to take lunch in the orchard. Trestles are brought out, linen is draped over them and assorted chairs are assembled. Flagons of wine and vases of flowers from the rose garden are placed on the tables. The wine flows. There is a toast to Tom, then another and another. Speeches are made. There is a toast to William Cartwright; another to Tommy Aldcroft; another to Ely. More wine flows. More speeches are made. As the debris from the meal is cleared away, three musicians from the village arrive and start up some Breton jigs. There is dancing, after a fashion.

Late in the afternoon and with a hazy heat still in the sun, the ten revellers splinter into smaller groups. In the distance, they hear the faint sound of the musicians, leading staff who live out in an impromptu parade back to the village. Nearby, bees hum happily in the flower borders and hedgerows. Jean sleeps soundly in a wicker chair. Mellie and Lavinia lie in adjacent hammocks and tell each other stories about their very different lives since schooldays. Marie-Anne, Nathaniel and Eleanor speak fluently in French to one another. Jem and Harriet walk arm in arm into the meadow beyond and disappear from view. Martin and Tom look on, pleased with their work.

'We did it,' says Tom.

'We did. Thank you.'

✑

In October, Jem and Harriet check into the Hotel Bristol in Paris for a few days. They attend Bizet's new opera, *The Pearl Fishers*, at the Theatre Lyrique on Place du Chatelet. The following day, they walk in the parks, stroll the boulevards and stop in cafés for coffee and cognac. In the afternoon, they buy each other expensive presents in the boutiques on the rue du Bac. They dine at Maison Dorée.

'Look at us,' Harriet says. 'We are almost like a couple.'

THIRTY-TWO

In the Final Furlong
La Celle-Saint-Cloud and Paris, France
London and Ascot, England
1864

2 Ferry Lane
Norwich

Dear Eliza

I hardly know what to say. Martin visited us this morning and what a pleasant young person he is. It would have been wonderful if you had been with him, but we are used to your absence now and have grown accustomed to it. Please don't concern yourself on our account. Your poor dear parents have little time left and we are just grateful for any small mercies that come our way.

Anyway, Martin was the perfect gentleman and I suppose he has learned all these fine manners from growing up with princes. He is on some search or other. He was very vague about the details and what he did say quite bewildered your poor father and me, but I'm sure he will resolve things as he seems a very clever young man. *I've no idea where he acquired his intelligence, although, of course, he inherits his looks from you.*

I suppose it would be quite pointless of me to ask when you might visit us, but I will, nonetheless. Please let me know when you are next in England. Your poor father and I dream of the day you might be with us again.
Mama

﹌

Château de Beauregard
La Celle-Saint-Cloud

Dearest Mama
Thank you for your lovely letter. It was a joy to hear from you. Martin is making his own way in life now and is very much his own man. I am very proud of him, as you might imagine. I know you are very disparaging about Tom Olliver, but he has been the most marvellous friend and advisor to Martin and I cannot thank him enough. As you know, Martin has reached his twenty-first year and will be striking out independently from now on. I am sorry that I have no plans to be in England soon. I very much hoped that you would join me here, but, of course, it is your choice to stay where you are. Mellie is a tremendous comfort to me and we spend a great deal of time talking about the old days.

God bless you.
Your loving daughter.
Eliza

❧

At the Château de Beauregard, Jem is a regular visitor. He and Harriet are still taking things slowly, as if they must go through the phases of courtship all over again. It is Jem who eventually moves things along, arriving one day with a more than usually serious look about him. He seems preoccupied, nervous even. It becomes clear that he has a script prepared.

'No more excuses. No more arguments. No more games. I am here for good, if you will have me. The fault has been mine. You have always been true. I know that now.'

'I want you to be sure,' she says. 'There is no going back. We have one chance.'

'I know it. I am sure.'

'Should I see this as a proposal on your part?'

❧

Martin spends the summer in England. He judges that he will best serve progress by keeping a low profile and letting things take their course. For the first time, he enjoys the English "summer season". In late May, he visits Epsom for the Derby with Tom. Ely is judged slightly short of a gallop after bruising a knee and doesn't take his place in the field – Tom deciding he will be better suited by Ascot. It is a sunny, shimmering day and a swelling multitude, including the Prince of Wales, makes their way to the track. Every carriage, cab, trap, dogcart and van is pressed into service to take racegoers along the dusty road over Banstead Downs, while thousands more people spill out of the trains arriving every ten or twenty minutes from London. Here is a seething mass of humanity, intent on seeing the best horses from the best possible vantage points. All across the scene, there are flags, tents, booths, fairground rides, parked vehicles and crowds of spectators. Endless crowds. Hampers of all shapes and sizes spill out picnics. A great noise swirls around the racecourse: costermongers pitch their wares; gypsy women hawk lucky heather; bookmakers shout out the odds. The hubbub rises to a roar and echoes through the grandstands, as the big race approaches.

Before the race, Tom and Martin both pick out Blair Athol, a tall, flaxen chestnut colt with a broad white blaze – bred, owned and trained by William l'Anson from Malton, Yorkshire. Despite his appearance and the knowledge that his dam is the great race mare Blink Bonny, who won the Derby seven years earlier, they are put off by the fact he is having his first ever run and he is unfancied at 20/1 on the bookmakers' lists. The race is delayed by several false starts and when the runners eventually break Blair Athol is slow into his stride and is towards the back of the field in the early stages. His jockey, James Snowden, rides a patient race, steadily making ground and moving in behind the leaders at Tattenham Corner. In a move that reminds them of Ely's win in the Champagne Stakes, the favourite, General Peel, goes clear entering the final furlong and appears the likely winner, until a confident Snowden, in the blue and gold colours, produces Blair Athol with a late challenge and sprints away to win easily by two lengths from General Peel, with Scottish Chief third.

'That's a lesson learned. Never be put off your own judgement,' says Tom.

'Agreed. If there is a better horse in training, I haven't seen him. Even Ely would not have lived with him today. This is a horse worth following.'

The two men are greatly amused when the newspapers carry a story about their old adversaries, Count Lagrange and Fille de l'Air, winners of the Oaks.

The Times, Monday 30th May 1864

OAKS SCANDAL AT EPSOM

The Count Lagrange's Fille de l'Air had an easy victory at Epsom. She won the Oaks in a walk and the numerous visitors on Ladies Day witnessed an unusual scene of excitement, uproar and violence. The mare, it will be remembered, was heavily backed for the "Two Thousand" at Newmarket, but was supposed to have been "pulled" according to orders and consequently the ease with which she, directly afterwards, carried off the French Oaks and Epsom ditto caused such a strong feeling among British sportsmen that the Count deemed it prudent to beat a hasty retreat to native land; it required all the practical energy of hired pugilists to protect the French quadruped, her jockey and trainer from Lynch's law on Epsom downs. Whether the English racing world is more honest and straightforward than Bonaparte's aristocracy may be open to argument, but that the Queens's lieges don't like to be "done" by the polite Mossoo was roughly testified at Epsom. We

*have been assiduous in teaching our neighbours the high
arts of horse racing, cricket and other sciences and they
prove apt scholars, but if all be true which we hear of
Monsieur le Comte and his stud, we must deplore the
fact of French noblemen so speedily acquiring the dirty
habits of English vagabondism on the turf.*

∽

At Royal Ascot, the fine weather continues. Martin acts as
unofficial assistant trainer to Tom for the week. He finds
Ascot rather genteel by comparison with Epsom, but this,
as Tom points out, may be more to do with the fact that he
confines his movements to the saddling boxes, the parade
ring and the Royal Enclosure. Smartly attired, in black silk
top hat and morning coat, he moves in elevated circles.
Out on the heath, there is no escape from the noise and
the crowds, as if the whole of the metropolis has gone
racing.

Ely wins the Prince of Wales Stakes, again beating Fille
de l'Air, and "the Syndicate", comprising Tom, Martin, Strode,
Mocquard, Princess Mathilde, Lavinia Lampard and Jem,
make another successful foray into the betting market. The
Prince of Wales himself makes the presentation. Martin is
invited to the Royal Box after racing and joins the guests at
Windsor Castle later in the evening. Queen Victoria, who
forgoes the races on account of a twenty-hour journey from
Balmoral the previous day, is sufficiently rested to make
an appearance. Martin is mystified when Her Majesty asks
him how the parterre garden at Beauregard is looking and

requests that he convey her regards to his mother. In the same week, Blair Athol wins the Triennial Stakes and the Syndicate is again fully invested. Tom and Martin work well together. Before the week is out, Tom suggests a joint business venture, working with horses in England and France.

∽

Martin attends Goodwood races in July, at the Duke of Richmond's invitation. The sun shines. Blair Athol wins the Gratwicke Stakes: the Syndicate collects. Martin wonders why life cannot always be so uncomplicated. He takes in Henley regatta, although he has very little idea who is rowing against whom. He attends Cowes week, but the hot weather finally breaks and some of the yacht racing is cancelled due to rough seas. Martin makes a pilgrimage of sorts to Carisbrooke School, the scene of Harriet's escape attempt. There is, of course, no trace of Harriet ever having been there and she does not feature in the list of illustrious alumni, etched in gold leaf on a board in the reception hall, but he does sit on the mounting block, where she waited for the milk cart some twenty-odd years earlier.

∽

At the end of the summer season, Martin meets Nathaniel Strode in London to discuss his financial arrangements, before he returns to France. Martin turns down direct assistance from his mother, but the proceeds of his wagers, on Ely and now Blair Athol, sit untouched in the bank and

Strode is keen to set them to work. Martin explains that he and Tom have a business proposition they are working on together.

'Tom thinks there are opportunities. Jem has agreed he will work with me. They will both put money in. William Cartwright is also in. We would like another investor to spread the risk, even though we are confident. I think you would say we are being prudent if I have understood my lessons correctly.'

'You are a quick learner. I will solve this for you myself. I will be the last investor. Let me know the figure when you are ready. I think that concludes our business for today.'

'I meant to ask you something else. I didn't know Mama was so well acquainted with the Queen.'

'Your mother has friends in the highest places; I can assure you of that.'

'So it seems. You knew about it?'

'I did. There is a great deal about your mother that you don't know. She has asked that I provide you with answers if you have any questions.'

'But first I have to know which questions to ask.'

'Indeed. I think you have developed a good instinct, though. The need for secrecy is gone and Harriet wants to set things in order. You will not need to be patient for much longer. I think everything will become clear.'

∽

In France, things take their course, much as Martin and Tom hope. Jem moves to France and joins Harriet at

Beauregard. Jem retains his house in St John's Wood and Martin takes possession of a set of keys, so that he will have a base in England. Mellie moves into the cottage in the grounds at Beauregard, once it is suitably redesigned and redecorated to suit the needs of a lady. Martin rents a townhouse in Versailles to be close to La Celle but not in the way. It is a sort of mutually beneficial merry-go-round. Lavinia and Mathilde soon invite themselves to the London house, as a bolthole, so that when they are not busy terrorising the eligible bachelors of Paris they can turn their attention to the wealthy, unattached gentlemen of London. Parties, the more lavish the better, are the order of the day, where Lavinia and Mathilde are concerned. Harriet and Jem sometimes accept an invitation in Paris and trail in their wake, but they are usually home by midnight at the latest.

Nathaniel Strode visits Beauregard for one of his regular reviews with Harriet. She is keen to resolve the remaining issues concerning her divorce from Trelawney and to make some adjustments to her will.

'I will have the paperwork drafted,' he says. 'I will ask the lawyers to send you the documents for signature.'

'I am looking forward,' she says. 'I will draw a line under the past and look towards the future.'

'Very good. I am always keen that those I advise make changes as soon as they have made decisions. It is a sensible precaution. Too many people let things run on. We cannot know what will happen tomorrow.'

⁂

Back in France, Tom stays with Martin at Versailles. Tom has horses to buy and money to spend. Jem and Martin already have a shortlist of horses they have tried out. Provided Tom is happy and the horses are passed by the vets, deals will be struck. When the talk of horses is finished, Tom asks about Harriet and Jem.

'Is everything going well?'

'I hesitate, but yes. I think we can say we are entering the final furlong.'

'Let us hope they can stay the course.'

THIRTY-THREE
Reconciliations
La Celle-Saint-Cloud, France
Wroughton, England
1864

The Syndicate, with the exception of one reverse, when Blair Athol is beaten by the French horse, Vermout, at Longchamp, continue their successful season. Tom takes charge of the commissions when Blair Athol wins the St Leger at Doncaster in September. It is one of those years when virtually everything goes their way. A party is held at Beauregard, almost exactly a year after Ely's victory at Doncaster. Jean Mocquard sends apologies, but everyone else is present and Princess Mathilde is in rampant form. There is a star-strewn, moonlit sky and the evening culminates in an impromptu midnight cross-country race over the post and rails and hedges of the estate. Lavinia wins, riding side-saddle. Tom and Jem fall off their mounts – admittedly, they are riding bareback. No damage is done. The anaesthetic qualities of several more flagons of wine mean that only pride is dented. At one point in the evening, Martin sits alongside Tom. He has been observing proceedings.

'Is there something between you and Lavinia?' he asks.

'There was once, a long time ago.'

'Could there be again?'

'Who knows?' Tom shrugs but he can't conceal a smile.

'You old rogue. I see you are ahead of me.'

The party continues long into the night. The church clock strikes twice before the carousers give best. It marks the end of an idyllic summer in England and France.

∽

Autumn at La Celle sees Harriet and Jem immerse themselves in the charms of the château. The long, hot summer and the continuing mild weather mean Beauregard has never looked better. They are still making improvements, but the changes are minor and cosmetic, rather than substantial. There are some days when they wake without a plan, so they spend the day deadheading late roses in the garden or cleaning tack or mending fences. After everything that has gone before, the unexceptional normality of daily life is refreshing. They are often to be found at the races at Longchamp, whether they are involved with runners or not. They never tire of the Paris parks: the Parc Monceau, the Jardins du Luxembourg and the Tuileries Gardens all have a special place in their shared history and they visit often. A mood of reconciliation pervades their relationship. It is an enchanted existence; they both feel it. There is, though, still something unresolved between them, something they are avoiding. Jem broaches the subject.

'We need to talk about Martin,' he says.

'Yes, we do.'

'Do you have something you would like to tell me?'

'You seem to get on well.'

'We do. I count him a good friend. I think he feels the same. But if there is something more, he deserves the truth.'

'And you?'

'I cannot rewrite history and you have taught me not to live in regret. It cannot change anything now. Can I make this easy for you?'

'I don't think I follow you.'

'Martin and I discussed it between us recently. Frankly, it was impossible not to, given the time we spend together. We are as certain as we can be that Martin is my son. We understand that you had reservations about admitting this in the past, we are sure for good reasons, but there can be no point in maintaining the mystery now. The only secret is that everyone around you still pretends to you that they don't know.'

'Everyone?'

'Mellie, Lavinia, Mathilde, Tom, Nathaniel, me. Is that enough?'

'You have discussed it between you?'

'I am afraid so.'

'When was this?'

'After the party. You went to bed first. Everyone else stayed up. Mathilde started it. You know what she is like. She would not be denied.'

'I don't know what to say.'

'Just say yes. Then we can all relax.'

'Yes.'

The tears that follow reflect relief rather than sadness, as if a great weight has lifted from Harriet's shoulders. All those years spent searching for the right moment and now it has been taken out of her hands.

'I have a lot to thank you for,' she says. 'I see that I have made myself hostage to a habit I could not shake off.'

'That puts it very well. Your friends would not stand by and let you stay like that. Martin and I had already talked about it, but it was Mathilde who brought it into the open.'

∽

Martin, Tom and Jem become established as business partners, based at the Château de Beauregard. They stand two stallions, board mares and foals; take horses for pre-training, prior to sending them on to the training centres at Saint Cloud and Maisons-Lafitte; source new horses for owners and trainers; and provide stabling for English-trained runners, when sent over for French races. Strode is their accountant, as well as an investor. There is no repeat of the excesses under Captain Trelawney's stewardship. It is a profitable business, run on strict commercial principles. Strode sees to that. Beyond the professionalism, though, there is the gift that the three main partners share for horses. It is a winning combination.

∽

In the wider world of politics, everything seems to be going well, although Harriet rarely has cause to think much about the grand alliance between France and England, preferring to concentrate on matters closer to home. For all the reservations about Emperor Napoleon III, the British Government, under Lord Palmerston, feel vindicated by their role – not that they would admit anything – in his extended stay in power. True, he is fixed on his vanity project in Mexico, thankfully now free of British involvement, but he is persuaded by Lord Russell to follow Britain's lead in staying out of the American Civil War and he resists the temptation to meddle in German, Italian or Russian affairs – for the moment, at least. There is nervousness about the emergence of Bismarck's Prussia as a major power again, but, Denmark aside, there is a prevailing calm in Europe and Palmerston judges that peace is best achieved by maintaining the status quo. Besides, he has an election coming up in the following year and the more he can exude stability and calm, the more certain he will be of victory.

Lord Cowley visits Harriet, after another very long absence, to ask her if all the "arrangements" agreed with Palmerston are satisfactory. She thinks it an odd thing to happen, but, reading between the lines, it seems that Queen Victoria has been asking about her and, as usually happens, Cowley is dispatched by Palmerston to make sure Harriet is behaving herself.

✂

Harriet and Jem's enthusiasm for the château and for each other is undimmed as winter envelops La Celle. In Paris, they attend a preview of Offenbach's new production, *La*

Belle Hélène, at the Théâtre des Variétés. One day, at the Jardin des Plantes, with snow on the ground, they realise they are reprising a scene from many years ago. Harriet recalls their conversation.

'Do you remember... I said everything would be alright?'

'Some would say we have taken our time.'

'They would be correct.'

'It was worth the wait.'

'There is one more thing I must do,' she says. 'I have made so many excuses not to visit my parents. It is another habit that needs to be broken. I asked them to come here, but they are set in their ways and won't be moved. I must go to them before it is too late. I must see for myself that they are provided for. Then, when I return, our life together stretches out before us, uninterrupted. Everything will be resolved.'

'Would you like me to come with you?'

'We have decided that it will just be two of us: Mellie and me. We will see Mellie's mother in London. She does well, by all accounts, but we will make sure she is settled and looked after. Besides, you have much to do here. You and Martin are in charge of the arrangements for the new paddocks.'

'Very well. I shall pine for you here.'

∽

Life has a habit of casting clouds, just when all seems positive. Jean Mocquard dies on 12th December 1864, after a sudden and unexpected illness. Harriet weeps long into the night at the loss of her friend. Jean-François-Constant Mocquard, to give him his full appellation, leaves his wife, Marie-Anne, daughter, Marie-Emilie-Hortense, and son, Amédée. Jean's son is already a successful lawyer and on good terms with Martin. Indeed, the Mocquard and Howard families have become very close over the years. Harriet would like to attend the funeral, but she knows that Louis and Eugenie will be there and everyone agrees that this is probably best avoided. Mellie and Martin attend in Harriet's place.

⚜

A few days after the funeral, Nathaniel Strode receives a telegraph to say that Harriet's father is in hospital in Norwich. Strode has a long-standing arrangement with a local churchwarden, who lives close by the Harryets, to alert him urgently if any difficulties arise. It has never been needed, until now. He sends his own physician up from London and waits for news. He decides not to inform Harriet until he knows the extent of the illness. When he receives the diagnosis, it is, thankfully, not as serious as first feared. Apparently, Joseph fell down the stairs at the cottage and Elizabeth could not move him. He complained of chest pains and she called for help. The neighbours, fearing a heart problem, took him to the hospital. By the time Strode's physician, Dr Clements, arrived the next day, Joseph was sitting up in bed. He was suffering lacerations around his face, but a thorough examination and a discussion with Elizabeth revealed the likely cause of the fall as an excess of alcohol and the likely cause of the chest pains as indigestion, following an overindulgence of roast goose. Dr Clements finds it hard to hide his irritation and this is rather reflected in the invoice that arrives on Strode's desk the following week.

∞

There is a third, and more serious, dark cloud gathering. The next time Martin and Tom meet at Wroughton, Martin expresses his concern.

'Jem is not well. I'm not sure how long they will have,' he says.

'I have been bothered about Jem's health for a long time now. I don't expect him to live into old age, but I thought he seemed steady enough when I saw him last. Has something changed?'

'He has lost weight. He coughs all the time. I don't like the look of him at all. I noticed it much more recently, when I hadn't seen him for a few weeks.'

'What did Jem say?'

'Initially, he made nothing of it; he said he felt fine, but eventually the truth came out.'

'What truth?'

'He is carrying an illness, but there is something else. You remember I spoke to you about Nicholas Sly's murder. I said the finger pointed at Francis Mountjoy-Martin. That is not the case. It was Jem.'

'I can hardly believe it. Are you sure?'

'It is not something he would invent. It is a heavy burden.

At any time, there could be a knock on the door. Mountjoy-Martin was very accommodating in laying a false trail, knowing he had an alibi. He was at a regimental dinner with two hundred officers available to verify his whereabouts. Nevertheless, the worry remains.'

'I didn't even know Jem and Mountjoy-Martin were acquainted.'

'I don't think anyone does. Jem sought him out and asked for his help. Mountjoy-Martin was happy to oblige. I think both of them felt their relationship with Mama was doomed, but with their help she could be rid of Sly at least.'

'Have you spoken to Harriet about it?'

'She is preoccupied with going to England at the moment. I understand that. She needs to see her parents. Jem puts on a good show in front of her. It seems to me he doesn't want to worry her. I am not sure she should ever know about this.'

∽

Château de Beauregard
La Celle-Saint-Cloud

Dearest Mama

I am so sorry that Papa has been unwell, but relieved to know that he is well on his way to recovery. Please tell him we are all thinking about him here and send our best wishes.

We have enjoyed the most delightful summer here at La Celle. The sun seems to have shone every day, right through into September. Even the recent months have been tolerably kind to us and we are preparing the house for Christmas as I write. It is not such a tradition, here in France, but we like to keep a little of England at Beauregard and our friends all seem to enjoy seeing the house dressed and joining in the old games we played as children.

Martin is now established in his stud business and doing very well. He does seem to have a real talent for it. I am sure he will call in to see you, the next time he visits Newmarket.

We have endured one great sadness this year, as our dear friend Jean Mocquard died earlier this month. We all miss him awfully and life will never be the same without him.

As soon as New Year is behind us, I am coming to England. I will be with you as soon as I can. I know I have neglected you so terribly and I can only ask for your forgiveness.

God bless you.
Your loving daughter.
Eliza

⤨

2 Ferry Lane
Norwich

Dear Eliza
Thank you for your note. I know you won't take

it the wrong way when I say that we will believe it when we see it. Of course, it would be lovely if you could visit, but please don't put yourself to any trouble.

       Mama

THIRTY-FOUR
Falling at the Last
Norfolk and London, England
La Celle-Saint-Cloud, France
1865

B ad weather in the English Channel through the early part of the year thwarts travel plans for Harriet and Mellie, but eventually they arrive in England at Tilbury. They travel first to London and stay overnight at Clarendon Place. Mellie goes in search of her mother; she has an address, but she has not heard from her for several months. Harriet continues her journey to Norfolk. However, instead of going straight to Norwich, she makes a detour to the north coast. She books a stay at the George Hotel in Cley-next-the-sea. It marks a nostalgic return to the home county of her childhood. She remembers summers on the beach at Brancaster and sometimes at Cromer. She remembers gazing in wonder at the sails of Mr Lee's windmill, just by the hotel. By the time she reaches Cley, the light is fading and she opts for an early night, with the prospect of a dawn start in the morning. The next day, sleeping in longer than planned and after a leisurely breakfast, she crosses over onto the coastal path from the hotel, briefly follows the coast road west, then branches out across the marshes and along by the ruins of Blakeney Chapel. Turning left, she looks out towards Blakeney Point. A coastal breeze blows the clouds across the sky, casting rippling ribbons of shade across the sunlit green and brown strips of the marsh landscape.

In Blakeney, she stops on the quayside. There are some children with fishing lines set out to catch crabs in the creek. She sits on a bench and looks across the marshes, mesmerised by the changing colours as the sun moves higher. A marsh harrier glides above her, searching for prey. Her thoughts turn inevitably to the meeting with her parents. She imagines how it will be. She rehearses the things she will say, the apologies she will make. There will probably be tears. There may be some harsh words. That is understandable. Ultimately, though, her reconciliations will be complete. She will soon be at peace with herself and the people she loves most in the world: her parents, Martin and Jem. She will be happy. She hopes so. The shouts of the children jolt her from her thoughts. A bucket tips over and the tiny crabs make their bid for freedom.

She walks up the lane past the fishermen's cottages and meets the coast road at the crossroads by St Nicholas church. She goes through the woodland beyond the churchyard and strides back across the fields at Wiveton. She walks over the green, past the vicarage and crosses the old Wiveton bridge. Soon, another wide green opens out in front of her and she walks up to Cley church, St Margaret's. She recalls this was her mother's favourite Norfolk church. She spends time here, wanders among the headstones and then she goes inside. She says a prayer. Beneath the east window of the south aisle, she finds two boards dated 1772, one of which displays the Ten Commandments. Memories flood back. This is where her mother explained them, along with a strict exhortation that she must obey them always. Harriet thinks she was probably about eight years old.

Further along the south aisle, she finds the medieval, stained-glass windows containing the images of eight female saints, all martyrs: Cecilia, Agatha, Sithe, Catherine, Petronilla, Barbara, Faith and Apollonia – each with their own story. As Harriet recalls, she asked endless questions, as children of a certain age will, about why the women were martyred, which stretched far beyond her mother's ability to answer. Mama seemed to find no irony in the fate of the women, martyred, as it appeared to Harriet, for their devotion to the exact Christian principles she was endorsing. Needless to say, this apparent contradiction was not voiced, but it did rather shape the view in Harriet's mind that the Ten Commandments might not be all they were cracked up to be – this last, a new phrase, picked up from the gypsy children, travelling with the fair at Cromer. These children, with whom Mama forbade her to mix, even though they seemed to have more fun than those with whom she could play, helped sow doubts in her mind. She thought, even then, that she might need a more pragmatic set of guidelines than the Commandments for the way she would live her life.

Now, she sits for a long time, lost in thought. Eventually, she wanders along the back lane through Cley, walks through the loke into the lane beside the hotel and runs up the stairs to her room.

In the evening, she takes another stroll, this time turning right past the windmill and down the lane to the shingle beach. Here, just as she remembers it, is the big, red Norfolk sky, hanging above the greying sea. She watches as a charm of goldfinches spirals across the shingle, tossed by the wind. A sparrowhawk comes out of nowhere and leaves a tiny puff of yellow feathers and a fine mist of blood. She is surprised to be so shaken. She understands the wild and the reality of nature. Sparrowhawks must eat, she tells herself. She hastens back to the hotel and cancels her supper. It is a long time before sleep overtakes her.

⚬∕∕⚬

The next morning, Harriet makes her way from Cley to Norwich. The coach takes the coast road via Cromer, striking south through North Walsham and skirting the Broads into the town from the north. A bright, blue sky frames the majestic outline of Norwich Cathedral. She knows she must have been here as a child, but she can barely remember it. As she travels closer, she is awestruck by the vast size and scale of the building. Arriving at the Erpingham gate, she attaches herself to a group of schoolchildren being guided around the town and cathedral. The astonishing height of the spire, the extraordinary vaulted ceilings and the extreme length of the nave are all explained, but the detail is too much for her. She cannot take it in. Her thoughts are interrupted by last-minute changes to what she will say to her parents. She excuses herself and makes her own way. She lingers in the cloisters, losing count of the number of turns she takes. She goes over what she will say one more time. She knows she is delaying.

Finally, she walks out into the Close and onto Ferry Lane. She turns the corner and there is her parents' house: a double-fronted, three-storey, flint and brick cottage, with large sash windows and tall mock-Tudor chimney stacks. It looks much as she imagined it from Strode's description and from the little snippets she has gleaned from her mother's letters. She takes a deep breath and knocks on the door. If anything, the cottage is larger than she expected. Strode has done well, she thinks. Inside, Harriet finds her mother surprisingly little changed. Greyer, definitely, and affecting a vague stoop, but facially youthful and alert. Harriet is effusive about her mother's appearance and congratulates her on the beautiful home she maintains. If she was hoping for some reciprocal blandishments, however, she is disappointed.

'I hardly recognise you,' says her mother. 'I thought you would never come.'

'I thought so, too. I am sorry. There is so much to say…'

'How is Martin?'

'He is well. He has a promising future before him.'

'I am pleased. He was delightful when he visited us.'

'He very much enjoyed his trip here. He spends much of his time in England. I am sure he will visit you often. He has many friends in Newmarket.'

'I hope so. We have missed your presence here. He is some compensation.'

'Are you sure you will not join me in France? You would see Martin more often there. Would that not be compensation also?'

'You have our answer on that.'

'Will you reconsider?'

'Please don't mention it again. It upsets your poor dear father.'

'Where is Papa?'

'He is in the garden. He prefers it there.'

'Will he come in or should we go to him?'

'As you wish.'

They make their way into a neat courtyard garden. In the corner is a small bower, adorned with early pink clematis and underplanted with hellebores and anemones. Her father sits on a bench, squinting as if puzzled by something. He is a pale shadow of the father Harriet remembers, but the blue eyes still pierce when they focus on her. Harriet and Elizabeth sit beside him on wooden chairs.

'Papa, I have missed you.'

'Hmmm.'

'Will you not give your daughter a kiss?'

'Hmmm.'

She turns to her mother. 'Is he always like this?'

'No, I am not always like this, if you must know,' he says. 'You ignore us for twenty years and then expect to be greeted like the long-lost favourite. It will not do. It just will not do.'

'The fault is mine, I know. I am sorry. Will you forgive me?'

'And salve your conscience?'

'I hoped we could be reconciled. It is my one remaining wish.'

'You have poor judgement. Even Carisbrooke School

could not help you. We tried our best for you, but you always fought it.'

'I was a trouble to you. I know that. I am here to apologise and to make amends.'

'It is too late for that. You still surround yourself with scoundrels and vagabonds. I told your mother that no good would come of it.'

'I have managed well enough. I am sorry you don't approve of the way I live. It is my life now.'

'Please don't justify yourself with me. I won't have it. Why have you come here?'

'I am trying to make things right between us. I have neglected you, I know. Things have not been easy for me. I cannot tell you all that has happened. I have tried to look after you and Mama, and to bring up Martin as well as I could. I have not always done the right thing, but I have always tried to do the right thing.'

'Is that so?'

'I hope you live comfortably here. If you need anything else, please tell me.'

'I see. You are here to make us grateful and have us beg if we wish for more.'

'That is unkind.'

'Unkind, you say. I will tell you what is unkind: abandoning your own parents to fend for themselves, living a life of debauchery among foreigners and letting your son grow up a bastard. That is unkind.'

'What do you want me to say?'

'I want you to say nothing. Why don't you go? I wish never to see you again.'

Harriet sits back in her chair.

'Mama, is that what you want, too?'

'She will not say it,' he says. 'She was always too soft with you.'

'Papa, you wrong me. I wanted to explain…'

'I won't hear it. Go back to France. Stay there with your fancy friends and their fancy manners. Cavort with rogues and ruffians, if you must. Leave us in peace. Let us die quietly in England, without being sullied by your influence.'

'I only ever wanted the best for you.'

'Did you ever ask us what we wanted?'

'I am asking you now. Please don't punish me.'

'Yes, you ask us now, when it is all too late. You have been selfish. Harriet Howard is all you care about. You were so ashamed of us, you would not even keep the family name. How do you think we felt? Our daughter has disowned us. The neighbours laughed at us.'

'I meant no harm by it. I took advice. It is a good name for an actress.'

'It is a good name for a harlot.'

Harriet chokes back tears. Her mother leads her back into the cottage.

'I am sorry. These thoughts have been festering for a long time,' she says. 'I had no idea they would come out as they have. He likes getting things off his chest. Perhaps he will be calmer now. I will talk to him.'

'I must make arrangements for London. I will come again soon.'

When Harriet arrives in London, she begins to relate her experiences in Norfolk. She tells Mellie about the Ten Commandments, as she once promised she would, in Lyon. But it is clear that Mellie has more important news. Her visit has not gone well, either, but for different reasons. She finds that her mother is no longer at the given address. What she tells Harriet is not an unfamiliar story. Mellie's father died in debt. Her mother made the best of things and encouraged her daughter to find her own way in life. Nathaniel Strode's intervention was perfectly timed when he asked if Mellie would join Harriet as her travelling companion, on their trip to Nice, some ten years past. Mellie sent money home and her mother found a small income, working in a laundry. Pride kept her going and a string of letters with a largely fictional account of her life persuaded Mellie that all was well. The truth was very different. When she is found, Mrs Findon is in the workhouse. Worse still, she is seriously ill and not expected to live.

By the time Harriet arrives, any prospect of moving her to a hospital is judged pointless. Harriet and Mellie nurse their patient for forty-eight hours. The stench of disease is everywhere. Harriet thanks God she has been spared such a life. Mrs Beatrice Findon dies the next evening. The official cause of death appears on the certificate as pneumonia, but the haste with which the medical authorities insist on her burial leaves doubt. Only Harriet's intervention saves her from a pauper's grave. When the funeral is over, Harriet asks Mellie what she wants to do.

'There is nothing for me here now,' she says.

'Nor I. Let us make speed for France.'

⤬

They find a ship leaving from Tilbury. The crossing is not particularly rough, but Harriet and Mellie are both sick almost immediately after embarkation. By the time the ship sails into Dieppe, their condition causes concern. The ship's doctor prescribes potassium and advises them to drink plenty of water. The captain finds them the best coach and horses he can and sends them on their way. They both rally briefly during the journey, but by the time La Celle is reached the two women are in a wretched state. At Beauregard, Mellie improves for a good night's sleep and manages to eat some thin soup. The colour comes back to her. Harriet worsens and becomes delirious. Dr Villeneuve is called. He makes a thorough examination.

'I have seen the symptoms before,' he says. 'It is cholera.'

THIRTY-FIVE

Something to Live For
Le Chesnay, France
Norfolk and London, England
1865

The Times, Monday 21st August 1865

COUNTESS DE BEAUREGARD DIES

The Countess de Beauregard, perhaps better known by the name Harriet Howard in England, died at her château in La Celle-Saint-Cloud, near Paris, on 19th August 1865, after a brave fight against illness. She leaves an only son, Martin Harryet, Count de Béchevêt. It is widely believed that he is the son of Emperor Napoleon III of France, although this has never been verified.

Born Elizabeth Anne Harryet on 10th August 1823, she adopted the stage name of Harriet Howard during a brief but successful career as an actress on the London stage.

She achieved fame and not a little notoriety as the consort of Louis Napoleon. Speculation that she would become Empress, when Louis Napoleon became

Emperor Napoleon III of France, proved unfounded when the Emperor married the Spanish Countess of Teba.

In later years, she lived quietly at the Château de Beauregard and involved herself in local charities.

She will be remembered both for her great beauty and her vivacious charm. She was also very well regarded in hunting circles, as a fine rider across country. She married Captain Clarence Trelawney in 1856, but the marriage was dissolved earlier this year.

∽

The newspaper also reports that President Andrew Johnson signs a proclamation, declaring that "Peace, Order, Tranquillity and Civil Authority Now Exists in and Throughout the Whole of the United States of America". The American Civil War ends. Naturally enough, this dominates the news coverage and rather overshadows Harriet's obituary. Nevertheless, when Lord Palmerston, fresh – if such can be said of a man in his seventy-ninth year – from his general election victory, meets Lord Cowley the same day, it is Harriet Howard he wants to talk about. Palmerston, who makes little secret of the fact he would have preferred a Confederate victory in America, ignores Cowley's attempt to engage him on the subject of the proclamation.

'Damn the proclamation. They'll be invading Canada next. Mark my words. Anyway, dear Miss Howard has left us. Did you see it?'

'I did, indeed. She was a complicated person. I never quite got to grips with her, so to speak. Normanby was a great advocate of hers. I thought you were rather ambivalent about her.'

'That I could never be. I never met a woman like her.'

Palmerston blows hard into a purple handkerchief.

'Damn this cold,' he says.

Yet Cowley can see it is not a cold that afflicts the old man. He is fighting back tears.

∽

Harriet's funeral takes place at Le Chesnay. Jem, who refuses to leave Harriet's side during her illness, suffers from exhaustion and sickness and Dr Villeneuve gives strict instructions that he must be isolated and must not under any circumstances attend the funeral. Martin, a recovered Melliora Findon, Tom Olliver, Nathaniel Strode, Lavinia Lampard and Amédée Mocquard are the six principal mourners. There are, perhaps, another twenty people from the village who come to pay their respects. Rain overnight soaks into the ground and muddies the pathways. As the temperature drops, hail blows in and covers the graveyard. Everyone present is invited back to Beauregard for lunch. Tom and Martin's attempt to lift the sombre mood is appreciated, but, almost inevitably, fails.

The next day, Nathaniel Strode reads out the will for an assembly of interested parties. The details are much as expected and reflect promises made and agreements reached in Harriet's lifetime. The Château de Beauregard is left to Harriet's parents, whereas the Italian estate, together with the Villa Danetti in Nice, is left to Martin.

∽

In September, Nathaniel Strode goes to see Harriet's parents. It is not something to which he looks forward, but he feels he owes it to Harriet to see it through himself. He doesn't really know Joseph and Elizabeth Harryet. He visited the cottage once, before they took up residence. He follows in Harriet's footsteps in Norwich and arrives in Ferry Lane around midday. A wisteria, not much more than a twig when he was first there, is now grown into an impressive structure, stretching over the left-hand windows and above the front door. He meets Elizabeth at the cottage and goes in. Her husband is still in bed and he shows no signs of emerging.

'He has not spoken since we heard the news,' she says. 'He has taken it hard.'

'I understand from Miss Findon that Harriet and her father argued when she came here.'

'It was not so much an argument. Joseph was angry with her. He said some very unkind things. Of course, I am sure he regrets it now.'

'Yes, it is a shame. We never know the future. Once said, things cannot be unsaid, even though we might wish it.'

'We cannot turn back the clock, either, although I wish we could. If she had not come to England, she would still be alive.'

'You must not think like that. Harriet was determined.

She had to come. She was putting her life in order. And she wanted to see you.'

'I see that. Mr Strode, did you know my daughter well?'

'I knew her very well. I was her financial and legal advisor, and I managed her affairs for her. I flatter myself we were friends as well.'

'Did she talk about us, Joseph and me?'

'You were forever in her thoughts. She talked about you often.'

'And our living here, our financial rescue, as you might say. Was that all due to Harriet?'

'It was.'

'Thank you. All the stories about her… were they true?'

'That is not easily said. I think there were many stories. I cannot answer to them all.'

'I think you know what I am asking… as her mother.'

'I understand. I would say that Harriet was much maligned. My own experience of her was that she navigated her way through difficult waters with great courage, integrity and strength. It is not my place to say it, but I think you should be proud of her.'

'I appreciate the sentiment. I sense there is a great deal you are not saying.'

'I suppose it doesn't matter now, just between us. Harriet was in the employ of the British Government.'

'Assisting at the embassy?'

'I think it was rather more than that. I would say she did not accept the role willingly. There were threats to the people she loved. She had very little choice. She made the best of things and I hope I helped her in some small way.'

'Thank you. I am grateful for your replies. I will ask no more. Now, I assume you have not come here simply to express your condolences and to answer my questions, although it is kind of you and very much appreciated. How can we help you?'

'There are, perhaps, some issues for discussion, concerning Harriet's will.'

'I assume so. I hope we will not be unduly affected. We would like to carry on here if that is possible.'

'Quite the contrary. You and your husband are the main beneficiaries of Harriet's will. It is probably appropriate if you are both present for this part of the discussion.'

After a while, Joseph Harryet shuffles into the room and stares blankly into the middle distance. His face is grey and he has not shaved for a few days. Little tufts of white hair sprout randomly around his cheeks. His eyes are rheumy and he shakes visibly. Beside him, Elizabeth Harryet is the stronger, but Strode can see from the knitted brow and the pursed lips that she is only just holding herself together. Strode reads out the will, slowly and with particular emphasis here and there. When he is finished, he gathers up the papers in front of him and takes off his spectacles. He waits for them.

'You will forgive us if we understand the details imperfectly,' she says. 'We are not as sharp as we once were. Can you summarise for us?'

'Of course. With the exception of some specific bequests to Mr Martin Harryet, Miss Melliora Findon, Mr Thomas Olliver and Mr James Mason and myself, Mr Nathaniel Strode, the rest of the estate falls to you and your husband, with the provision that the Château de Beauregard be held in trust by you, to live in during your lifetimes if you wish, but to pass to Martin on your deaths.'

Elizabeth asks for a little time alone with Joseph to digest the implications, but she doesn't detain Strode long.

'Thank you for explaining everything so clearly. It is a generous arrangement. We don't want the château. It is not for us. Can we give it straight to Martin?'

'If that is what you wish.'

'It is.'

'Very well. I will put things into effect as soon as I return to London. Is there anything else I can help with before I leave you?'

'Yes, there is one more thing I forgot to ask.'

'Of course.'

'Was our daughter happy? I mean, before she came to England.'

'I never saw her happier.'

∽

When Strode returns to London, he visits Jem, now installed back at Clarendon Place. Strode hopes to see him looking better, but he is disappointed. Jem looks shrunken, wizened. In short, Strode thinks he looks awful. There is no doubt that Jem is ailing, but it is hard to know what is due to the illness and what should be attributed to the effect of his bereavement. He is bitter about the circumstances of Harriet's death. As will often happen in such cases, those left behind cannot help but look for blame. It is a natural part of the grieving process.

'Mellie is sure that the presence of cholera was well established in that area of London,' he says. 'Yet the authorities did nothing.'

'I am sorry; she is right. The government is suppressing the figures. There is fear in many parts of town. Another epidemic is only a matter of time.'

'Should I make other arrangements?'

'You are safe enough here, but there are many places I would advise you avoid. I am having a list of areas of the city drawn up. I will send it on.'

⁂

Strode's next task is to see Martin back in France; they meet at the townhouse in Versailles. Strode is quick with the news.

'Jem is in a bad way. You should visit him.'

'I will travel back with you, if that is alright.'

'Of course. I have seen the Harryets as well.'

'How are they?'

'As well as can be expected. It is hard for them. They want you to have the château. It will be yours when the lawyers have completed their work.'

'Joseph and Elizabeth didn't need to give up Beauregard, surely?'

'They are glad to pass on the responsibility. They live very simply, although I encourage them that they can spend more if they wish. They will never spend their money. They have never quite become used to the idea that Harriet provided for them so well. It is a great sadness that the old man reacted so badly when Harriet went there.'

'I blame myself for not picking that up when I visited. He was an old curmudgeon, but I never suspected he was harbouring such vitriol. When Mellie told me Mama's account of what he said, it shook me.'

'There is, perhaps, a lesson for us all.'

❧

As the year draws to a close, Tom visits Clarendon Place. Jem does his best to respond to his old friend, but he finds it impossible to shake off a deep depression. Tom cannot console him.

'I am so sorry, Jem.'

'I needed something to live for. Now, I have nothing.'

'Martin needs you.'

'That is a romantic thought, but it is not so. He has managed all his life without me. He is his own man.'

'He would still benefit from your guidance.'

'He has you to guide him. And Nathaniel Strode. He cannot improve on that – even you will not argue the point.'

'You are correct, of course. I am trying to say the right things, but it doesn't come easily. How can I help you best? Can you tell me?'

'There is nothing. I've always valued your friendship. That is enough. You and Strode made me see sense. I'm thankful.'

THIRTY-SIX
One Day
Wroughton, England
1873

Autumn is late this year. It is the beginning of November and red and orange flamed leaves hang on stubbornly to their hosts. I was thinking the other day that it is ten years since we landed the gamble with Ely at Doncaster. How we celebrated. It seemed to go on forever, but, of course, none of us knew what was around the corner. I'm afraid my old alias, Black Tom, is more accurately Grey Tom these days. I don't move so well lately and there is a downstairs room in the house I have converted to a bedroom. There is an attached sitting room, with a small terrace outside. I can see into the yard, here at Wroughton, and I still maintain the pretence that I am the boss, even though I rely more and more on my staff to train the horses. I gave up riding about five years past when my knees started to seize up and my assistant, Tom Leader, drives me up onto the gallops in an old growler – a hansom cab in Bath in a former life.

Of course, Jem is no longer with us. The cancer took him, just over a year after Harriet left us. At least he didn't suffer for long and I think it was nothing to him, compared to the loss of Harriet. He stayed on at Clarendon Place, with nursing care, in his final months and I saw him there as often as I could. He was well looked after and all his old racing friends rallied round. There is much I could say about Jem, but *The Sporting Life* put it best. I keep this cutting folded up in my pocket. I read it often.

The Sporting Life, Saturday 27th October 1866

DEATH OF JEM MASON

Modern hunting men, whose talk is of horses and who seldom care to note how Guilder held the line over a dusty fallow, or how Grappler turned short to the left while the whole body of the hounds flashed to the right, differ very widely about riders' merits. There seems, however, to be one point upon which the older school seem pretty well agreed: that James Mason, in getting to the end of a run and as a steeple-chase professional, had scarcely a peer in England. A lath-like, elegant figure, beautiful seat and hands, and a very quick eye, combined to make him quite the doyen of the steeple-chase field, though his great rival, Tom Olliver, was a much harder man and a stronger finisher.

What struck you so in "Jem" Mason was the perfect absence of anything like effort or fuss. The right thing to do came to him by intuition and he did it instantly. Poor William McDonough, in his hot haste, might take the ridges slantways, but Jem would just gallop along the headland and then come straight and leave him and The

Nun in hopeless distress, like a gunboat in a gale. We know of no exact parallel to his handling of a horse. The last steeple-chase which we saw Mason ride was more by way of a lark than anything else, at Hendon, and he did not even condescend to take his cigar out of his mouth. The more a hunt approximated in pace and distance to a steeple-chase, the better he liked it.

He was equally at home over Leicestershire or Northamptonshire, or the doubles of the Vale, but, as for killing the fox, he was much of Mr. Holyoake's opinion; "It's perhaps best killed, if it's any satisfaction to the master of the hounds, but it's none at all to me". He liked to have a horse of perfect manners and in perfect condition, on which he could take the lead and sail away, but he had no idea of persevering if he was beaten and generally pulled up at once with "an appointment in town". He did not care to buckle on his spurs to "make a scraw stir" or to nurse a third-class horse through a long run, simply for the honour of getting to the finish. He will forever be remembered in Mr. Elmore's "light blue and black cap", carried by Lottery, when winning the Liverpool Grand National Steeplechase. We will consider ourselves fortunate, indeed, if we ever see his like again.

∽

Martin visits when he can, although not so often in recent years. The Comte de Béchevêt title suits him well and he is married now with four young children. Aunt Mellie lives with the family and helps to look after the children. I'm not sure how much of my advice helped him, but when Martin found the right girl, Marianne-Joséphine-Caroline de Csuzy, he didn't prevaricate. Martin sold the château at Beauregard. I think there were too many memories there. And, without Jem, his heart went out of the stud business, although he and I still dabble in a small way – more as a way of keeping in touch than anything. He lives in Compiègne now. He follows a career as a diplomat, which has a certain irony, but his education and charm have helped him succeed. He still rides out in Chantilly and rides in the occasional amateur race.

He was able to spend some time with Jem before the end came. They rode out together, went racing together and enjoyed each other's company. They had a lot to talk about. The funny thing was that after the drunken party at Beauregard, when Mathilde got us all talking about Jem and Martin, it was never discussed again. I think we all thought it was understood between us and it didn't need underlining.

∽

As we get older, our world shrinks into itself; life exists inside our heads as a patchwork of memories. I spend a lot of time looking back on things nowadays. Living in the past becomes a habit. Different scenes flit in and out of my thoughts: an urchin on a coloured pony, galloping across the Grafton countryside; a beautiful woman riding side-saddle, ghosting into view down a mist-shrouded drive; a slim, elegant figure on a bay horse, jumping the last fence clear at Liverpool, neat as a cat; a young man walking into my yard at Newmarket, with questions on his mind; a nerveless jockey, sitting motionless at Doncaster, as the horse in front goes four lengths ahead, only to sweep past a few seconds later. In more recent years, I think about what wonderful times we all had at the Villa Danetti: Nathaniel Strode and Eleanor; Martin and Marianne; Amédée Mocquard and his sister, Marie; Mellie Findon and her good friend, Sarah Clare; Princess Mathilde plus one, but never the same one; and the lovely Lavinia Lampard. Harriet would have enjoyed it.

I think about the people who shaped Harriet's life: Palmerston, Normanby, Sly, Mocquard – all gone to meet their maker. I think about those who are still with us, somewhere. What happened to Captain Clarence Trelawney? He managed to repeat the feat of marrying a beautiful woman with money and spending the lot, before disappearing again. Rumour says he went to America. And Colonel Francis Mountjoy-Martin? He never came back from India, as far as I know. I often wonder about him. He is no longer listed as a serving officer, but perhaps he stayed on and made his fortune, as he hoped. Even Louis Napoleon died earlier this year. I think he missed Jean Mocquard's wise counsel and, like his uncle before him, his reputation faltered. Finally, his reign collapsed in ignominious defeat at Sedan. He lived out his days in exile at Camden Place in Chislehurst and is buried near there. He and Eugenie, who survives him, eventually became on good terms with Queen Victoria, who has the great good grace to always see the best in people. We are fortunate to have her. We know politicians cannot be trusted. At least we have our monarch to provide some stability.

∽

Nathaniel Strode calls in to see me. He is full of surprises. He quite embraced horse racing after our adventures with Ely and Blair Athol, and he is something of a man of the turf these days. He likes to come up on the gallops with me and talk about which horses are working well and what plans I have for them. I have a lovely horse called George Frederick, bred by my old friend, William Cartwright, and named after Queen Victoria's grandson. He is the best since Ely and I have great hopes for him. I always thought Strode quite a cold sort, but as I've come to know him better I realise he has a lighter, more quixotic side to him.

'Not all accountants are dull,' he says. 'It is not a requirement, although it does help.'

We talk about Harriet, as we always do. He fills in some details if I press him. I ask him how he managed to be in Harriet's company so much and not be seduced by her charms.

'Not easily,' he says. 'She was the mistress of the bewitching smile and the appealing glance. I pride myself on keeping a professional distance from my clients. I think I managed it very well for a long time in Harriet's case. The time she was in England, staying at Camden Place, to see Lord Palmerston provided the greatest challenge. Palmerston was physically rattled by her and she positively glowed after the encounter with him. It was intoxicating. Suddenly, I had invited her to the theatre and to dine with me. Nothing else mattered at that moment and I didn't even think about the consequences. Fortunately, my fiancée arrived unexpectedly and that brought me to my senses. I was almost lost.'

He tells me about his friendship, in later years, with Louis Napoleon.

'It has always gone unspoken between Louis and me, but I sometimes wonder if everyone around Harriet knew what was going on except her.'

'You think he knew that Harriet was being funded by the British Government?'

'I think it's possible – with the benefit of hindsight, of course. I don't think Louis questioned it too much. Why would he? An attractive woman with no shortage of finances was making herself available to him, without strings attached. I think he went along with it happily.'

∽

I know, above all things, that life is fundamentally unfair. Harriet and Jem deserved better.

In the year following Harriet's death, six thousand people died of cholera in an epidemic in the East End of London. All the deaths, including Harriet's, were avoidable. I know that, by comparison, I've been lucky. I get a bit melancholy sometimes, but then I find myself up on the gallops in the early morning, just as daylight breaks. The mist clears slightly and I hear the thud of hooves on turf and see a group of thoroughbreds thunder past me. Then, the sun burns through and the skylarks start to sing and lift into the air. It always brightens the morning and it usually puts me in a good mood for the rest of the day.

Lavinia lives with me here and we get along pretty well. She is a wonderful person and I'm thankful to have her company. Harriet is the link between us and I never tire of Lavinia's stories about her, Harriet and Mellie in their time at school on the Isle of Wight, all those years ago. She talks about Harriet's dream of becoming a famous actress. Her dream came true, I suppose, but it didn't last. Of course, we all need to hold on to something. I dream that one day a horse will come along that can take me to Epsom and win the Derby. It is what keeps me going. George Frederick might be that horse. I pray God I'll live long enough to see him there.